D. MA.

PENGUIN BOOKS
From Here to Maternity

Sinéad Moriarty lives in Dublin with her husband and their son. *From Here to Maternity* is her third novel.

www.sineadmoriarty.com

From Here to Maternity

SINÉAD MORIARTY

PENGUIN
IRELAND

For Hugo

PENGUIN IRELAND

Published by the Penguin Group
Penguin Ireland, 25 St Stephen's Green, Dublin 2, Ireland
(a division of Penguin Books Ltd)
Penguin Books Ltd, 80 Strand, London WC2R ORL, England
Penguin Group (USA) Inc., 375 Hudson Street, New York, New York 10014, USA
Penguin Group (Australia), 250 Camberwell Road,
Camberwell, Victoria 3124, Australia (a division of Pearson Australia Group Pty Ltd)
Penguin Group (Canada), 90 Eglinton Avenue East, Suite 700, Toronto, Ontario, Canada M4P 2Y3
(a division of Pearson Penguin Canada Inc.)
Penguin Books India Pvt Ltd, 11 Community Centre,
Panchsheel Park, New Delhi – 110 017, India
Penguin Group (NZ), cnr Airborne and Rosedale Roads, Albany,
Auckland 1310, New Zealand (a division of Pearson New Zealand Ltd)
Penguin Books (South Africa) (Pty) Ltd, 24 Sturdee Avenue,
Rosebank, Johannesburg 2196, South Africa

Penguin Books Ltd, Registered Offices: 80 Strand, London WC2R ORL, England

www.penguin.com

First published 2006

1

Copyright © Sinéad Moriarty, 2006

The moral right of the author has been asserted

Set in 13.5/16 pt Monotype Garamond
Typeset by Rowland Phototypesetting Ltd, Bury St Edmunds, Suffolk
Printed in Great Britain by Clays Ltd, St Ives plc

A CIP catalogue record for this book is available from the British Library

ISBN-13 978-1-844-88109-3
ISBN-10 1-844-88109-1

Acknowledgements

Thank you to Patricia Deevy, my wonderful editor, and Michael McLoughlin, Cliona Lewis, Brian Walker and all the team at Penguin Ireland for making the publishing process so enjoyable.

A big thanks to all in the Penguin UK office, especially Tom Weldon, Becke Parker, James Kellow, Naomi Fidler and the fantastic sales team.

Sincere thanks to Gillon Aitken, my agent, Sally Riley, Ayesha Karim and all at the agency for their hard work.

Thanks to my friends for their loyalty and enthusiasm.

I want to thank my nephews – Mikey, James, Jack and Sam – all inspirations for Yuri. Warmest thanks to my sister Sue and brother Mike, and their spouses Jim and Audrey, for being so selflessly supportive, loyal and enthusiastic.

Thanks also to Mum and Dad, for always cheering me on and making a fuss of every achievement, however small.

My biggest thanks go to Troy, my soulmate, for always being there – and to Hugo for making me smile every day.

Hello, I'm Emma. I'm a thirty-six-year-old makeup artist. I married James five years ago. He's a rugby coach, which means that I spend a lot of time standing on the sidelines of rugby pitches in the lashing rain and howling wind. After a happy first year of marriage we decided to have children. Unfortunately Mother Nature was not on our team, so after a couple of years of post-sex gymnastics followed by fertility treatments – all of which failed – we decided to adopt.

Then we spent a year and a half sitting through a very intense adoption course where everything about us and our relationship was dissected by social workers – including how often we had sex. We were eventually approved and a month ago we flew to a children's home at the back end of Russia to meet our little son Yuri, with whom we both fell in love at first sight.

We are now on our way back to Russia to make the adoption official in court. Then we can bring Yuri home to Ireland with us and begin our life as a family.

Oh, and by the way, I've just found out that I'm pregnant. Seven weeks. Needless to say I'm in shock. I told James last night . . .

Chapter 1

The day after my best friend Lucy's wedding I woke up to find James staring at me.

'What? Do I have dribble on my face?'

'Was I dreaming last night or did you tell me you were pregnant?' asked James.

I shook my head and smiled. 'Nope. I am. Can you believe it, James? After all this time and all those horrible tests and IVF, and now that we finally have a son I'm pregnant! It must have been all the distractions of the adoption. I must have stopped obsessing about getting pregnant and then it just happened. Isn't it amazing?' I flopped back into my pillows, grinning.

James leant over and kissed me. 'You do realize this means we're going to have two children in the space of seven months.'

'I know – isn't it wonderful?'

'Absolutely! I'm still in shock. How about you?'

'I've actually been feeling really sick lately, but I just presumed it was nerves and stress, with all the adoption stuff. It never crossed my mind that I might be pregnant. If Jess hadn't asked to borrow my Tampax, I'd still be none the wiser.'

Jess is my other best friend. She has two kids – Roy, named after Roy Keane, her husband Tony is a big Man U fan, and Sally, named after Meg Ryan in *When Harry met Sally*, which is Jess's favourite movie.

Jess, Lucy and I had all been at school together, and Jess and I were Lucy's bridesmaids. The guy she married, Donal, is James's best friend and the captain of the Leinster rugby team that James trains. So James was best man at the wedding. I had set Lucy and Donal up on a blind date and, although their relationship had a tempestuous start, they eventually fell in love, which culminated in their wedding. I took full credit for my matchmaking skills.

Anyway, the day before the wedding, when Jess and I were supposed to be doing helpful bridesmaid stuff but had actually snuck off to have a drink as far away from Lucy's overbearing snob of a mother as we could get, Jess had asked to borrow some Tampax. I suddenly realized I hadn't had my period in ages. Normally I knew my cycle inside out, but I'd been so distracted by the adoption that I'd clean forgotten about it. I told her I didn't have any with me and went up to my room to look at my calendar. I was over four weeks late! I was shocked.

I nipped down to the local chemist and bought two pregnancy tests. They were both positive. I couldn't believe it. I'd been praying for this moment for so long, but now that I was pregnant, I felt completely numb. It was only when I told James the next day and saw his face that I grasped it was true and we were actually going to have a baby.

'Gosh, it's going to be some year. We'll have a ready-made family by summer,' said James, shaking his head.

'I know,' I said, imagining us walking in the park, James and Yuri ahead while I strolled behind with a little brother or sister in the pram.

'It'll be tough going, though. Especially for you, being pregnant and looking after Yuri all day.'

'Are you planning on going somewhere?'

'No.'

'Well, then, why will I be on my own with Yuri?'

'Because I'll be at work.'

'James, you're going to have to spend less time at the club this year. Delegate more to Jonjo.'

Jonjo was James's assistant coach at the Leinster rugby club and, from what I could see, he did sod all. James had coached the team to victory in the European Cup a few months earlier, no thanks to Jonjo, who seemed to spend more time socializing with the team than coaching them.

'Jonjo does his bit. But, Emma, I'm going to be pretty tied up. We're defending the Cup. We don't want to give it back.'

'OK – you can take Yuri to training with you. Get him used to rugby from an early age.'

'I think ten months might just be a tad *too* young to start him. You do have to be able to walk to play rugby. Mind you, it would be wonderful if he ended up playing for England some day.'

'You mean Ireland,' I said, reminding him of where he lived. James was English, but had lived in Dublin for the past nine years.

'If he's good enough, I'd like him to play for England – with an English father he can declare for them any time.'

'But my dad will be devastated. Yuri has to don the green jersey and play for Ireland.'

'Darling, England won the World Cup last year. I'd rather he played for them.'

I rolled my eyes. As if I didn't know that England had won the bloody World Cup. For at least three months after the team's victory in Sydney, every time I walked into the TV room, James was watching replays of Jonny Wilkinson's winning drop goal and shaking his head in admiration. I thought at one point that he was in love with Jonny.

'He might hate rugby and be brilliant at tennis,' I countered. 'I'd much rather go to Wimbledon than Twickenham. We could sit in the family box, drink champagne, eat strawberries and hang out with the Duchess of Whatsit, Sue Barker and John McEnroe. Mind you, with his Russian roots Yuri might be more keen on ballet.'

'No,' said James, sharply.

'What do you mean, no?'

'No son of mine is going to ponce around in a pair of tights with his balls round his neck.'

'Ballet's beautiful – so expressive.'

'Exactly.'

'And athletic! You should see the way they leap about.'

'He can jump around the rugby pitch.'

'I hope you're not going to go all macho, James. I want Yuri to explore the creative side he's bound to have inherited. The Russians are very arty.'

James groaned. 'Emma, please tell me you're winding me up. You're not going to start booking him into dance classes, are you?'

'I might –'

There was a knock on our door. It was my sister Babs. Lucy had invited my whole family to the wedding – my parents, Sean, my younger brother by eighteen months, and his fiancée Shadee, and my brat of a sister Babs, the afterthought, twelve years younger than me. We'd all spent the night in the same hotel.

'Helloooooo, are you decent? I'm hiding from Mum, let me in.'

James scurried off to have a shower and I let Babs in.

She was wearing a tiny T-shirt that barely covered her bum.

'Have you no shame? Where's your dressing-gown?'

She shrugged. 'Dunno, and I'm too hung over to care. I just tried to order breakfast but they said it was too late, and I've eaten everything in my mini-bar so I've come to raid yours.' She bent down to pull out the Toblerone. Thank God James was in the shower, I thought, as I got a full flash of her arse.

'Hey, what's this?' she said, as she threw her wrapper into the wastepaper basket, which was empty except for –

SHIT! My pregnancy test.

'Emma?' she said, looking at the positive result and then at me.

I groaned and covered my head with the pillow. I wanted to get used to the idea myself first. James had only known for about twelve hours – nine of which he'd spent in a Guinness-induced coma.

'Look, I've only just found out and I'm still in shock. Don't tell Mum, OK?'

'Don't tell Mum what?' asked my mother, coming through the bedroom door, which Babs had left wide open.

'It's like Central Station in here. Well, what a wedding! Did you have fun, Mum?' I said, trying to distract her.

'What is Barbara not supposed to tell me?' she asked, glaring at me suspiciously.

Babs, helpful as ever, waved the pregnancy stick in front of her face and shouted, 'Emma's preggers!'

'What?' said Mum, staring at me. 'Is she joking? Are you?'

I was suddenly overcome with emotion as I saw tears well in my mother's eyes.

'Oh, Emma,' she said, reaching over to hug me. 'What a wonderful surprise. How long have you known?'

'I've literally only just found out.'

'Well, you won't need to go to Russia now.'

'What do you mean? Of course we're going to Russia. Yuri's our little boy and this is just an incredible, miraculous bonus.'

'But you don't need to adopt somebody else's child, you've your own on the way now.'

'MUM! We love Yuri, we want him to be our son and we're adopting him officially in five days' time. Nothing's changed.'

'You need to think about it, Emma. He might feel a bit left out now that you're going to have a baby. He'll always be adopted and the other child won't.'

'Mum, Yuri's our son in every way. We adore him and I don't want to hear any more of your opinions. We're leaving tomorrow to bring him home, so just drop it – OK?'

'Lord, there's no need to bite my head off. It must be your hormones. Lie back now and calm yourself. It's not good for a woman in your condition to be getting het up. You need to mind yourself, Emma. There's a high risk of miscarriage in older women.'

'I'm not old,' I said, gritting my teeth. It never ceased to amaze me how easily my mother could make my blood boil.

'Well, you're no spring chicken either.'

'Who's no spring chicken?' asked Dad, wandering into the room.

'Me apparently,' I said.

'Emma's pregnant,' said Mum.

Dad looked at me. I smiled and nodded.

'Jesus, I think I'm having a heart-attack. There's never a dull moment with this family. Oh, Emma, love, that's the best news I ever heard,' he said, hugging me.

'What is?' asked Sean, coming in to join the family.

'Emma's pregnant and Dad's getting all soppy,' said Babs, taking a large bite of the Toblerone.

'*What?* Really? Oh, Emma, that's fantastic,' said Sean, taking over from Dad in the hug department. 'It's going to be an exciting year for the family. Emma's two babies and my wedding.'

'What about my job?' demanded Babs.

'Nose job or real job?' asked Sean, referring to the nose job that Babs had recently undergone, transforming her from an attractive blonde with a great figure but a large, hooked nose – we're talking Barbra Streisand, Barry Manilow, Seabiscuit, Shergar, you get the picture – into a very good-looking blonde with a lovely nose.

'I'm referring to my job as a television presenter,' said Babs, flicking her hair. She had landed a job selling crappy products on BFL – the Buy For Less channel in London – and thought she was the new Oprah.

'What are you selling again? Gardening tools and wooden spoons?' asked Sean, winding her up. Thankfully, before a fight broke out, James came strolling out of the bathroom in his towelling robe.

'Congratulations,' said everyone, descending upon him.

Chapter 2

Lucy woke to a knock. Still half asleep, she grabbed a robe and opened the door to be greeted by a fresh-faced waiter, wheeling a table laden with food. 'Good morning, madam, I hope you'll find everything here that you need,' he said, as he positioned the trolley at the end of the bed.

'Thanks,' said Lucy, and fumbled for her purse to tip him while her new husband snored beside her.

When he had left, Lucy prodded Donal's back. 'Did you order this?' she asked, staring at the full Irish breakfast, Danish pastries, toast, muffins, smoked salmon and scrambled eggs, cereal and fruit.

'What time is it?' asked Donal, rubbing his eyes.

'Ten. Donal! Look at all the food – it's obscene.'

Donal sat up, smiling. 'Ah, yes, I couldn't decide what I fancied for breakfast so I ticked all the boxes on the menu. I was ravenous after my night of passion. God, you were a tiger last night – you had me worn out. If this is what married life's going to be like, I'm a happy man.'

'Very funny,' said Lucy, squirming, as she handed him a cup of coffee. 'Sorry about last night. I think the tiredness just caught up with me.'

'I come out of the bathroom in my red silk underpants, ready for action, to find my beautiful bride face down in her wedding dress.'

'Which I woke up in at six o'clock this morning. I'll make it up to you on our honeymoon, I promise.'

'All the lads said that once you marry them, women stop putting out. I should have listened. I wonder could I get an annulment and trade you in for a young one with more energy?' said Donal, winking at her as he shovelled a large slice of bacon into his mouth.

'Right! That's it. Come here, Mr Brady, till I show you how energetic us oldies can be.'

Later that day, as they waited to board their flight to Thailand, Lucy called me to say hi. James and I had checked out of the hotel early to go home and pack. We were heading to Russia the following morning and we needed to get all the baby paraphernalia ready for Yuri and pick up our visas from the embassy.

'Hi.'

'Hello, beautiful bride. Oh, Lucy, you were stunning and it was such an amazing day. Did you enjoy it?'

'I loved every second of it. Thanks for being such a brilliant bridesmaid. We're about to board our flight so I wanted to say good luck with Yuri. I'll be dying to see him when we get back. It's so exciting, Emma – I'm so happy for you.'

'Thanks, I'm sorry we had to rush off this morning, but it's all a bit manic. I'll have the photos developed for you when you come back. James took some really nice ones. Oh – and, Lucy?'

'Yes?'

'I'm pregnant.'

'What? Oh, my God! Really?'

'Yes, I can't believe it.'

'But it's just incredible. I'm actually shaking here. After all this time, it's unbelievable.'

'I know, we're in total shock.'

'I'm so pleased for you,' she said, voice wobbling. 'Oh, Emma . . . it's . . . so . . .'

'I . . . *knooooow* . . .'

'. . . wonderful . . .' she croaked.

'Thanks.' I sniffled.

I could hear Donal calling Lucy in the background. 'I have to go,' she said. 'I wish I could see you to hug you. God, Emma, so much is happening, it's fantastic. Wait until Donal hears – he'll be chuffed.'

'Go and catch your flight and have a wonderful time, I'll see you in two weeks. *Bon voyage!*'

Lucy ran on to the plane and told Donal the news. He was thrilled. He knew how much Emma and James wanted children and had been instrumental in helping them with the adoption process by acting as one of their referees. 'We'll have to start thinking about nippers ourselves,' he said.

'We've been married for twenty-four hours. It can wait,' said Lucy, and began to blow up a round object.

'I don't want to leave it too late. Look at how long it took Emma and James,' said Donal, but he was distracted by the sight of Lucy's puffed cheeks. 'What on earth are you doing?'

'It's a neck pillow, vital for long-haul flights. I bought one for you too. Here,' she said, handing it to him.

'Lucy, there's no way I'm sitting on a plane full of people with a dinghy wrapped round my neck. Anyway, back to the children issue, I think we should set to.'

'I'm thirty-six, not forty-six, and yes, it's something we need to address over the next year or two but, if you don't mind, I'd like to enjoy my honeymoon without stressing out about getting pregnant. Now, put these on,' she said, handing him a pair of knee-high socks.

'Are they pop socks?' asked Donal.

'No, they're anti-DVT socks.'

'DVT?'

'Deep-vein thrombosis. It's a blood clot that develops in your leg, can stop blood flow and kill you. Long-haul flights can trigger it. These socks are preventive.'

'What are the symptoms?'

'Swelling of the leg, redness or just pain that gets worse when you move around.

'Jesus, Lucy, why couldn't we go to the west of Ireland for two weeks?'

'Because it's the middle of winter and I don't fancy getting rained on every day of my honeymoon. Thailand will be amazing.'

Lucy had booked the honeymoon. She knew that if she hadn't she'd have ended up in a cottage in the west of Ireland – all very well for two sunny weeks in the middle of July, although in Ireland two sunny weeks would be considered a miracle – but it was winter, and she wanted sun, sand and luxury. So, she'd booked fourteen days in a top hotel on the island of Koh Samui.

'These seats are made for midgets,' said Donal, trying to get his six-foot-four frame into a comfortable position. 'Considering I've to spend the next twelve hours with my legs wrapped round my neck, in a pair of tights – not to mention the dinghy round my neck – it better be worth it.'

While Lucy nodded off, nestling into her neck pillow, Donal sat bolt upright, convinced that every twinge was a blood clot in his leg making its way up to his heart. Every half-hour he got up and walked around, stretching his legs this way and that. The elastic at the top of the socks was digging into his calves and he was convinced that it alone would give him a blood clot. Were they swelling? he wondered, as he looked down at his calf muscles bulging out of the socks. Had Lucy said redness was a symptom? He shook her.

'What?' she grumbled. 'I was asleep.'

'Did you say redness was a symptom of that DMT thing?'

'DVT. Yes.'

'Right, that's it. I'm off to have a word with the pilot. My legs are killing me and they've definitely swollen up – look, the socks are giving me a blood clot, not preventing it,' he said, shaking a leg in front of her.

'Shut up and go to sleep. Your leg looks exactly the same to me.'

'Well, if you want to be widowed after one day's marriage that's fine with me.'

'Donal,' hissed Lucy, 'you're imagining it. The socks prevent DVT, they don't cause it. Now blow up your neck pillow and close your eyes.'

'Fire ahead, Florence Nightingale, get your beauty sleep. Don't mind me. I'll just sit here with the circulation cut off from my knees upwards,' said the resident hypochondriac, as his not-so-young bride curled up and went back to sleep.

They spent the first week with Lucy sizzling herself under the hot sun while Donal sat under a palm tree, swatting flies. He read the newspapers daily, giving Lucy a running commentary on what was going on in the world, something she had specifically travelled halfway across the globe to avoid.

'Donal,' she said, after a particularly long tirade on the

state of Liverpool Football Club had interrupted her day-dream of winning the lotto and how she would spent the millions.

'Yep?'

'Would you mind not giving me a blow-by-blow of the sports section today? I'd really like to chill out without having to listen to how Steven Gerrard's talents are being wasted by that no-good, greasy Spaniard.'

'Fair enough. I'll stick to politics.'

'No, thanks all the same, but I don't want to know anything topical. I want to switch off. That's why I travelled here to Thailand – to get away from the news.'

Donal sighed. Lucy could see he was bored. He didn't like the sun: he just went red and burned. He complained constantly about the humidity, and the fact that every time he got out of the shower he started sweating. She knew he was itching to get back and start training for the new season, which would probably be his last. He was thirty-four now, which was old for a rugby player, particularly a wing forward, and he was beginning to really feel the tackles. But when they won the European Cup last year, it had been the proudest day of his life and he told Lucy that, as captain, he was determined to defend the title this year and keep the Cup at Leinster.

'Why don't you go for a swim?' she suggested.

'Maybe later. I'll go and ring Annie, see how she's doing. I'll meet you in the bar in an hour.'

Lucy sank back on her sun-lounger. Annie was Donal's niece and the bane of her life. Before Donal's sister Pam and her husband were killed in a car crash six years earlier, they had named him as Annie's legal guardian. She was now almost sixteen and was constantly causing havoc between him and Lucy. Last year she had even managed to break them up for a few days, shortly after they'd got engaged.

Annie hated Lucy because she thought she was going to steal Donal from her. Having been orphaned at ten years of age, Annie had some serious abandonment issues. Lucy had bent over backwards to be kind to her, but Annie had been consistently horrible and eventually told Lucy she wished she'd get cancer and die, at which point Lucy had snapped.

Unfortunately Donal had only heard Lucy's side of the conversation and had berated her for losing her temper with an innocent teenager. They'd had a huge argument, which had ended in Lucy packing her bags and going to stay with Emma and James. Donal was so heartbroken that he almost single-handedly lost the semi-final of the Cup by playing the worst match of his life.

However, when she saw how dejected Donal was without Lucy, Annie had realized her mistake in breaking them up: she had come clean and confessed to Donal what a wench she had been to Lucy behind his back. She had apologized to Lucy, and Lucy and Donal had got back together. Although Lucy was still a little wary of Annie, she had to admit that the girl had made a big effort and had almost managed to crack a smile on their wedding day. She hoped things would improve. She would have liked to be friends with Annie and for them to get on well for Donal's sake. That was another reason why she didn't want to get pregnant straight away. She was worried about Annie's reaction. She wanted to get to know her better first and maybe then introduce the idea.

Now Lucy pushed Annie to the back of her mind. She'd worry about all that later. For the moment she wanted to enjoy herself and think of no more than getting a tan. They were a week into the holiday already and she was getting a lovely colour.

When she went to meet Donal in the bar for lunch, he was waving a brochure at her and beaming. 'I've a great surprise for you.'

'What?' said Lucy, warily. She hated surprises, especially Donal's.

'Well, I think we've had enough of this lying around so I've booked us on a five-day jungle trek in northern Thailand. We fly out the day after tomorrow and head off into the jungle with a guide.'

'Are you insane?'

'I thought you'd be pleased. This hotel is lovely but I could tell you were getting restless with all the sunbathing – sure it's fierce boring. Come on, it'll be fun and I booked the best one they had.'

Lucy realized that this was the first test of her marriage. Donal was restless and he wanted to do this trek. She could be selfish and tell him to sod off, or she could agree to go and try to enjoy it. After all, he had spent a week doing what she liked. She took a deep breath. 'OK, but it'd better be a nice trek – no sleeping under the stars or anything.'

'Don't be silly.'

Four days later, Lucy was cycling through the jungle with three Australian tourists and Donal, feeling exceedingly grumpy. In the past few days she had endured having snakes wrapped round her neck, she had trekked for five hours through a jungle full of nasty creepy-crawlies, and now she was cycling uphill in the sweltering midday sun, having been savaged by mosquitoes in the hut they had slept in the night before. The three Aussie blokes were in their early twenties and mad keen to do everything. Donal, in a testosterone-fuelled attempt to keep up with them, had turned into Tarzan, Lord of the Jungle, and was outdoing himself. The day before, despite the fact that he was sunburnt and exhausted, he had insisted on staying up all night drinking with them and playing cards while Lucy lay awake under a torn mosquito net and watched herself being eaten alive. This was not her idea of a honeymoon.

When she finally reached the top of a particularly steep hill, Donal was waiting for her alone. 'Hurry up, slowcoach, the others have gone on ahead. We've been waiting for you for at least twenty minutes. Come on, it's all downhill from here.' With that he turned his bicycle round and took off down the hill.

Lucy followed him and tried to keep up, but she was going too quickly and when she hit a large crater in the road her bicycle wheel buckled and she fell over the handlebars, landing with a thud. At first she thought she was dead, but when she got her breath back and managed to sit up, she realized that no permanent damage had been done and nothing was broken – although the cuts and grazes on her arms and legs were extremely painful. She could see a navy dot in the distance – Donal was miles ahead: he'd never hear her. She'd have to walk the rest of the way.

Half an hour later, she limped into the campsite. Donal was drinking beer with the Australians. He jumped up when he saw her. 'There you are! I was wondering what was keeping you. Beer?'

'Donal!' Lucy snapped. 'A word in private, please.'

'Looks like you're in trouble, mate,' said one of the

Australians, laughing. If Lucy had had the energy she'd have thumped him.

Donal came over to her. 'Where's your bike?'

'My fucking bike is in a paddy-field where I threw it after it threw me over the handlebars. The blood running down my legs and arms is the result of that fall and if you do not get me out of this hell-hole and into a ten-star hotel by nightfall we'll be annulling the shortest marriage in history.'

'Thank God for that. I'm too old to be Tarzan. Come here to me, beautiful,' said Donal, lifted her up and carried her back to the hut to clean her grazes and pack their bags.

Chapter 3

I read through my checklist one more time: bottles and teats (I had an array of sizes because I didn't have a clue which would be right for Yuri as he was small for his age), blankets, vests, Babygros, socks, pyjamas, warm jacket, hats, gloves, a range of outfits in powder blue, navy and red; stripy outfits, denim dungarees, white snowsuit, hundreds of nappies, a small changing mat, baby wipes, powdered formula milk, baby shampoo, soap, lotion, powder, baby toothbrush, toothpaste, comb, thermometer, baby Tylenol, Calpol, small plastic cups, bowls, spoons and bibs, not to mention a suitcase full of toys and a travel cot. This obviously did not include any of my or James's things, which were in a pile in the corner.

James came into the room – which I had painted in an attempt to turn it into a nursery – and surveyed the mess surrounding me on the floor. 'We can't take it all, Emma.'

'We have to,' I said firmly. 'Alexander said we needed to be prepared for all eventualities.'

Alexander ran an agency called Help Is At Hand based in Georgia, in America. When the Irish Health Board finally approved us to adopt, I had gone looking for an agency to match us up with a Russian child and Help Is At Hand appeared to be the most highly regarded. Alexander had matched us with Yuri and given me all the information for our trips to Russia.

James picked up my Jimmy Choos – my beloved only pair. 'I really don't think you're going to need these.'

'I want to look my best when we go to court.'

'It's winter in Russia too. You do realize that they're also in the northern hemisphere? Snowboots would probably be more appropriate. I think the judge will be rather alarmed to see Yuri's mother in strappy sandals in the snow. It could work against us.'

'The judge will appreciate my efforts to look nice in his courtroom. Besides, I looked up the weather in Novorossiysk and, because it's two thousand miles south of Moscow, it's actually quite mild at the moment. Now I'm packing your good suit and shoes too. I want us *both* to look our best for the judge. I'm going to wear this,' I said, holding up a cream wrap dress.

'Emma, you'll catch pneumonia and what good will you be then?'

'Alexander said that the Russians consider the woman as the primary care-giver so most of the court's attention will be on me. I have to look nice. Besides, women are used to freezing for fashion.'

We were both nervous about the trip but neither of us wanted to admit it so we spent the next two hours focusing on trying to squeeze five suitcase-loads of baggage into two. Things came to a head when I jumped on the case to help James close it.

'Jesus Christ,' he roared, 'what are you doing?' He held up a throbbing index finger.

'I'm trying to help, you grumpy old fart.'

'Maiming me is not helping. I asked you to lean on the case, not leap on it.'

'Well, it's closed, isn't it?'

'With half my finger in the lock.'

'Oh, stop being so dramatic.'

James began to breathe deeply via his nostrils – it was a really annoying habit he had when he was angry. He sounded like a rhinoceros. 'Perhaps it would be better if you left the packing to me,' he growled.

'No, I want to help.'

'I'd rather you didn't.'

'Well, tough, because I'm going to.'

'Emma, just let me do it alone. You're not helping.'

'Not helping?' I wailed – I was the hyena to his rhino. 'After everything I've done! Who found Alexander? Who sprinted round Dublin getting all our documents together for the adoption? Who went out and bought all the things Yuri will need when we pick him up? Who bloody well started this whole adoption thing in the first place? I think, James, you'll find it was me.'

James sighed. 'OK, darling, you're right, it was you, and I'm sorry I said you weren't helpful. Now, calm down. You shouldn't be getting yourself into a state. It's bad for the baby.'

'And that's another thing,' I said, crying now. 'I'm worried that Yuri will feel left out when the baby comes. What if he feels like an outsider because he's adopted and the baby isn't?'

'He's ten months old. He won't know he's an outsider.'

'But later on when we tell him he's adopted? What if he feels it then and runs back to Russia when he's eighteen to find his real mother?'

'Are we going to worry about this for the next seventeen years?'

'Probably.'

'By the time he's eighteen Yuri'll be more interested in

getting laid than finding his biological parents – so will you please not get yourself into a state about it now?'

'Do you think he's going to be a heartbreaker?'

'A total stud, just like his father.'

'James?'

'Yes?'

'It'll be OK, won't it? We'll make it work out with Yuri and the baby, won't we?'

'Of course we will, darling. Now, come on, I'm putting you to bed. You need to get a good night's sleep before the flight tomorrow.'

'James?' I said, as he tucked me into bed. 'Do you think Yuri will remember us? A month is a long time in a baby's life.'

'I don't know about me, but there's no way he could forget the first foxy redhead he ever saw,' he said, ruffling my hair.

The next day, Mum and Dad came to drive us to the airport. I felt sick – I don't know if it was morning sickness, pre-adoption sickness or just plain nerves, but I hadn't slept a wink and couldn't face breakfast. I was a wreck.

'You look wonderful, James. Emma, on the other hand, is very peaky,' said Mum, turning around in her seat to examine me.

'I'm fine.'

'Very peaky – isn't she, Dan?'

Dad glanced at me in the rear-view mirror and winked. 'She looks all right to me. It's not as if she was ever sallow,' he said, chuckling.

'She doesn't look well, James. I'm not sure about this long flight to Russia,' continued Mum, acting as if I were deaf or had been abducted by aliens and was no longer sitting in the car.

'It's all right, Mrs B, I'll look after her.'

'Oh, I know you will, James. Sure aren't you marvellous? You've the patience of a saint.'

I counted to ten and bit my tongue.

'She needs to calm down, though. She can't be gallivanting about the place in her delicate state.'

'I'm not gallivanting around the place. I'm going to Russia to adopt my child – and will you please stop referring to me in the third person?' I said.

'What did I tell you? She's totally stressed out,' said Mum. 'Pale, tired and worried. It's no good at all.'

Before I could explode, Dad defused the situation by asking James about the Leinster team and who he was going to pick for the first game of the season. The rest of the car journey was spent with the two men talking rugby, me fuming and Mum tut-tutting to herself.

When we got to the airport we all hugged, and as I was saying goodbye to Mum, she slipped a little bottle of holy water into my hand. 'To bless our little grandson and to bring you all luck.'

I cried into her shoulder, too overcome with everything to speak, while she patted me on the back and James and Dad shuffled about uncomfortably behind us.

What seemed like an eternity later, we landed in Sheremetyevo-2 – Moscow airport to you and me – and were met by the driver we had had the last time. His English was no better than our meagre few words of Russian so a heated political debate was not on the cards. We drove in silence to the domestic airport an hour away. There, we boarded the same decrepit plane we had been on four weeks earlier and spent the next two and a half hours flying to Gelendzhik, near Novorossiysk. Olga, our translator, was waiting for us. It was only when I saw her that I really felt the knot in my stomach begin to unwind. We were here, nearly with Yuri, and Olga was smiling and reassuring us that everything was OK and Yuri was well and the court date was still set for two days' time. Considering that Olga hadn't cracked a smile throughout the whole of our last visit, I felt this was a good omen.

We drove through the trading port of Novorossiysk to the three-star Hotel Novorossiysk. On our last visit we had stayed with a lovely Russian family – the Vlavoskis – in their apartment, but it was a single bed, and while doing the spoons in single beds looks romantic in the movies, in the real world it had meant that I slept with my nose pressed up against the wall and James's backside was hanging out the other side all night. Besides, this time we'd have Yuri with us on the last night, so the hotel seemed a better idea.

Despite being absolutely exhausted, we were desperate to see Yuri so we dropped off our bags and went straight to the children's home. We sat in the draughty reception area waiting for the director to fetch our baby. I gripped James's hand and tried to suppress the sob that was rising in my throat.

The door opened and our beautiful little boy was placed in my arms. His big brown eyes, enormous in his pale little face, looked up at me and blinked. I had to hand him to James because the tears streaming down my face were threatening to drown Yuri. I was just so relieved to see him, and to know that he was still ours. The first time we'd met him he'd been crawling across the floor in a blue romper suit, concentrating on getting to the other side without being trampled by the other children. We had fallen in love with him there and then, so the last four weeks without him had been torturous.

I watched as James gently rocked him back and forth beaming at him and, as Yuri's hand reached up to grab James's finger, I saw my husband's chin quiver. He was as overcome as I. The only time I had ever seen James cry was when he first held Yuri, and now he looked like he was about to do it again.

After we'd spent an hour cuddling and playing with Yuri, the director said it was our son's bedtime. Very reluctantly we said goodnight to him, smothered him with kisses, then went back to the hotel, where we slept properly for the first time since we'd left Russia previously. We were so relieved that he was OK and that everything was still on track.

We woke up early the next day and went straight back to the orphanage to see our son. We spent the day with him and were ridiculously excited at every little movement he made and his reaction to the toys we had brought him. Needless to say, we had treats for all the children, but had kept the best ones for our boy.

When he swayed to some classical music we cheered and whooped. When he didn't finish his lunch, we worried about his appetite. He was quiet with us at first, but after a day with two adults beaming at him, clapping every time he moved and kissing him at any opportunity, he seemed to relax and, once or twice, he even smiled. Not a big broad smile, a quiet, sad sort of smile, but it was enough for us. We talked of nothing except Yuri on our way back to the hotel for the last night we'd ever spend without him.

*

The next morning I was up, dressed and ready for court at seven. We weren't due for another four hours, but I was too nervous to sleep. This was the final hurdle in our four-year journey to become parents, and I just wanted it to be over. I wanted to hear the judge say, 'Emma and James, congratulations, you are now the proud parents of a little boy.' I was worried about the questions the judge would ask me, so I woke James by opening the curtains and asked him to run through the list that Alexander had sent.

James sat up. 'I assume there's no chance that if I asked you nicely you'd close the curtains and let me sleep for another few hours?'

'None. Now, come on, ask me the questions.'

James sighed and looked at the list. 'All of them?'

'Yes. Alexander said they're the likely ones to be asked, although they'll probably only ask a couple of them, but I want to be prepared. Fire ahead.'

'Do you recognize the authority of this court?' said James solemnly.

'Yes, Your Honour.'

'OK. The next question is for us to give our names and address, where we were born and our occupations.'

'OK – move on.'

'What is your educational background?'

I answered thoroughly, although James pointed out that the Russian judge wouldn't really need to know about Mrs Farelly's playgroup when I was three.

'Describe your house, the rooms, the surrounding area et cetera.'

I described it, exaggerating a little when I said our garden was forty feet long when in fact you could barely swing a mouse in it, it was so small.

'You're going to be in court, I really don't think you should lie,' said James.

'I'm not lying, I'm just bending the truth a little. The Russians are used to big open spaces and they'd be shocked if they saw our postage stamp. Anyway, it's not as if the judge is going to turn up on our doorstep to inspect it.'

'All the same,' said James, 'I'd rather you were honest. Just say it's a compact garden, perfect for babies and toddlers.'

'Fine. Next question.'

'The next few ask if we've met the child, what age he is, are we aware of his medical records and will we do everything required for his medical needs.'

'Yes, ten months, yes and yes.'

'Why are you adopting from Russia?'

'Because there are loads of orphans here.'

'Um, I'm not sure about that. I think we should say that, as Europeans, we decided to adopt a child from Europe, and after extensive research we chose Russia because of its wonderful cultural heritage and because of its excellent relationship with Ireland.'

'Brilliant. Next.'

'Why are you adopting and not having a biological child of your own?'

'I'm doing both,' I said, grinning.

'I don't think we should tell them you're pregnant. It could go against us.'

'OK, I'm adopting because unfortunately I haven't been able to get pregnant naturally and I desperately want a family. I think of Yuri as my own child and I couldn't love him more. Adoption to me is just another form of childbirth – it takes longer and is a lot more complicated, but the end result is exactly the same. The joy of motherhood.'

'Good answer, darling,' said James. 'The next few questions are about our hopes for Yuri and how we plan to raise him.'

'We hope that he will have a normal, happy childhood in Ireland and we will give him every opportunity we can.'

'Will you teach him about his heritage?'

'Yes. My husband and I have been learning Russian and we plan to spend all our summer holidays in Russia.'

James grinned. 'That might be a little over the top. Why don't you just say that we plan to educate him about his country of origin throughout his life?'

'Good one.'

'What religion will you raise him in?'

'Catholicism.'

James raised his eyebrows. 'Really?'

'Yes,' I said, surprised that he seemed surprised. 'He's going to be living in Ireland and going to the same school his uncle Sean went to, and it's bad enough that he's adopted without being non-Catholic too. I want him to blend in, not stick out.'

'What about Church of England, like his father? And since when did we decide what school he was going to? I seem to have missed that conversation.'

'James, you never go to church. Nor have you ever shown the slightest interest in anything religious since I first met you, so don't start sticking your oar in now. Besides, Sean's school is perfect for Yuri and it's only down the road.'

'As the boy's father, I'd like to be consulted on decisions involving his religious upbringing and education, but we can go into that later. Next question, what do your family and friends think of this?'

'Well, my mother tried to rugby-tackle me off the plane,

my sister's more interested in her new nose than her new nephew, and my brother is about to marry an Iranian so he's kind of distracted too.'

'This might be the time to practise some of that truth-bending you're so good at,' said James, laughing.

We met Olga and the director of the children's home outside the court. My Jimmy Choos were totally unsuitable and my feet were turning blue as we walked inside. Still, at least the judge couldn't say I hadn't made an effort to dress up. We went into the courtroom, to find the court clerk, a doctor from the Department of Health, a prosecutor and a steno-grapher. A moment later the judge swept in and I was relieved that she was a woman. She had a kindly face and good child-bearing hips – which, hopefully, meant she had a brood of kids at home and would be sympathetic to our cause.

She flicked through our dossier, and then the children's home director gave a short speech in support of our adop-tion. (Olga translated quietly to James and me.) The judge turned her attention to me and asked me if I had seen the child and what age he was. I answered as rehearsed, although my voice was shaking, while Olga translated. Then the judge asked, 'Who will look after your child in case of your death?'

James forgot to ask me that one. I looked at him in panic. I had no idea. Christ, we'd only just found Yuri and the last thing I'd been thinking about was what we'd have to do if James and I were killed in an accident. Give a girl a break – could I not have even five minutes of official motherhood before having to contemplate Yuri being orphaned again and who to leave him to?

James hissed, 'Henry and Imogen.' Henry was his brother

and Imogen his dreadful sister-in-law, but now was not the time to remind James of how much I loathed her.

'My brother-in-law Henry and his wife. They have three beautiful children so they would be the perfect choice,' I said, hoping that this was not going to be an irreversible decision, set in stone in the courts of Russia.

The judge nodded, then asked about the ten-day waiting period and if we wanted it waived. We said we did. The director of the orphanage stood up and said he thought it necessary because Yuri needed medical attention. This was not strictly true – a considerable bending of the truth, in fact – but Alexander had told us that it was the best way to have the ten-day wait eliminated and the director had been happy to help: he said he did it all the time. If the judge said no, we'd have to stay in Novorossiysk for ten days in limbo before the adoption decree became absolute. During that time it could be appealed by the prosecutor – Alexander said it happened rarely, but we didn't want to hang around to find out. I crossed my fingers and prayed that the judge would agree.

She stood and left the room. For the next twenty minutes James and I sat holding hands and praying to God, Buddha, Allah and every other holy representative out there. This was it, the final hurdle. If the judge signed the decree, Yuri was ours for ever. No more waiting and worrying. We could put behind us the years of being scrutinized by gynaecologists, fertility specialists and social workers. We'd be free to get on with the rest of our lives.

The judge came back in. She looked very stern. I thought I was going to faint. James squeezed my hand. She spoke and we listened as Olga translated. I seemed to be swimming under water – everything was in slow motion and Olga's voice was muffled. I looked at James, who was beaming at me.

'It's over, darling, it's finally over. He's ours!' said the besotted father, as I collapsed into his arms.

Chapter 4

We hugged each other, then Olga and the director. I even lunged at the prosecutor – I was ecstatic. When the judge had written up the decree we went to get the adoption certificate and Yuri's new birth certificate, which named us as his parents. We then had to go to the local police station to have Yuri released from the adoption register, and finally we went to the passport office to get his new official passport. After that we raced back to the children's home to see Yuri and pack his things.

He was waiting for us, dressed in the blue Babygro we had first seen him in a month ago, freshly washed and groomed. The carer handed him to me and I held him so tightly that he began to cry and James told me not to smother him. We looked around for his things, but the director said Yuri had no real possessions. Everything in the home was shared between the children, even their clothes. The only thing he said we could take was the tatty little grey elephant that Yuri slept with every night. It was the only thing his mother had left with him when she'd dropped him off at the home.

I have to confess that I was tempted to leave it behind so that Yuri could start completely afresh. I didn't want him clinging to some toy his biological mother had given him – I'd rather he clung to me – but it was important that he had a keepsake, so I said nothing. James and I took pictures of the home so that Yuri would know where we had found him. We photographed his cot and the toys he played with and the other children in the orphanage, and James put a handful of soil from the garden into his handkerchief for Yuri. The director handed us a sheet of paper with notes on Yuri's sleeping habits and what food he liked. Then, finally, we bundled him into his new white snowsuit and headed back to the hotel – parents at last.

Yuri cried all night. We cuddled him, bounced him on our knees, tucked him into the bed with us and fed him milk that he kept throwing up. The director had said that he drank tea laced with sugar when they had no milk – which was quite often, apparently. I was loath to continue to give a baby tea, but we decided to give it a go – anything to calm him down. While James boiled the kettle, I played Yuri the Mozart CD we had brought with us. He continued to howl.

'Do you think he wants to go back?' I asked, as I wiped the big salty tears from his cheeks.

'No, he's just a bit frightened by the unfamiliar surroundings. It'll probably take him a while to adjust. It'll be better when we get him home.'

'How long do you think?' I wanted James to say days. I wanted him to lie to me. I was exhausted – emotionally and physically. I needed reassurance.

'I'd say it could take a while, a couple of months or so.'

I suppressed the urge to join Yuri in a wail. The kettle whistled.

'How much sugar?' asked James.

'It says here he likes three spoons,' I said.

'That can't be good for him. It'll rot his teeth. Maybe we should try it with just half a spoon.'

At this point Yuri had been roaring for over three hours

and the people in the room next door had banged on the wall several times and shouted at us in Russian. It's amazing how similar 'Shut the hell up' sounds in all languages. I was beginning to panic at Yuri's distress.

'James! This is not the time to start weaning him off sugar. Add an extra spoon, for God's sake, anything to calm him down. I don't care if the few teeth he has fall out. He'll grow new ones. Now hurry up.'

James faffed about with the tea, blowing on it and making sure it wasn't too strong or too milky. Eventually I grabbed it from him and placed the bottle to Yuri's lips. He sucked and swallowed. The silence was wonderful. James and I smiled at each other. Yuri didn't want to go back: he was just hungry and cranky.

Eventually we all fell asleep on the bed, fully clothed. I woke up four hours later to the sound of gurgling. I rolled over and saw Yuri snuggled up on James's chest, his huge brown eyes staring at his new father in wonderment. I basked in the beautiful sight. Sensing that he was being watched, Yuri turned his head, looked at me and started to cry.

Twenty-four hours later, having flown to Moscow to pick up Yuri's visa from the Irish embassy, and another fitful night spent with him in our bed – when we got three whole hours' sleep – we were on a flight home. The plane was crowded with other recent adopters and a handful of unfortunate businessmen, who were subjected to the howls of Russian babies unused to their surroundings. Having been removed from their familiar orphanages, the babies and toddlers were now sitting in a big, noisy metal bird with strangers trying to feed them unfamiliar food. They were not a happy lot and I was reassured to see that the other new parents were all looking extremely frazzled too. We smiled and nodded at each other in sympathy.

An hour into the flight and Yuri threw up yet another bottle of milk, so we ended up feeding him more sweet tea to keep him calm. When he continued to cry, we changed his nappy again and bounced and cuddled him as best we could. I had managed to buy some *kefir* (some kind of Russian yogurt, which looked particularly unappetizing), which the children's home director had listed as one of the main foods fed to the children. I spooned it into Yuri's open mouth and prayed it would stay down. The poor little fellow was probably starving.

Thankfully, it seemed to satisfy him for a while and he fell asleep in my arms. At this stage I felt utterly shattered – between being pregnant, the emotional rollercoaster of finalizing the adoption and the lack of sleep over the past two nights. I turned to James: 'You know the way everyone goes on and on about how having a baby changes your life and nothing can prepare you for it and you won't believe the tiredness, blah blah blah?'

He nodded.

'Well, I think I'm beginning to understand. It's only been two days and I feel more tired than I ever have before. I'm a bit scared,' I whispered.

'Don't worry, darling,' said James, squeezing my hand. 'It'll get easier.'

'When?' I asked, trying not to panic.

'Emma, it's only been two days. It's not that bad. Here, give him to me and try to get some sleep.'

I handed Yuri over and closed my eyes. But sleep was not an option – my head was spinning. Bed was my favourite place in the world. I loved my sleep. I'm a nine-hours-a-night girl. I had seen the state of my friend Jess when her kids were born – she was a wreck for months. She always looked exhausted. Was this it? Was it over for me and my bed? Suddenly the elation of motherhood began to fade. I hated myself for allowing negative thoughts to enter my head so soon. It was ridiculous: I was over-emotional and pregnant to boot. It'd be fine. I took deep breaths and told myself to get a grip. But what was going to happen when James went off to work and I was on my own? What if it took Yuri a year to settle in and he just cried all day? I'd have to get help. Mum would help and Jess, and maybe we could get a child-minder for a few hours a week.

We had been so focused on the adoption that we hadn't thought about afterwards. Granted, we had bought a buggy, a changing mat and a cot, and I had painted the room a yellow that had looked nice and soothing in the tin but was a lot brighter on the walls. The fact that it was streaky and looked like a bad DIY job didn't help. I hoped Yuri wasn't averse to yellow. What if he grew up, hated Ireland and buggered off back to Russia as soon as he could? Would he feel left out now that we were going to have a baby of our own? I looked over at him sleeping in James's arms. His little eyebrows were knitted, as if he was concentrating very hard on something. He was such a serious little fellow . . . My heart melted. I would bring laughter to his life. I would make my beautiful son beam with joy. I'd sing and dance and stimulate him in every way I could, so that he never even thought about the miserable old orphanage. James was right: Yuri just needed time to adjust.

When we landed, James collected our luggage and I changed Yuri's nappy, then dressed him in little navy dungarees with a white and blue checked shirt. He looked adorable. Mum and Dad were waiting anxiously for us when we came out of Arrivals. They bounded over to us, and when they saw their beautiful new grandson, they both welled up. Dad began coughing and pretended he was sneezing into his handkerchief as he wiped his eyes. Mum held Yuri and, with tears rolling down her face, she cooed and rubbed his back. He stared at her and gave her one of his half-smiles. Dad took his grandson's little hand and kissed it – I had to turn away because I was sobbing.

As we drove home, Mum pointed out landmarks to Yuri, who was fast asleep in my arms, worn out after the long flight. When we arrived into the house, the fridge was full of organic baby food, and two baby books lay on the kitchen table.

'Oh, Mum, you're a star,' I said.

'Well, you can thank Jess, really. She told me what to buy and she insisted on lending you those books. She said this one in particular is the Bible for modern mothers,' said Mum, rolling her eyes. 'I'm not sure about all these books with their rules and regulations, but if it lives up to its name I suppose it's worth a read.'

I glanced at it – *The New Contented Little Baby Book*. Good old Jess. I'd read it as soon as I had the energy to open it.

'You look worn out, pet,' said Mum. 'Why don't you both go for a lie-down? We'll mind the little fellow for a few hours. You need your rest.'

She didn't have to ask twice. At that moment I loved my mother more than ever before – I was dying for sleep. James and I almost sprinted up the stairs.

Chapter 5

While we were in Russia, Babs had gone to London to meet her new employers and move her things into Sean's apartment. She wasn't starting until January, but the company had asked her to come over just before Christmas to see the set-up and sign her contract. She was staying with Sean and Shadee while she found her feet. Sean lived in a gorgeous two-bedroom apartment in Putney, overlooking the Thames. He had moved to London fourteen years earlier, after graduating from university, to work as a lawyer at Brown and Hodder. Then, four years ago, aged thirty, he announced that he had been made a junior partner and would now have to work twenty hours a day instead of the usual eighteen.

Like me, Sean was ginger – but more of the carrot-and-big-orange-freckles variety – and historically hadn't been lucky in love: he tended to get trodden on. He had a terrible habit of falling in love with beautiful, over-confident women and inevitably got shafted when they found someone else. That is, until he met Shadee, who was a sweet, very pretty maths teacher, who adored him. I was thrilled that he had finally found someone who made him so happy, and although Mum and Dad had been alarmed at first to discover that she was of Iranian origin, they had accepted it now – well, Dad had. Mum was still a work in progress.

Thankfully, Mum had now read more about the culture

and history of Iran and stopped basing her views of the Iranian people on the movie *Not Without My Daughter*. In the film, Sally Field is locked up by her Iranian husband and forbidden to go back to America with their little daughter. It is, to say the least, a very unflattering portrayal of Iran. Also, Shadee had come to visit us in Dublin and had been utterly charming. Sean was still working on persuading Shadee's parents – who were not happy that she was engaged to an Irishman – that he did not have a drink problem and was not, nor ever had been, a member of the IRA.

Babs was still only twenty-four and had spent a year after college swanning about, trying to persuade Dad to pay for a nose job. Eventually, out of sheer boredom, she had tagged along with me to work to see what makeup artists did and whether it was an easy way to earn some cash before she became the Hollywood star she knew she was destined to be. Babs had never suffered from lack of confidence, even with the big nose.

My main job was doing the makeup for Amanda Nolan, the presenter of *Afternoon with Amanda*, Ireland's version of *Oprah* without the famous guests. Amanda was a very glamorous forty-plus – no one knew exactly how old she was – who had never got married and had no children. She thought kids were the scourge of society and claimed that all her friends had changed from interesting, energetic career-women into guilt-ridden, sleep-deprived messes, who got nothing but abuse from the children they so adored and for whom they had sacrificed so much. As far as Amanda was concerned, motherhood was the most thankless job a woman could have, so why bother? She had plenty of affairs and was always dating high-flying businessmen, but never settled down – she was far too used to her independence.

Within an hour of meeting Amanda, the unstoppable Babs had managed to persuade her to run a piece in her show about plastic surgery and to use her as the guinea pig. Babs was happy to have a nose job live on air, if the show paid for it. The producers loved the idea and Babs got her long wished for new nose free of charge. Meanwhile my mother, horrified by the idea of Babs shaming the family on national television, had tried to contact MI5 and the FBI to ask about entering the witness protection programme. It was Babs's exposure on Amanda's show that had landed her the job on the Buy For Less shopping channel.

My mother ended up staying in Ireland, although she did go around wearing dark glasses and a headscarf for a while.

'What do you think?' asked Babs, twirling around in a black micro-mini dress and knee-high black patent boots.

Sean rolled his eyes. 'It's obscene to have that much flesh on show at seven in the morning. Go and put some clothes on. It's a shopping channel, not porn.'

'Piss-off, you bore. Shadee, what do you think?'

Shadee, who clearly didn't want to get drawn into a family argument, was diplomatic: 'You look lovely, but it might be a little too glamorous for a breakfast meeting.'

Babs snorted. 'No offence, but what would a maths teacher know about fashion?'

'If you're going to shoot down our opinions, why bother asking?' snapped Sean. Babs could be a real handful – and seemed to be getting worse with age.

'Would you like something to eat?' asked Shadee.

'No, I don't do breakfast. I'll grab a coffee on the way. Speaking of which, can you lend me some money?'

Sean glared at her. 'What about the money Dad told me he gave you?'

'Duh, you're looking at it,' said Babs, pointing to the dress. 'And please spare me the lecture on wasting money. Just lend me forty quid. I'll give it back as soon as I get paid.'

Sean sighed. He didn't want to fight with Babs on her first morning in the apartment. He'd tackle her later about her spending habits. 'Here,' he said, handing her some cash. 'Call me later to let me know how you get on. Remember what I said. Do not, under any circumstances, sign the contract until I've read it. I did a background check on the company and they don't seem very stable.'

'OK, Granddad. Anything else?'

'Yes. Wear a coat – you'll catch cold.'

Babs hopped on to the tube. The studio was seventeen stops away. Bloody hell! She'd have to find somewhere a bit closer to live or she'd spend her whole time commuting. Still, it would be handy to live rent-free for a month or two, and Sean's place was nice, although he had turned into an old fart. Almost an hour later she arrived at Tower Bridge and within five minutes was strutting through the studio doors. 'Hi, I'm Barbara Burke,' she announced to the receptionist, as if she was Cameron Diaz herself. 'I've got a meeting with Billy Garner at nine.'

'Take a seat,' said the receptionist, not remotely impressed.

Babs sat down and looked around her. It wasn't exactly cutting edge. The reception was a bit shabby – it needed a good lick of paint and some new furniture. Still, they were a relatively new station so they were probably putting all their money into production costs. Babs had only watched the BFL station once and that was the day before when she had arrived at Sean's apartment – she couldn't get it on the TV at home in Dublin. In the few minutes she had watched, two young girls had been modelling necklaces. They were quite attractive – but not a patch on her – and they weren't selling the products as she would be: they were just standing there, smiling inanely into the camera. Billy had said Babs would be talking, modelling and selling.

Ten minutes later, a harassed-looking woman came down to fetch her. She introduced herself as Suzie, Billy's assistant, and showed her upstairs to the boardroom where Billy was waiting. He was in his mid-forties, about five eleven, thick black hair and very fit. But it was his eyes that struck Babs: they were deep blue and slightly slanted, which gave the impression that he was constantly amused. They bored into Babs as she sashayed into the room, brimming with the confidence of youth.

'Hello, Billy, I'm Barbara Burke. Everyone calls me Babs.'

'Hi, Babs, grab a seat,' said Billy, taking in the short skirt and boots.

'It's great to be here. I've always wanted to work in television. It's been my dream since –'

'All right, Babs, love, no need to lay it on so thick. You've got the job. I just wanted to meet you in person and get the contract sorted. I was impressed with you on that Irish show – feisty. We like feisty birds here at BFL.'

'What are the terms of the contract?' asked Babs, trying to sound as if she had done this before.

Billy laughed. 'The terms are – you work when I tell you to and for as long as it takes. This is not a nine-to-five job

43

so you'll be on call twenty-four hours a day, seven days a week. If you're sick, late, bolshie, rude or unhelpful, you'll be fired.'

'What's my job description?'

'You'll make tea when we ask you to, wear and sell what we tell you to, and if after three months you're still here, we might consider renewing your contract.'

'How much do I get paid?' asked Babs, deciding to be equally direct.

'Fuck-all,' said Billy, roaring laughing. 'We'll pay you two hundred quid a week and then, if you're a very good girl, we might throw in some free products.'

'But that's only eight hundred a month.' said Babs, unable to hide her shock. There was no way she'd survive on that.

'Take it or leave it, darling. I have younger, fitter girls than you begging me for jobs. Now, are you in or out? I've got a meeting to go to. Sign here.'

Babs was going to tell him that her brother wanted to look over the contract first, but she knew that Billy would probably kick her out. She hadn't expected him to be so blunt – or good-looking, for that matter. It was a pretty crappy job, but everyone needed to start somewhere and she'd use it as a stepping-stone to getting a proper presenting job on MTV or Channel 4. The competition in London was fierce: she needed to get her foot in the door and some experience behind her. She'd have to live with Sean for a little longer than she had expected.

Billy pushed the contract in front of her and Babs signed.

'All right, Babs, see you in January – and wear something that covers your arse next time. A lot of old people watch our channel and we don't want to give them coronaries. It wouldn't be good for business. Can't buy anything if you're dead, eh? Nice legs, though,' he said, winking at her as he strode off down the corridor.

Later that morning Sean rang Babs.

'So how did it go?'

'Fine,' she told him.

'Do you have the contract?'

'No.'

'What do you mean?'

'It's no big deal. It was very straightforward so I signed it.'

'You what?'

'Keep your hair on. It's only for three months.'

'I specifically told you not to sign anything. These guys could be total bandits. What are the terms?'

'I dunno, just the usual – work hard and get paid weekly.'

'How much?'

'Um,' said Babs, wondering if she should lie, but deciding not to as she needed to stay in Sean's apartment. 'Well, it's a bit scabby – two hundred a week.'

'You idiot,' said Sean. 'That's daylight bloody robbery. It probably won't even add up to the minimum wage. Why don't you listen? Did they cut your brain off along with your nose?'

'Oh, relax, will you? It's just for a few months. I'm not planning on staying long at some stupid channel selling earrings. It'll be fine.'

'And how are you planning to pay rent and live in London on that enormous salary?'

'Well, it looks like I'll just have to stay with you guys for a bit longer.'

'Oh, Christ,' Sean groaned.

Chapter 6

Yuri didn't appear to like his yellow room. Every time we tried to put him down in his cot, he screamed blue murder, so we moved it into our room and he seemed much happier. We had tried several times to give him a bath, but this had caused utter pandemonium. He wriggled, squirmed, kicked his legs and freaked when we put him into the water, so we had to take him out and soothe him. It had now been a week and the only wash he had had was with a wet sponge that I rubbed over him in five seconds flat each morning. We were due to visit the paediatrician in two days' time and I was ashamed to be bringing an unwashed child to see her. I was beginning to feel like a failure. Yuri seemed pretty miserable and I was worried that I was doing everything wrong.

I decided to read the books Jess had left me. I opted for *Secrets of the Baby Whisperer* by Tracey Hogg – *How to Calm, Connect and Communicate With Your Baby*. I'd get to *The New Contented Little Baby Book* later. Right now I badly needed to calm and communicate.

I flicked through the first part until I got to the what-type-of-baby-you-have section. Angel baby – no; textbook baby – no such luck; touchy baby . . . yes! My God, it was as if the author was describing him in person. Ultrasensitive . . . flinches at loud sounds . . . cries for no apparent reason (Tell me something I don't know, Tracey!) . . . has difficulty falling asleep . . . Tracey said that the touchy baby needed to be snuggled and you had to make a sound like sh-sh-sh so he thought it was the splashing of fluid in the womb. Hang on, I thought. Yuri's been out of the womb for nearly eleven months. He won't remember what it was like, and all he's heard since we brought him home is sh-sh, but not because I was trying to re-create swooshy womb noises – because I was trying to get him to stop crying.

Mmmm. I flicked ahead in the book. Oooh, I like this bit. Tracey says that us new mums shouldn't be hard on ourselves. She says we're shocked, exhausted and frightened – too right I am, Tracey – and loving our babies takes time. Hurrah, I'm not alone.

I was feeling marginally better, when the phone rang. 'Hi, how's it going?' asked Jess.

'Actually, I'm finding it all a bit hard.'

'Welcome to my world,' she said. 'Don't worry, it gets easier. Listen, I wanted to see if you'd be keen to join my mother-and-baby group. It's just a few of the girls, and the babies range from three months to two years old, so Yuri will fit right in.'

I had met some of Jess's baby-group friends before – Sonia and Maura. They were incredibly smug, and when I had told them I was in the process of adopting they had more or less implied that adoption would be like wearing someone else's cast-off clothes and they could think of nothing worse than bringing up another person's child. They kept telling me I was very brave. Did I really want to spend time with witches like them? Then again, maybe I'd found them so awful because I was sensitive at the time, and it'd be nice for Yuri to meet other kids: he probably missed his mates from the children's home. Besides, they couldn't all be like Maura and Sonia: the other mothers must be normal, or Jess wouldn't still be going, would she? Also, maybe I'd pick up a few tips on how to bathe your child without social services calling round because they could hear him howling three miles away.

'Um, yeah, OK. That sounds nice.'

'Great. By the way, did you read those books I left you?'

'I'm actually in the middle of *The Baby Whisperer* now.'

'No, Sally you can't watch *Shrek*, it's nap time,' said Jess, to her little daughter. It had always driven me mad when I called her and she spent half the time talking to me and the other half to her children. I never felt she was concentrating on the conversation.

'Sorry, Emma. *The Baby Whisperer* is good, but if you want to get Yuri into a proper routine you need to follow Gina Ford's *Contented Baby* book.'

'OK, I'll try to get to that later – *Stop*, Yuri,' I squealed, as my little boy stuffed my lipstick up his nose. 'Sorry, Jess, gotta go,' I said, beginning to understand Jess's distracted phone behaviour a little more each day.

I plonked Yuri and the ten million toys we had bought him into his playpen – I know some people don't approve of them, but it was the only way I could get anything done and make sure he didn't crawl into the fire or electrocute himself or something. After putting on the third wash of the day – how on earth could one child create so much laundry? No wonder poor old Mrs Walton looked so tired up there on Walton's Mountain with no washing-machine and a brood of kids – I opened *The Baby Whisperer* and tried to find something about bathing your child.

I found it: a ten-step guide to bathtime. I'd been doing it all wrong. Tracey said you need a warm room and some nice music. Fill the bath two thirds full, only slightly warmer than body temperature, and then there was a complicated bit describing the correct way to hold and lower the baby . . . It was clear that I needed help for this, so I read on and waited for James to come home. He had gone out three hours previously, saying he was just popping down to the club to sort out some paperwork. He had sprung this on me while I was changing Yuri's nappy and hightailed it out of the door before I could give him a list of things to do and buy.

When he finally arrived back I was waiting for him. 'Right. Come on,' I said, handing Yuri to him. 'Bathtime.'

'Any chance I could take off my coat first?'

'You've been gone for four hours, during which I have managed to find a solution to the bath problem – not to mention washing clothes, feeding and changing Yuri and attempting to play stimulating games with him.'

'How did they go?'

'Disaster. He ignored me and sat chewing the cardboard box. Anyway, never mind that. Come on, upstairs,' I said, and ushered him up to the bathroom. I had put on my favourite Norah Jones CD and turned the heating up so the bathroom was nice and warm. The scene was set. I handed James a list of pointers I'd copied from the book, and while the bath was filling I asked him to read me the instructions.

'OK, place the palm of your right hand on Yuri's chest and scissor your fingers so that three of them go under his left armpit and your thumb and index finger rest on his chest.'

'Not so fast,' I grumbled, trying to figure out the scissors manoeuvre as James leant over and prised my fingers apart. 'Ouch, what are you trying to do – break my hand?'

'You're going to drop him. Do a proper scissors.'

49

'I'm trying. Read on.'

'Slide your left hand behind the back of his neck and shoulders and gently bend his body forward, transferring the weight of the body on to your right hand. Now place your left hand under his bum and lift.'

I was never very good at following instructions. I had that problem where if someone said go right, I went left. I had sat my driving test six times before they eventually took pity on me and passed me. When we had first met, James thought it was cute. But that wore off when we took a trip down to the west of Ireland where I kept telling him to turn right when I meant left. We ended up being stopped by the police for driving the wrong way down a one-way street. He went from finding it endearing to finding it mind-boggling – he simply couldn't understand how someone could have difficulty differentiating between right and left. I said it was a curse I'd been born with and it was very cruel to be rude about someone's shortcomings.

'No, Emma.' He sighed as I shuffled Yuri from right to left, trying to scissors my hands and hold him under the armpits, the back of the head and the bum. How the hell could I do all three? 'Not left hand – right hand under his bum.'

'I'm doing my best,' I hissed, as Yuri's lip began to wobble. 'Please don't cry, sweetheart, please. I'm trying here,' I said, kissing his cheek as I almost dropped him in an arm-swap-scissors-style move.

'I've got an idea,' said James. 'Why don't you read the instructions and I'll follow them? I think it'd be much wiser.'

'No, I've got it now.'

'Emma, if you put him in like that, he'll drown.'

'Oh, you and your stupid lefts and rights. Fine, take him

and show me how easy it is, then,' I snapped, and handed Yuri over.

James did some swift hand movements and suddenly Yuri didn't look uncomfortable or miserable. 'Read on,' he said smugly, as I tried to hide my annoyance.

'Yuri should be slumped over your right hand in a sitting position, bent forward and lightly perched on your left hand.' Even reading my notes was confusing. Maybe I had copied the information down incorrectly. But when I looked up, James had Yuri in what appeared to be the right position.

'Slowly lower him into the bath in the sitting position, feet first, and then transfer your left hand to the back of his head and neck to support him. Ease him into the water. Your right hand is now free and you should be able to wash him.'

I was frankly amazed to see that he had done exactly as I told him and Yuri was sitting in the bath – not exactly looking ecstatic to be there but not crying either. James smiled. 'Piece of cake, darling. All you need to do is concentrate on the instructions. Pass me the sponge.'

I wanted to ram it up his condescending nose, but decided not to upset Yuri's first bath. 'I'll wash him. You just make sure he doesn't lurch backwards – and stop being so damn smug.'

'It's really not difficult. The instructions are foolproof. You'll get the hang of it.'

'Are you implying that I'm a fool?' I snapped, while softly sponging water over Yuri's hair.

'Of course not. Following instructions is just something men are better at. Mind his ears.'

'I am minding his ears. Just hold him steady.'

'Mind his eyes,' said the ever-helpful, self-appointed expert.

'Will you please stop telling me what to do? I'm the one who read the bloody book and wrote down the instructions while you were shuffling papers at the office.'

'Language, darling,' said James, choosing this of all moments to remind me that we had agreed never to curse in front of Yuri.

'You annoying, irritating, infuriating –'

'And Daddy loves Mummy too, Yuri,' said James, kissing me mid-tirade. 'Particularly when she gets all hot and bothered and rants at him for reminding her of the non-cursing rule she insisted upon.'

Yuri was clearly unimpressed and whimpered so I decided to quit while we were ahead. 'OK, lift him out slowly and I'll wrap the towel round him.'

James lifted Yuri out, talking to him as he did, reassuring him that it was over. I wrapped the warm towel round his little body and he gurgled as James rubbed his back.

James let the water out of the bath while I got Yuri dressed. He looked so sweet in his stripy pyjamas, and as I held him to me, inhaling the scent of body lotion, he snuggled into my neck and I felt a surge of love – it was almost an ache. James looked around and smiled at us.

'I'm sorry for being such a grumpy old cow, but you know how frustrated I get about lefts and rights. It's like a handicap and I don't think I'll ever get the hang of it and I'll never be able to give him a bath on my own and it's just ridiculous because I'm his mother,' I said, getting upset at the thought of my endless failings.

'Emma, it's all right. I'm not going anywhere. We'll do it together until you get the hang of it. However, you might have mentioned that you were handicapped before we got married – a fellow should know these things before he says, "I do."''

Chapter 7

A few days later, James, Yuri and I were sitting in Dr Liz Costello's surgery. She was the paediatrician who had reviewed the video of Yuri we had received before our first visit to Russia. After studying it and looking at his medical records, she had told us that as far as she was concerned he seemed like a healthy little boy – small for his age, but a lot of children who had been institutionalized were under-weight. His senses appeared to be in good working order and he seemed alert. We had been reassured enough to go to Russia and accept Yuri as our match, so she seemed like the perfect person to consult now that Yuri was home.

James and I watched her examine him.

'All his bits are in the right place,' she said, smiling, as a naked Yuri wriggled about under her touch. 'Head circumference proportional to body . . . responds well when spoken to . . . seems very alert . . . good movement, good muscle mass. OK, I'm going to check him now for a range of conditions.'

'Like what?' I asked, suddenly anxious. Although Yuri looked fine, he might have some hidden disease: the social workers had warned us of this possibility, but I had blocked it from my mind.

'Anaemia, strabismus, rickets and HIV, hepatitis A and C. I'll need to draw some blood. James can you hold him steady for me?'

James held Yuri's skinny little chicken leg, while Dr

Costello cleaned his heel with alcohol, then punctured it with a sterile needle. She collected a blood sample, then covered the scratch with a plaster. The brave little soldier didn't even cry: his eyes just widened and his face went a shade paler. James picked him up and soothed him when it was over.

'Good boy,' said the doctor, patting Yuri's head. Then, turning to me, she said, 'We'll send the blood sample to be analysed. I'll know more in a few days. The main problem with children from Russia tends to be based around their diet. The orphanages simply can't provide a balanced one. Often the milk is diluted, lessening the concentration of nutrients. Vitamin D and iron are consistently missing. But don't worry yourselves until we have the results. He looks well anyway, although you two are clearly tired. You look particularly peaky, Emma. How are you feeling?'

I told her I was pregnant and that most food made me want to throw up at the moment, but I was sure it'd pass once I got over the three-month mark. It felt strange to talk about my pregnancy. It still didn't feel real. I was so preoccupied with Yuri that sometimes I forgot about it.

'It's important that you get plenty of rest. The first trimester is key. How many weeks are you?'

'I'm not sure – I think about eleven.'

'You really should go and see your obstetrician for a scan. I'll have these blood-test results for you in three days. I'm closing the surgery for Christmas week, so I'll let you know Yuri's diagnosis before then. Now, go home and try to get some rest. Happy parents equal happy babies.'

We bundled Yuri up and left, feeling nervous but strangely reassured. The blood tests would show up any horrid illnesses that he might have, but Dr Costello had said he looked healthy, so hopefully he would be OK. James went off to supervise a training session and I decided to call in to my mother. 'Helloooo,' she cooed, as she lifted Yuri out of my arms at the front door. 'How's my little grandson today?'

Yuri beamed up at her. I had to confess she was brilliant with him and he seemed to adore her. 'Now, let's take off your coat. Lord, what was your mummy thinking dressing in you in those clothes? She must have been half asleep,' continued Mum. I bristled: I'd spent ages choosing a nice outfit for Yuri to wear to the doctor's. I thought he looked adorable in his little Baby Gap hoodie. When he was settled in his high chair, she turned her attention to me. 'Well, how are you, pet?' Before I could answer, she did it all by herself. 'You look awful – big black sacks under your eyes and as pale as a ghost. You need your rest, Emma. You have to look after yourself now that you're pregnant.'

I wasn't particularly thrilled to be told how crappy I looked. I was well aware of it. Every time I glanced into the mirror I got a fright at the haggard woman staring back at me. 'I know I'm a state, Mum, but Yuri's taking time to settle in. He wakes up at least four times a night and I have to soothe him back to sleep. What can I do? I can't ignore him.'

'No, but you can't give in to his every cry. Sometimes babies cry for no reason and you have to let them at it. He'll fall asleep again in no time. Still, I suppose the last few weeks have been a shock to him. Poor little fellow.'

'We were just at the doctor's having him checked out.'

'And?'

'She thinks he's fine, but she won't know for sure until the blood tests come back.'

'He looks grand to me.'

'I know, but there are a lot of illnesses that children from Russian orphanages can have.'

'Poppycock.'

'No, Mum, it isn't. They told us on the course that it's one of the realities of adopting.'

'Well, at least you won't have to worry about any of that with number two,' she said.

'True.'

'You'll have to do something about your appearance, though, Emma. You can't be letting yourself go just because you're pregnant. Those old jeans are awful on you.'

'Mum, I got about four hours' sleep last night, on top of which I was worried about Yuri's tests. Planning my wardrobe was not the first thing on my mind this morning.'

'Surely you could have found something nicer than that jumper? Why didn't you put on that nice pink shirt you have and tie up your hair. You look like you've been dragged through a bush. It's a well-known fact that if you make the effort, you feel better. Anyone who saw you now would think you'd lost interest in your appearance – and it's not good for a marriage to have the wife going round like the dog's dinner. Mark my words, many's the marriage that went askew when children came along and the wife stopped looking after herself. The husband's eyes start to wander.'

'Well, that's great. Thanks a lot. I called in for some TLC and I end up getting a lecture on how appalling I look and that James is going to leave me, wiry-haired, pregnant and with an eleven-month-old child. I feel so much better now, Mum. You're a real tonic.'

'Dear, oh dear, Yuri, Mummy's very touchy today. It must be the tiredness that has her so grumpy. I hope she's not snapping at your daddy like this.'

'Can you please not do that?' I hissed.

'Do what?'

'Talk to me through Yuri. I hate when people do that. It's incredibly annoying.'

'There's no pleasing you today.'

'Why couldn't you just say, "Hi, Emma, how are you? Sit down there and have a cup of tea and tell me how it's all going," like normal mothers do.'

'Oh, I see. So it's my fault that you adopted a child who won't sleep and it's my fault that you're exhausted? I knew I'd get the blame sooner or later.'

'That's not what I meant. It's just – oh, forget it.'

'Fine,' said Mum, sniffing. 'Have you heard from your sister?'

'She called briefly the other night, but I couldn't really talk because Yuri was acting up. Besides, she only rang to ask me for some money.'

'I'm worried about her. Selling things on the television – what kind of a job is that?'

I decided to go with this conversation – anything to get her off the subject of me, my marriage (which apparently was under threat due to my frizzy hair and tatty jeans), and motherhood. I was quite happy to talk about Babs.

'It's a stepping-stone for what she really wants. If it works out she could end up presenting *Panorama*,' I said, trying to keep a straight face.

'Mmmm, somehow I don't see that Terence McDonald quaking in his boots at the thought of Barbara taking over.'

'Trevor.'

'What?'

'It's Trevor McDonald – and he doesn't present *Panorama*.'

'And how's Sean?' asked Mum, ignoring me. Trevor would for ever be Terence to her, like Gwyneth Paltrow was Glynice Parow.

'Again, I only spoke to him briefly, but he sounded a bit cheesed off. I'd say Babs is driving them mad.'

'What do you mean? Does Sherie not like Barbara?'

'It's Shadee, Mum, and, no, that's not what I said. Babs is a handful – as you well know – and I'm sure it's not easy having her living on top of them.'

'Well, they shouldn't be living in sin before the wedding. You know my thoughts on that one,' said Mum, pointedly. She had not been happy when James and I had moved in together before getting married, although for once – miraculous though it might seem – she had held her tongue because she was so shocked that I had met someone nice, normal, good-looking and successful (truth be told I was a bit shocked myself). However, Shadee's background – i.e. the fact that she was raised Iranian and Muslim (although not practising) – was still something Mum was trying to get used to. Initially she had told her friends that it was a casual thing, that Sean was just experiencing other cultures 'over there in London', but when they'd got engaged, she'd had to change her story. She was now telling her bridge cronies that Shadee was English with a drop of foreign blood. Just as Shadee's parents were probably telling their friends that Sean was Irish but had lived in London most of his life.

'Any news on the wedding? He tells me nothing any more,' she continued, probing me for information. Sean had told me that they were going to have it all booked before he came home for Christmas next week, but I decided to remain vague. I didn't fancy having to listen to a tirade of

'Why couldn't they get married in Ireland? Was it not good enough for them?'

'I think they're still looking around. I'm not sure, really.'

'And would they not look around here? With all the beautiful castles and churches they could have a spectacular wedding. Oh, no, I suppose it's not good enough. It has to be some fancy place in England. I don't know why he wouldn't even look at your cousin Pat's hotel in Wexford. It's a lovely spot.'

Cousin Pat's hotel in Wexford was a dump. Mum had tried to strong-arm me into getting married there, but when James and I had gone down to check it out, the stench of boiled cabbage and the nylon sheets on the beds had been enough to send us hurtling out. Mum thought everything should be kept in the family and I admired her loyalty – but there was no way I was getting married there and neither would Sean.

'Mum,' I said firmly, 'you should be thanking your lucky stars that they aren't getting married in Tehran. Leave it be and don't stick your oar in.'

'I never interfere in my children's lives,' said Mum, looking genuinely put out as I choked on my tea. She fussed over Yuri for a bit, then asked, 'And will all her relatives be coming over from Iran covered with the big black sheets?'

'I don't know.'

'I suppose there's no chance she'll convert to Catholicism?'

'Highly unlikely.'

'But Sean won't become a Muslim, will he?'

'No, Mum, he won't.'

'Well, then, what'll the wedding ceremony be?'

'I have no idea. Maybe a blessing of some sort.'

'In a Catholic church?'

'Or a mosque.'

'A mosque! Lord save us and bless us, that Taliban crowd and your man Osama bun Ladle will be turning up next.'

'Mum!'

Chapter 8

A few days later when James came home from work, he found me on my hands and knees with my finger in an electric socket. 'Wouldn't a bottle of sleeping pills be a more civilized way to go? Less messy,' said our in-house comedian, as he threw himself onto the couch and kicked off his runners.

'Stop, please, you're cracking me up,' I said, poking my little finger further in.

'All right, let me guess. You read that electrocution restores energy to the body. Am I right?'

'No. To cut a long story short I was ironing in the kitchen with Yuri sitting on the floor playing with his toys when the next thing I knew he had his head in the cupboard under the sink, had pulled out the bottle of bleach and was sucking the cap. Once I had recovered from the shock I realized that this house is a danger zone. Tracey says that –'

'Who's Tracey?'

'Tracey Hogg, *The Baby Whisperer.*'

'The what?'

'The book, James! The one that gave us the instructions about bathing Yuri. Anyway, she said that once the baby is crawling, your house must be childproofed and that the best way to do this is by crawling around on your hands and knees and seeing what your baby sees at his level. Apparently there are loads of things we need to be careful of – poisoning, which we almost had today, airborne pollutants, strangling, electric shock, which I was testing when you came in, drowning, burning, falling and bashing into things with sharp corners.'

'Airborne pollutants?' said James, trying not to laugh.

'Yes, James, and I would imagine they include the toxic smell of your sweaty socks, so please either put your runners back on or wash your feet. After that you can prove your prowess at DIY. I have a bag full of clips that need to be attached to all the cupboard doors.'

James groaned. 'Mercy, please. I've just spent three hours at a training session.'

'Well, why on earth did you have to train with the team? You're the coach, for goodness' sake. I doubt Alex Ferguson jogs about in his tracksuit with the Manchester United squad.'

'He's in his sixties and, besides, it's good for me. It keeps me fit. Do we have anything decent to eat? I'm starving.'

'I'm afraid I spent half my day pulping food for Yuri so I didn't cook. You do, however, have the choice of mashed banana, stewed apples and pears or chicken and pasta, also mashed.'

'I'll order pizza.'

'No. I'll order pizza. You get out the screwdriver. Oh, and, James?'

'Yes?'

'You're not planning on leaving me any time soon, are you, because I look like a bag of hammers?'

'I don't know, darling. Between your handicap and your loss of looks, I have strong grounds for annulment.'

'Seriously, though, do I look that bad?'

'I presume I owe this latest attack of paranoia to your mother?'

'The one and only.'

'Emma,' he said, getting down on his hands and knees to talk to me at eye-level, 'with my airborne pollutants, I'm in no position to complain.'

The next day Lucy called in. She was back from honeymoon and, aside from some nasty grazes on her arms and legs, she looked great and was as brown as a berry. I felt like a washed-out ninety-year-old beside her. She rushed in, hugged me, then ran to Yuri, who was sitting in his playpen looking angelic.

'Oh, Emma,' said Lucy. 'He's perfect. Can I hold him?'

'Sure, but I've just fed him so he may burp on you.'

'Who cares?' she said, lifting Yuri and kissing him. She bounced him up and down in her arms and then, as if on cue, he threw up all over her.

'Oh, shoot,' I said, taking him from her and handing her a towel.

'No problem,' she said, as she tried to wipe vomit out of her hair. Lucy was an only child and had no nephews or nieces. Babies were as alien to her as they had been to me – until I found Yuri.

I cleaned him up and put him back into his playpen, surrounded by at least thirty toys. I was hoping for twenty minutes with Lucy before he started acting up. 'So, how was it?' I asked.

'Brilliant,' she said, grinning.

'Oh, God, you're all loved up, and brown and skinny and stunning. If you weren't my best friend I'd hate you. Tell me all. Sex three times a day, cocktails served in coconuts, dinner at sunset on the beach . . .'

'Pretty much all of the above until Donal got bored and decided to book us on a jungle trek.'

I began to laugh. 'Oh, God, how bad was it?'

'Well, these scars on my arms and legs are the result of being flung off my bicycle while I was hurtling down the side of a mountain – the same mountain that I had just cycled up, in one hundred degrees heat.'

'You? Cycling?'

'I know. But I kept thinking, marriage is about compromise, so I agreed to it. Mind you, we left the camp immediately after my fall and booked into the most luxurious hotel in Thailand. So we ended on a high note. Anyway, enough about me, how are you? How's motherhood?'

'It's amazing, and he's such a little dote. I honestly can't remember what it was like before he arrived. I can't believe we have him. He's as much our own child as the next one will be,' I said, getting a little emotional.

'Oh, Emma,' said Lucy, squeezing my arm. 'It sounds perfect.'

'It is – but you know the way you always hear mothers going on about how exhausted they are and how nobody could possibly understand the tiredness unless they'd experienced it first hand?'

'God, don't remind me,' said Lucy, rolling her eyes. We had always thought Jess was exaggerating when she droned on about how tired she was all the time and how we couldn't understand it . . .

'Well, I'm sorry to say that it's true. I never could have imagined how wrecked I feel. My brain has turned to fuzz.'

'Is it really that bad?'

'Mind-blowing,' I said. 'Honestly, Lucy, I hate to be a

bore, but it's true what they say. Mind you, the fact that I'm pregnant as well probably makes it worse. I'm up at least three times a night with Yuri.'

'Your pregnancy is just the best news. I'm so pleased for you,' she said, hugging me again. 'But you need your rest. Aren't babies supposed to sleep all night after a month or two?'

'Apparently, but I think he's unsettled because he's been transported to unfamiliar surroundings.'

'Will he settle down soon?' said Lucy, asking the exact question I wanted answers to myself.

'No idea. But I hope so.'

'What's it like – you know – when you look at him and stuff? I mean, do you just think, Oh, my God, there's my son, I couldn't love him more. Is it really love at first sight?'

'Between you and me, sometimes I want to send him back to Russia on a one-way ticket. Like at four o'clock this morning when he started crying for the third time and I was so tired I wanted to scream. But then he'll smile, or snuggle into you, or sigh, or yawn, or just look at you in a certain way and, I swear to God, your heart just stops. It's overwhelming.'

'Wow. Donal's mad keen to start trying,' admitted Lucy. 'Are you?'

Lucy shook her head. 'Not yet. I want to enjoy our first year or two of marriage without the pressure of trying to get pregnant. I know I'm thirty-six and my biological clock's ticking and all that, but I don't feel ready yet. Besides, I'm not sure how I feel about kids. You know? Sometimes I think I'd like to have one, but other times I don't. One would definitely be enough for me but Donal wants the bloody Von Trapp family.'

'Well, don't do anything until you're ready. Take your

time. Because, honestly, Lucy, once you start, before you know it, you'll be consumed by it.'

'That's just it. I've seen Jess popping them out like a rabbit, and you had such a struggle and it took over both your lives. It took me a long time to meet my Mr Right and get married. I'd like to enjoy it before complicating it with children. Besides, my mother was pretty bad at parenting and my dad did a runner when I was five, so who's to say I'd be any good at it?'

'Lucy, no one's born to this. From what I can see, everyone's just winging it. I think I'm useless at it, but I'm hoping that I'll get better as time goes on. You'd be a brilliant mother, but don't rush into it until you feel ready. Tell Donal to relax.'

She nodded thoughtfully and I looked down at Yuri, who was merrily chewing on Lucy's powder-pink suede Prada bag. He had dribbled all over it and bits of banana were stuck to the side. I reached into the playpen and grabbed it, which made Yuri bawl at the top of his lungs.

'You'll never want kids now,' I said, handing Lucy her soggy bag.

'Don't be silly. I'd better go anyway,' she said, backing out of the door and trying not to examine the damage to her bag in front of me. I waved her off, and sighed. I remembered well calling into people with kids and only being able to last about fifteen minutes before wishing I could leave. I'd have to meet Lucy at night in future. It was important to remember that just because I was besotted with Yuri it didn't mean anyone else was.

When Lucy got home, Donal was back from training.

'How'd it go? Is he gorgeous?'

'Mmm, very sweet,' she said, leaning down to kiss him.

'Jesus, what's that stink? I hope it's not some new perfume.'

'No, it's the lovely scent of baby puke,' said Lucy, grinning.

'Ha-ha! Did he throw up on you?'

'Oh, yes, and then he proceeded to eat my new bag.' She waved the evidence at him.

'He sounds like a great fellow altogether. High spirits – that's what you want from a kid. How's Emma getting on?'

'She looks the worst I've ever seen her. She's utterly exhausted and completely distracted. She says it's all worth it and she's clearly mad about Yuri, but I actually got a fright when I saw her. She obviously hasn't slept in ages. I don't know, Donal, this motherhood lark is definitely not all it's cracked up to be.'

'Well, she's been through a lot in the last couple of years. You'll have no problems – you'll be pregnant straight away. My super-sperm will see to that. We'll have a brood of kids in no time.'

'Donal, you do realize I'm thirty-six, so the chances of us even having two kids are slim?'

'Ah, I reckon if we got going now we'd squeeze at least three in, maybe four.'

'One baby a year might be pushing it.'

'We're bound to have twins. My father's a twin.'

'Donal, I'd be quite happy with just one.'

'One? But sure that's no good. Only children are always spoilt and selfish and loners. There was an awful fellow in school with me who . . .' Suddenly Donal realized what he was saying.

Lucy raised her eyebrows. 'Go on.'

'Obviously there are exceptions to the rule – like you.'

'So I'm not selfish, spoilt or weird?'

'No, not at all. You do like to get your own way, though.'

'Like when?'

'Like when you fecked your bike in a bush and demanded to be taken out of the jungle.'

'And you almost knocked me over in your eagerness to leave.'

'I was only trying to keep you happy.'

'Yeah, right. Anyway,' said Lucy, sighing. 'I like my job.'

'Where did that come from?' asked Donal, looking confused. 'I thought we were talking about the jungle.'

'I've spent fourteen years working my arse off to get to where I am and I'm really good at what I do. I like being respected and being successful in a man's world. I don't want to give it up,' said Lucy, who was a high-flying management consultant.

'But it'd only be for a few years until the kids were in school.'

'Donal, if you take more than two weeks' holidays in my profession, you risk losing your edge.'

'Kids need to have their mothers around.'

'Or fathers.'

'What?'

'Why do I have to give up work? You said yourself you're getting too old for professional rugby and that this'll probably be your last season. Why don't you stay at home and mind the baby?'

'Me? Stay at home? Like a big girl? Lucy, fellas don't do that.'

'Why not?'

'Because they don't.'

'That's your argument?'

'Lookit, girls are naturally maternal. They know how to look after babies – it's instinctive.'

'Bullshit. They get lumbered with it. I can tell you now, Donal, I don't think I'm very maternal. If I do ever have a baby I know I won't want to give up work. I love what I do – it's a huge part of who I am.'

'When it's your own kid, you'll feel differently.'

'I won't. But if you feel so strongly about it, why can't you be man enough to stay at home and mind the baby?'

'Name me one fella you know who minds the kids while his wife works.'

'Be a shepherd not a sheep.'

'Lucy, can you focus on the conversation, please?'

'I am. Why can't you be the first guy we know to do it? Lead the herd.'

'Why don't you join the flock and stay at home like Flossie and the gang?'

'Because, Donal, I'm a shepherd. Are you man or mouse?'

'I thought I was a sheep.'

'We'll get a nanny,' said Lucy.

Chapter 9

Sean and Babs flew home from London on 23 December. James, Yuri and I went to the airport to pick them up. Sean rushed over to hug me and to see his nephew for the first time. He swung him round awkwardly, then sort of patted his back. Babs lagged behind, busy chatting up a good-looking guy carrying a guitar. When they had swapped numbers, she finally trundled over to say hi. 'What do you think?' she asked, nodding towards the aeroplane guy. 'He plays in a band. Cute or what?'

'Hi. This is my son Yuri — the one I've adopted from Russia. Would you like to say hello or are we going to have to analyse some leper you just met on a plane for the next hour?'

Babs rolled her eyes. 'It's good to see that motherhood has really chilled you out.' Then, turning to Yuri, she took his hand. 'Cute kid. Lucky for him he's adopted or he could have been a redhead.'

'Thank you, Babs,' said James, laughing, while I fumed. 'That's the nicest thing anyone has said. You really have a way with words.'

Babs shrugged. 'I'm just being honest. Who wants a ginger baby? I hope the next one,' she said, pointing at my stomach, 'doesn't get Emma and Sean's redhead genes.'

'Well, as long as they don't inherit your nose they'll be all right,' I snapped.

'You can't wind me up about that any more, Emma,' she said, 'it's all in the past.' She wriggled the new one at me. I was tempted to punch it, but didn't want Yuri to witness violence at such a young age.

'Lucky you,' I said, turning to Sean, 'having Babs in your apartment twenty-four-seven. It must be heaven.'

'Joy, the like of which I never knew existed,' said Sean. 'She's a regular ray of sunshine to wake up to in the morning.'

'Not to mention considerate and generous.' I giggled.

'Never stops giving. She was born selfless.'

'Oh, shut up,' said Babs, as the rest of us roared laughing.

On the drive home to Mum and Dad's house, I warned Sean that Mum was sniffing around for information about the wedding. He said it was all booked and paid for, with no room for change or manoeuvre and he'd fill us all in on the details later.

'They might as well be married now,' said Babs. 'They're so dull. I thought they'd take me to all these cool bars and clubs, but all they do is sit in cooking dinner and watching movies or talking about wedding arrangements. *Boring!*'

'Why don't you go out and make friends?' asked James. 'I'm sure the English boys would find you most entertaining.'

'Well, I can hardly go out on my own and sit in bars like a slapper.'

'God, no,' said Sean. 'Someone might mistake you for the type of girl who sleeps with other people's older, rugby-playing boyfriends.'

James and Sean laughed at this, while I tried not to, out of loyalty to Lucy. To cut a long story short, last year, shortly after Donal and Lucy got engaged and had that huge argument about young Annie and Lucy had arrived on my doorstep, devastated because it was all off, Donal, who was equally upset, had gone out and got blind drunk. Unfortunately he bumped into Babs in a nightclub and one thing had led to another. I innocently called over to Donal's the next morning to pick up some work suits for Lucy only to find my little sister strutting about naked, except for Donal's rugby shirt. On hearing me shouting, Donal had woken up from his alcohol-induced coma and got the fright of his life when he realized what he'd done. Although I was furious with him, not to mention Babs, I had decided against telling Lucy as it was clear he regretted it and didn't, in fact, remember it. Besides, I knew he was genuinely in love with Lucy, and shortly afterwards they had sorted out their differences and got back together.

'In case you've all forgotten, he was the one with the fiancée, not me. So if you're going to give anyone a hard time, slag him,' retorted Babs.

'Believe me, I have,' said James.

When we arrived home, Mum and Dad were waiting for us with a lovely big fire burning and food and drink laid out. Dad loved Christmas, and every year the house looked more like Santa's grotto. Yuri was dazzled by all the lights and decorations. He sat on the floor cooing and the Christmas-tree lights flashed – much to my mother's disgust: she thought flashing lights were very tacky.

'Well, how are you both?' asked Mum.

'Great,' said Sean.

'Cool,' said Babs.

'How did the meeting go, Barbara? Did you sign your contract?'

'She stupidly signed her life away for two hundred quid a

73

week even though I told her not to agree to anything until I had looked it over.'

'It's only for the first three months. After that I'll get a raise. But until then I'm going to need you to help me out, Dad.'

Dad shook his head. 'You've bled me dry for twenty-four years and you're on your own now. It'll do you good to learn to budget.'

'*Daaaad!* There is no way I can survive on two hundred quid a week. It'll barely cover my tube pass. Do you want me to live in a hovel with no running water or electricity in some dodgy area *in London* and get mugged coming home at night after a long day's work?'

'I pity the poor fool who tries to mug you,' said Dad, grinning. 'Besides, the last I heard you were living in the lap of luxury with your brother.'

'Who has had enough of her, thanks very much,' said Sean. 'She's out on her ear in January.'

'Ah, Sean, would you not put her up for the first three months until she finds her feet?' pleaded Mum. 'That way you could keep an eye on her. I don't want her getting mixed up with a racy television crowd.'

'It's not just me. There's Shadee to consider, too.'

'Well,' sniffed Mum, 'maybe Shady could go home to her parents for a few months before the big day, like a good Catholic girl would.'

'First of all, it's Shadee – Sh-a-dee. Second, you're going to have to get used to the fact that she is not Catholic, nor ever will be. Third, you seem to have conveniently forgotten that Emma lived with James for two years before they got married.'

I decided to jump in before Mum started having a go at

74

me for being a loose woman pre-marriage. 'Speaking of weddings, any developments with your plans?' I asked Sean, as Mum bristled beside me.

'Yes, it's all booked. April the twenty-second at Abigail House near Brighton. It's a lovely old country manor over-looking the sea.'

'I thought Shady wanted to get married in Cornwall,' said Mum.

'We thought the drive would be a bit long for all the guests travelling from Ireland so we compromised and chose Brighton because it's only half an hour on the train from Gatwick. It's a lovely place, Mum, you'll like it.'

'Is the church close by?' asked Mum.

'What church?' said Sean, evenly.

'The church you're getting married in,' said Mum, digging her heels in.

'There isn't going to be any Catholic church. Shadee is Muslim.'

'She said she didn't practise her faith so I presumed, seeing as you do, it'd be a church wedding.'

'Mum, this may come as a surprise to you but I haven't been to mass in about fifteen years. It's fair to say that neither of us practises our religion, so we're just going to have a blessing.'

Mum looked at him blankly.

'We've found a Unitarian minister who's going to marry us in an open ceremony. We'll have a few general readings and exchange our vows. It should be all over in about twenty minutes.'

'Unitarian, did you say?' asked Mum.

'Yes.'

'Is that some kind of cult?'

'No. Unlike the Catholic Church, which spends most of its time damning other people for their beliefs and life choices, the Unitarian Church welcomes people of any faith, nationality, race and sexual orientation. It promotes freedom in religion, spiritual growth and social justice,' said Sean, sounding a bit like a brainwashed cult member.

Mum stared at Dad.

'I see. Well, that sounds great, but you've not actually joined this church, have you?' asked Dad. 'They haven't asked you to give them any money, have they?'

Sean groaned. 'It's *not* a bloody cult and, no, I haven't converted. It's just a good solution to our very different religious upbringing and it's supposed to keep everyone happy.'

'Shady's lot might be happy but I can tell you now that I'm not a bit of it.'

'You should see her in the apartment,' said Babs, stirring it up. 'She wears a big black sheet with two holes for her eyes and she's always kneeling on her prayer mat, chanting. The only book she reads is the Koran and she thinks Western women are sluts.'

'Well, she might have a point there,' said Sean, glaring at Babs.

'Does she really?' Mum asked, eyes almost popping out of her head.

'Oh, come on, Mum,' I said. 'Of course she doesn't. Babs is just winding you up.'

Mum didn't look convinced.

'Brighton's a great place to get married,' said James, jumping in to prevent a family punch-up. 'I was at a wedding there a few years ago, marvellous location.'

'Young Maureen Doherty's lost another stone on the

Weight Watchers – or is it Unislim? Anyway, like a super-model she is,' said Mum, in one last-ditch attempt to remind Sean that the lovely Maureen down the road – formerly fifteen stone – was now a svelte stunner.

'That heifer,' laughed Babs. 'She'll need to lose another three stone and have a face-lift before anyone would look at her.'

'It's not all about appearance, Barbara,' huffed Mum. 'Maureen's a lovely girl. Well-mannered, quiet, and she was always mad about Sean.'

'Quiet! She's practically mute,' said my charitable youngest sibling. 'She's barely said two words in her whole life – mind you, she was probably too busy shoving cream buns down her gob to work on her social skills.'

My shoulders shook, then Dad and Sean joined in. Babs, egged on, continued, 'And the only reason she's in love with Sean is because he's the only guy who ever spoke to her. All the others were sprinting in the opposite direction, afraid of getting crushed to death by the Michelin woman – but Mother Teresa here used to say hi to her because he felt sorry for her. Really, Mum, if you're trying to tempt Sean away from Shadee, I can tell you it's too late. All they do is stare into each other's eyes and hold hands on the couch. It'd make you sick. You'll need to come up with someone a bit more attractive than old Thunder Thighs from down the road to split those two up.'

Even James, who had never met Maureen – pre- or post-Weight Watchers – was laughing now.

Yuri chose this moment to crawl over to the Christmas tree and try to pull it down. I managed to swoop him out of the way before it fell and ruined all Dad's work. He bawled as I lifted him to the safer side of the room.

'Is that it?' Babs asked me.

'What do you mean?'

'Is that all he does – eat, shit and cry? Doesn't he do stuff, like walk and talk, yet?'

'He's not even one. What did you expect? A performing seal?'

Babs shrugged.

'Oh, and by the way, in case anyone's interested, Yuri got his test results and he's fine. He's anaemic and needs lots of iron over the next few months to build him up, but nothing serious. When you think of the list of conditions he might have had – Aids, foetal-alcohol syndrome, rickets – we're relieved.'

'Of course we were going to ask,' said Mum, 'I just got distracted with the others coming home. Didn't I tell you my gorgeous grandson was as healthy as the next fellow? Come here to me, pet,' she said, and took him from me for a cuddle. 'You're the only sane one in this room. I hope you don't give your poor mother as much trouble as these three have given me. Skitting at poor old Maureen and she starving herself on those milkshake dinners, staggering around the neighbourhood doing that power-walking with big weights attached to her ankles. Sure the poor girl can hardly lift her legs . . .'

Chapter 10

Lucy, Jess and I met up for a pre-New Year drink. We hadn't been out together since Lucy's wedding, so we were looking through her photo album.

'God, Lucy, you were just stunning,' I said, staring at a photo of her looking particularly radiant.

'Did you enjoy it?' asked Jess.

'Loved every second,' beamed Lucy.

'And how's married life so far?'

'It was all going swimmingly until Annie came home for the school holidays.'

'She's not being rude to you again, is she?' I asked.

'No, but let's face it, guys, she's never going to love me. She's polite and, in fairness to her, she's making a big effort, but she wants to have Donal to herself. She resents me being around all the time. And she's terrified we're going to have a baby. She keeps staring at my stomach and asking me if I feel sick or tired. I actually feel a bit sorry for her. She obviously thinks that if we do have a child, she'll be completely sidelined.'

'It must be hard on her, being an orphan,' I said, thinking of Yuri.

'Yeah, but she's lucky she has Donal and Lucy to look after her,' Jess said. 'Speaking of pregnancies, how's yours going? How have you been feeling?'

'Fine. Well, absolutely wrecked, to be honest, and still a bit sick – although strangely I feel worse in the evening than the morning. I don't know if the tiredness is Yuri not sleeping or the pregnancy. It's all a bit mind-blowing. I don't know if I'm coming or going.'

'How many hours is he sleeping?' asked Jess.

'It varies. Sometimes he might go six hours in a row, other nights he's up every two.'

'Have you tried the *Contented Baby* routine?'

'Oh, come on,' groaned Lucy. 'Spare me the bloody contented-baby-book chat.'

'Sorry, Lucy, but I'm desperate for tips. I need sleep. I haven't done the routine in that book, Jess, because it seems a bit draconian,' I confessed.

Jess raised her eyebrows. 'Well, if you want Yuri to sleep through the night, it's the only way. My entire baby group swears by it.'

The truth was that I had read Gina Ford's book and her plan had seemed – to put it mildly – Fascist. It went something like this: by seven a.m. the baby was supposed to be awake with his nappy changed and ready to be fed. But what if Yuri was asleep at seven – was I supposed to wake him up? Was she insane? Every second of extra sleep was vitally important to my sanity.

Then the book said that the baby's breakfast was to consist of a full bottle of milk, plus cereal and fruit. At eight a.m. he was to be encouraged to wriggle about on his play mat for twenty minutes, after which you washed and dressed him. But it took me ages to feed Yuri – he spat most of it out so breakfast lasted about an hour by which stage we were both covered with food and exhausted. I usually took him back to bed with me for an hour . . . besides which I didn't have a play mat. Wasn't a bed with lots of toys in it almost the same thing?

80

Then at precisely nine a.m. – not a minute sooner or later – we were supposed to settle the baby in his sleeping-bag in a darkened room with the door shut for thirty-five minutes. Well, I liked the sound of that, but if I put Yuri back in his sleeping bag and shut the curtains he'd go mental. Sure he'd only been up a short while. Maybe I was reading the instructions wrong. Maybe they were just a guideline. But Jess had said that you had to follow them exactly and Gina seemed to be pretty precise about how to manage your time.

At nine thirty-five you were to enter the room, open the curtains and undo his sleeping-bag. I wonder why she was so hung up on thirty-five minutes. Why not half an hour – or even forty minutes? Thirty-five is an odd number. Maybe it was an American thing.

By ten a.m. the baby was to be fully awake – did that mean you were supposed to spend the twenty-five minutes between the nine thirty-five and ten getting him to wake up because he was so sleepy? I was confused now. Then it was recommended to have the baby down again on the play mat for more kicking, or taken out for a walk. What about calling into a friend's house? Was that OK? It wasn't mentioned, so maybe that would mess up the routine. Did you get to go and meet people at any point? I read on.

At eleven forty-five you fed him again, then at twelve twenty you closed the curtains and shut the door again while he napped. At two thirty you were to re-open the curtains and feed him. At four fifteen you changed his nappy. How can anyone be so precise about changing a nappy? What if he had a big dump at three fifty-two? Did you have to wait the twenty-three minutes before you were allowed change the nappy? Seriously, this was like army camp.

We were told to feed the baby at five, give him a bath at six – whether ducks were allowed in the bath with him, I'm not sure. At six thirty the baby was to get a bottle and then at seven you put him down, curtains and door closed while he slept for a blissful twelve hours. Yeah, right, in whose fantasy world?

While I would welcome twelve hours' sleep a night, the timetable was so rigid that it left my head spinning. The day seemed to be taken up entirely with feeds, nappy changes, kicks in the air and the opening and closing of curtains and doors. I wondered if Gina had been GI Gina in a former life, or maybe she was a US Navy Seal. 'Maybe I'll try a milder version,' I said.

'No, Emma. If you're going to do it, do it by the book. It works. Gina Ford is a genius. There's a reason why it's a bestseller. Yuri would be happier if he was in a proper routine.'

'He is happy,' I said defensively.

'I know, but he'd be more settled if you created a properly structured day. It seems a bit haphazard.'

'Well, I'm still trying to figure out what he likes. Half of what I feed him – Gina Ford recommended or not – he pukes up.'

'I can vouch for that,' said Lucy, laughing.

'He spent the first ten months of his life in a children's home routine,' I continued, 'and suddenly he was reefed out and taken to a strange place, full of strange people, talking a strange language. He's just taking a while to adjust. He doesn't nap on demand. It's not so easy with adopted children. You can't force them – it has to be gradual.'

'But Gina Ford has dealt with all kinds of cases, Emma, and she still advocates a strict routine for babies.'

82

'Can we please stop talking about Gina bloody Ford and her routine? It's really boring,' said Lucy.

'I promise this is the last baby question,' I said. 'Is Cow & Gate the best baby food you can buy?' I asked Jess.

'Definitely. I swear by it. Most of the other mothers cook their own organic dinners and freeze them, but I'm lazy,' she said, a bit guiltily.

'Where and when are you supposed to find the time?' I asked, shocked that anyone would feel bad about not cooking meals. There wasn't a second in the day when I wasn't burping, playing, feeding, changing, washing or trying to stimulate Yuri. 'I've only ever really cooked fruit. By the way, did I tell you he got two new teeth last week. They're so cute.'

'Emma,' said Lucy, accusingly, 'you said you'd never turn into one of those mothers who talk about their kids all the time.'

'Sorry, but honestly, Lucy, if you saw him smile now you'd – OK, I'll shut up,' I said, suppressing my urge to describe in detail my son's two new teeth.

'Are they at the front or the back?' asked Jess.

'Kind of on the side.'

'I remember when Roy got his – it's such fun to see them all popping through – apart from the rivers of dribble that come with them,' she added.

'Somebody shoot me now. Come on, guys, give me a break. It's odd man out here,' groaned Lucy.

'You could join the club,' said Jess, grinning.

'Don't do that. Don't pressure me just because you've got kids and now Emma's got one too,' said Lucy, grumpily. 'The social pressure's bad enough. People in work and my mother keep telling me to hurry up and get on with it –

after all, I'm thirty-six, no spring chicken, biological clock about to shut down ... God, it was bad enough being considered a freak because I wasn't married and was heading towards my mid-thirties, but now that I've got that one sorted, I'm supposed to have kids ASAP. When do I get to enjoy being a newly-wed? I've waited a long time for this – I want to savour it for a while before I clutter it up with kids. Besides which – brace yourself, Jess – I'm not sure I want them. Which, apparently, makes me even more of a freak than a non-married mid-thirties career-girl.'

'But don't you think having a mini-Donal would be great?' said the earth-mother.

'Are you insane? One Donal's bad enough. Two would be a nightmare. Why does everyone assume that the minute you get married you're going to have kids? When does it stop? If I have one kid, everyone will want to know if I'm going to "go again". And then – God forbid – if I have two of the same sex, I'll be tormented about having another in the hope of producing a child of the opposite sex. And if – horror of horrors – I have another child of the same sex, people will feel desperately sorry for me and I'll become "poor Lucy with three girls, or boys". Not to mention that I'll have to give up my job, because you cannot do what I do at my level unless you're in the office ten hours a day, minimum. So I have to give up what is a huge part of my identity, to wipe noses and clean arses.'

Yikes! I'd had no idea how strongly she felt about it. I knew Lucy had reservations about diving into motherhood, but I hadn't realized how important her career was to her. She was a real high-flyer and I could see how hard it would be for her to give up that power and success. She was right about the pressure to have children: I had been tormented when James and I first got married and had found the questions invasive and annoying.

She continued to rant: 'I slaved to get where I am today. But apparently, because I'm "old", in fertility terms, I'm supposed not to care about my career. Well, I'm sorry but I do. Shallow though it may seem to you besotted mothers, I love my job. I love being successful and earning good money. But if I have a child I'll have to give it up or get a full-time nanny and never see the baby, which defeats the purpose of having it in the first place. Besides, I don't think I'd be very good at it. I do mind having puke and mushed baby food on my clothes. The thought of changing a nappy makes me want to gag and, I'm sorry, guys, but I find kids really boring until they can talk. And mothers who talk about their kids all day are equally so. But, as you can see, I don't really have an opinion on the subject,' she said, smiling ruefully.

'Oh, God, Lucy, have I turned into a bore already?' I asked.

'Well, no, but you're definitely heading that way,' she said, grinning as she waved a finger at me. 'And you promised you wouldn't.'

'What about me?' demanded Jess.

'No, you're fine too. In fact, you're normally really good because I only ever see you with Emma – who, until recently, wasn't interested in talking about kids either. But now that you both have children, I'm seeing another side creep in. Look, it isn't that I'm not interested, of course I am – your children are part of who you are – but after half an hour it gets kind of dull. At that stage I'd like to talk about other things. You'd feel the same if I talked at length about my job.'

'OK, no more baby talk. What'll we talk about instead?'
I asked, eager not to become a boring, one-dimensional
mother.

We tried to think of a subject.

'I went for my first scan the other day,' I announced. 'Oh,
sorry, baby talk again,' I said, realizing my faux-pas.

Lucy laughed. 'It's fine, I'm genuinely interested in hearing
about that. How did it go?'

'Are you sure?'

She nodded.

'It was great. I was really nervous, actually. I've been so
distracted with Yuri that I haven't focused on my pregnancy,
but when I was sitting in the obstetrician's waiting room,
I suddenly realized the enormity of it and got all emotional.
By the time he did the scan I was a sobbing mess – even
though all I could see was a fuzzy black blob. And then Dr
Philips let us hear the heartbeat, and that was when it became
real. Even James looked a bit choked up. I can't really
believe it's happening. We've been so blessed this Christmas,
it's almost scary.'

'Oh, God, don't do that Irish-Catholic-guilt thing,' said
Lucy. 'You deserve happiness. You went through hell to
adopt Yuri and to get pregnant. Enjoy it. What is it about
us that whenever things go really well we get the fear and
decide that something horrendous is about to happen? We
actually expect to get mown down by a passing car and spend
the rest of our lives in a wheelchair, instead of enjoying the
good things in a guilt-free oblivion.'

'It's the religion thing. You're constantly hearing how the
poor and downtrodden get to heaven first and the happy,
contented lot will be at the back of the queue,' said Jess.

'Speaking of religion, was Jesus really shagging Mary

Magdalene?' I asked, having recently read an article about *The Da Vinci Code* that claimed they were up to all sorts.

'Apparently so.'

'The local hooker?'

'Yep.'

'His mother must have been devastated – and her with the virgin birth.'

'I never really got that,' said Jess. 'I mean, Mary was married to Joseph, so how could she have been a virgin? Did the angel come down on their wedding night and say, "Hold that thought, Joseph, we need to borrow your wife's womb for a few months. After that she's all yours"?'

We giggled.

'Do you think they had kids after Jesus?' I asked.

'I'd say it's highly likely,' said Lucy.

'So there could be descendants of Jesus's brothers and sisters running around.'

'They'd have been half-brothers and -sisters because, as we know, Joseph wasn't involved in creating Jesus,' Lucy reminded me.

'Good point. But what if Jesus and the bold Mary Magdalene had kids? They'd be direct descendants,' I queried.

'Imagine Jesus being your father,' said Jess. 'The pressure on you to be good would be unbearable. You could never misbehave.'

'And your granddad would be able to see you wherever you were and whatever you were up to – because as we know . . .' I paused.

'God is everywhere!' we chanted.

Chapter 11

Two weeks into Babs's so-called job, and all she had done, apart from making copious cups of tea, was sell packets of ten 170-gram frozen steak burgers for £20.45, much to her embarrassment. She hadn't had her nose done and moved to London for that crap. She was thinking of complaining to Billy when she arrived into the office to find it in disarray. Sophie, the top salesgirl, had broken her arm while promoting a new trampoline and was now on her way to hospital. Billy was in a flap because they were due to sell a new range of blow-up beds and the American company – Sweetie Dreams – had specifically asked for Sophie to partner their male model, Randy, to shift the merchandise. Babs saw an opening and dived in head first. 'I'll do it,' she announced, as she was handing Billy a mug of tea. 'I look a bit like Sophie and, as my dad always says, I could sell ice to the Eskimos.'

'You've only been here a week and this is a scripted piece,' said Billy.

'Two weeks, actually, and how complicated can the lines be? I'm a college graduate, not some page-three bimbo.'

Billy wasn't sure. Babs was a bit of a live wire. Mind you, she did look like Sophie and she had a good personality and, more importantly, this needed to be filmed now or he was up the Swanee. 'OK, but don't vary from the script. Keep it nice and enthusiastic without being over the top. Go to Wardrobe and put on some pyjamas. I need you ready in twenty minutes.'

Babs skipped down the corridor. In Buy For Less TV terms, this was a big job. If she made a good impression today Sophie'd be out of a job by the time her plaster cast was off.

Twenty minutes later, Babs and Randy were lying on a large inflatable bed. Randy was one of those over-muscled, vacant-looking Californians with a thick-set jaw, sunbed tan and bleached teeth. He wouldn't have looked out of place on *Baywatch*, jogging alongside David Hasselhoff.

'Do you know your lines?' Billy asked Babs.

She nodded. She'd glanced at them while the wardrobe girl tried to decide between red, lilac or pink pyjamas. The script appeared to consist largely of oohs and aahs. No big deal.

'Follow Randy. He's an old pro,' instructed Billy.

Babs looked at Randy, who almost took her eye out by smiling at her. The reflection from his teeth was offensive. He was wearing a very tight blue T-shirt and spray-on red shorts. Babs was in pink fluffy pyjamas with bunny rabbits on them. She felt ridiculous. She had tried to persuade Billy to allow her to wear a skimpy little black négligé.

'Look, darling, I've told you before, our audience is largely made up of retired old fogeys or bored housewives. The oldies would be shocked by a display of so much young flesh and the housewives want to look at a safe, sweet girl-next-door, not some sexy vamp who's going to make them feel guilty about the plate of chocolate digestives they're about to scoff.'

'Well, maybe I could bring in a whole new audience of male viewers,' said Babs, raising an eyebrow suggestively.

'You're not that fit, love. Now, come on, on your back and don't forget to mention the product name as often as you can,' said Billy, grinning as she lay down on the bed.

'OK, you're on in ten, nine, eight, seven . . .' shouted Billy.

'Hi, everyone I'm Randy and this is Babs, and we're lying on the awesome new Slumber-Puff from Sweetie Dreams. The incredible air-mattress from America's top manufacturers. Isn't it comfortable, Babs?'

'Oh, it's just fantastic, Randy, I could go to sleep right now,' said Babs, hamming it up for the camera.

'When you have relatives come to visit, are you going to make them sleep on an uncomfortable camping mattress?' Randy asked Babs.

'No, Randy, unless you really dislike them, that is,' she said, as they both fake-laughed – although she wasn't sure that Randy *was* faking it: he looked genuinely amused.

'So, what *are* you going to do?' he continued, staring into the camera and shrugging. 'You don't have a spare bed and your storage space is limited. It's a serious problem.'

'Yes, Randy, it is. After all, you want your visitors to be comfortable and, let's face it, you can't put your in-laws to sleep on the floor,' said Babs, beaming into the camera.

'No, you can not, and that's where Slumber-Puff comes in. You simply inflate the mattress with this easy-to-use foot pump and the bed lifts you six inches *off* the floor.'

'Six inches!' said Babs, mouth open. 'No way! But that's impossible!'

'Not with Slumber-Puff,' said Randy, as he took out a measuring tape and showed the braindead folk at home that it really was six inches. Randy was as honest as the day was long.

'Wow!' exclaimed Babs, seizing the edge of the mattress. 'It's incredible! Slumber-Puff really does feel like a bed! You're so high up. It's not like sleeping on the floor at all.'

'Correct,' agreed Randy. 'No dust, bugs or germs are

going to get you up here. And the amazing part is that Slumber-Puff deflates into this compact piece of flat rubber,' he said, holding up a deflated version of the wonder-mattress.

Babs shook her head. It was too much good news in one go. 'It's so neat and easy to store.'

'No more cluttering up your closets with bulky foam mattresses or uncomfortable camping beds, Slumber-Puff deflates to an amazing thirty by thirty inches, so it'll fit into a regular drawer!'

'Far out!' exclaimed Babs, in an over-the-top imitation of one of the kids from *Fame*. 'And I have to confess, Randy, I'm amazed at how comfortable the Slumber-Puff is. It feels so firm.'

'It's as firm as an ordinary mattress, and I'd like to demon-strate that now for our viewers. So, Babs, why don't you lie down there and get some rest and I'll put the Slumber-Puff to the test?'

Babs lay down on the incredibly uncomfortable bed and closed her eyes, with an expression of ecstasy – she was determined to impress.

Meanwhile, in the corner, old Randy boy was limbering up, stretching and flexing his muscles. Babs was lulled into a false sense of security, thinking Randy was going to bounce gently on the bed while she 'slept' peacefully with her back to him. Randy, clearly a former interstate gymnast of some sort, came charging over from the side of the studio, threw himself into a cartwheel and landed feet first on Babs's hair, almost ripping it out of her head. It took every inch of her self-control not to scream. Then he proceeded to backflip several times as the blow-up mattress bounced violently up and down, almost throwing Babs overboard as she clung to

91

the side, pretending to be in a deep sleep. As Randy leaped, bounced and flipped about, determined to convince the viewers that this was a sturdy bed, he kept up a steady stream of breathless commentary.

'You see, folks, the Slumber-Puff mattress is so solid and sturdy that I can be doing all this while my girlfriend sleeps soundly beside me.'

As Randy saw the countdown for the ad break, he decided to outdo himself with one final giant backflip and, just as they cut to ads, crashed onto Babs's head. She shot up, grabbed him by the ankles and flung him on to the floor. As she stared at the clumps of her hair that lay in sorry piles in the middle of the mattress, she lost her cool. '*You fucking moron!*' she screamed, at the winded Randy. 'This isn't the bloody circus. You nearly took my head off, not to mind all my bloody hair. I'm practically bald! On top of which you landed several times on my right hand, which I now think is broken,' she said, peering down at it.

'All right, Babs, calm down. No need for violence,' said Billy, rushing over. 'You're doing really well. Just a bit more to go,' he said, smoothing what remained of her hair down and gently guiding her back on to the bed. We're back from the break, and ten, nine, eight . . .'

'Wake up, honey,' said Randy, shaking a still fuming Babs. 'Did you feel any of that activity?'

'No, it's awesome. I actually fell asleep,' said the future Oscar-winner, yawning as she smiled up at Randy, trying to ignore the throbbing in her head and hand. 'Were you beside me the whole time?'

Randy grinned into the camera. 'You see, folks? It's really that effective. And to prove it to you again, I'm going to ask Babs to join me in some jumping.'

With that, Randy grabbed her hands and jumped up and down like an excited kid with Babs in tow. 'Come on, Babs, higher,' he said. 'Isn't this fun?'

'Oh, Randy, I can't remember the last time I had so much fun. This Slumber-Puff mattress is the best,' said Babs, trying not to wince as Randy's full bodyweight thudded onto her feet.

'Do you think our viewers are going to be impressed?'

'I don't see how they couldn't,' puffed Babs. 'I'm going to order one now for myself, because I know these Slumber-Puff mattresses are going to fly out of the door, especially with the four easy payment options.'

'Exactly!' said the clumsiest acrobat in America. 'This incredible mattress – code five four three nine five two – can be yours for the unbelievable price of three hundred and forty-three pounds eighty, or eighty-five ninety-five per month, payable in four monthly instalments. With limited stock available I wouldn't wait around to order. Would you, Babs?'

'No way!' wheezed Babs, as her lungs threatened to explode. She hadn't done so much exercise in years. 'With our thirty-day money-back guarantee, it's a no-risk purchase. Besides, who could resist this bargain? Order now by phone, or for our interactive viewers, just press the red button on your remote control now.'

'Book now to avoid disappointment,' said Randy, as Billy called it a wrap.

Babs collapsed in a heap onto the bed. Thank God it was over. This selling lark was a lot more difficult than it looked.

'Well done, partner,' said Randy, holding out his hand.

'You big clumsy fool, you've crippled me for life,' snapped

93

Babs, and limped off the set to put ice on pretty much every part of her body.

Ten minutes later, Billy came in, grinning. 'What's so funny?' asked Babs.

'Those mattresses have been selling like hotcakes and we've had several calls to compliment our lovely new Irish presenter with the sweet smile and honest face. If only they knew what a little vixen you are.'

'I told you I was good at selling,' said Babs, cheering up. 'Do I get commission?'

'Don't push your luck, love. And next time try to be nicer to our American colleagues. Randy can't help being a bit thick. It's all the steroids he's been taking – they've fried his brain.'

'What time do you want me in tomorrow?'

'Come in for eleven. I've got some gardening products I need to shift. If you can persuade people to buy them, I'll give you Sophie's regular slot.'

Babs leant back in the chair and grinned. Things were looking up.

Chapter 12

Mid-January, I received a call from Amanda begging me to come back to work. She said my replacement was useless and made her up like a clown. She wanted me to come in and make her look fabulous again and she wouldn't take no for an answer. She even offered me a significant raise and had found some crèches near the studio where Yuri could go while I did her makeup.

I have to confess I was chuffed when she called – I'd been worried that the girl who'd taken over from me would be brilliant and that my contract wouldn't be renewed. I loved the job and I was getting a little bored hanging out with Yuri on my own all the time. The good thing about Amanda's show was that it aired between one and three, so I finished early every day, which meant I could spend most of the morning and the late afternoons with Yuri. But I was loath to dump him in a crèche seven weeks after moving him to Ireland, so I decided to ask Mum if she'd help out until he was more settled.

'Hi.'

'Hi, how are you? How's my favourite grandson?'

'Good, thanks. Actually, Mum, I'm phoning to ask a huge favour.'

'Oh?' she said, sounding suspicious.

'Amanda has asked me to come back to work – well, she begged me, actually – and has offered me a raise, which is great. But I think it's a bit too soon for Yuri to go to a crèche so I was wondering if you'd mind him between twelve and half three for me. It'd just be for the first few weeks and I'd pay you.'

'How much?'

I hadn't thought she'd accept payment. I had presumed she'd be delighted to spend time with Yuri. I'd only offered because I thought it sounded good.

'Oh, um, how about twenty euro a day?'

'Those poor children in the factories in Thailand earn more than that.'

'Twenty-five?'

'Thirty.'

What had happened to the doting granny? Suddenly I was dealing with a hard-nosed negotiator and was 150 euro a week poorer, which negated the pay rise and left me with less money than I was originally paid. Still, I didn't have a choice.

'OK, thirty, then,' I grumbled, 'but it seems a lot.'

'Believe it or not, I have a life, Emma. I don't just sit around here waiting to look after Yuri. I'll have to rearrange my Tuesday bridge meetings and my book club, so don't assume I'm a twenty-four-hour nanny service. If you want me to change my life round, you have to make it worth my while. I won't be taken for granted. I've raised my three children already, thank you very much. I'm doing you a favour here so don't begrudge me a few euro to help you out.'

I decided to jump in before I got the nobody-appreciates-me speech, which was an old favourite. 'OK, fine. I appreciate your help and I'm not taking you for granted and I don't mind paying you. I'm delighted you'll be looking after Yuri. He adores you and you're brilliant with him.'

'Yes, well, I was always good with children. I never had any help with you three, I raised you alone while your father was working and studying. It's important for a child to have its mother around for the first few years.'

'I know, Mum, but I'm only leaving Yuri for a few hours a day and the extra money will come in handy, especially after the adoption costing twenty thousand euro,' I said, playing my ace. Mum had been appalled: she thought it was disgraceful – as did I – that people who wanted to give orphaned children from other countries a good home should be charged any money, never mind an astronomical sum. I also thought it might make her back down on her daily rate.

'It's despicable that they charge to much. When I told my bridge-club girls they couldn't believe it. Shocked they were. You'd think the Russians would be paying you to give their little babies good homes. Anyway, when do I start my new job?'

'Monday, if that's OK.'

'That's fine. It gives me a few days to sort things out. And I'd like to be paid weekly, in cash.'

The next day Jess called to say that her mother-and-baby group was meeting at Sonia's house the following morning, and did I want to come? I decided to go along. I thought they might give me good tips on childcare options and what was best for young babies – crèches or one-on-one child-minders? I couldn't rely on Mum to look after Yuri long-term: it wasn't fair on her and, considering her rate, it was no bargain for me either. It'd be helpful to get some information from other mothers.

Sonia lived in a mansion with electric gates that swished back to reveal a long, pebbled driveway full of silver jeeps

– I had never seen such a variety before. You'd have thought we lived in the Kalahari desert, not the capital city of Ireland. Rangers living in safari parks would have considered those monstrous lumps of steel too big for their needs. I parked my small second-hand car in the corner of the driveway and took a deep breath. 'OK, Yuri, I'm not sure that this is such a great idea but, as they say, nothing ventured, nothing gained. And it'll be nice for you to hang out with people your own size for an hour or two.'

Yuri's serious little face stared up at me as he listened intently to me rambling on. He looked good enough to eat in his little denim dungarees and stripy blue top. I picked him up and hugged him. 'If we don't like it, we can always leave,' I whispered, as I kissed his cheek.

We climbed up the big stone steps to the front door and rang the enormous bell. A Filipina woman ushered us into a large, sunny living room that was softly decorated in cream and beige. Sitting on the cream sofas and chairs were five women, all dressed as if they were going out for a night on the town. Sonia, in a pair of brown leather trousers and beige halter-neck top – it was January, for God's sake – waved at me to sit down. Jess shuffled up on the couch and I plonked myself down beside her, wishing I hadn't worn jeans and a jumper. Jess was in her best wraparound dress and high heels. 'I thought you said casual coffee morning,' I muttered, under my breath.

'The others always dress up so I feel I have to.' She shrugged.

'Welcome, Emma. You know Jess, obviously, and we've met,' drawled Sonia. 'You've met Maura too, so it's just Juliette and Tamara you don't know.'

I smiled at the two svelte, overdressed women sitting opposite me. It was then that I realized Yuri was the only child in the room.

'Where are the kids?' I asked.

'Oh, Pam looks after them downstairs,' said Sonia.

'I see. Well, I'd better bring Yuri down.' I got up and went downstairs to find a bunch of children ranging in age from four years to three months. Pam was doing a great job of keeping them entertained. Some were painting, others played with Lego and one baby was fast asleep in his carry-cot.

Jess's little daughter Sally rushed over. 'Hi, Emma. My mummy told me you were coming today. Is this your baby?'

'Yes, it is. His name is Yuri. Will you look after him while I'm upstairs? I know I can trust you to make sure he's OK. Can you do that for me? And if he cries, come and get me.'

Sally nodded. 'I'll be his mummy.'

'Good girl, that would be great,' I said, smiling, as she bent down to pat Yuri's head. Yuri seemed delighted to be with little people again. His eyes were as big as saucers and he was smiling.

I went over to talk to Pam. 'Hi, I'm Emma and that's Yuri. He's recently been adopted so he might make strange with the other kids. If you have any problems, just give me a shout. You seem to be doing a great job here.'

Pam smiled. 'Well, I have five children at home in Manila, so I'm used to them.'

'How long have you been here?' I asked, shocked that the poor woman had had to leave her five children in the Philippines to come and work for a cow like Sonia. I hoped she was being paid my mother's rates.

'Almost two years. In another year I'll have saved enough to go back and send my children to proper schools and university.'

'God, you're amazing. Do you get to go back on holidays?' I said, unable to imagine leaving Yuri for two days not to mind two years. What a sacrifice this woman was making for her family.

'I go home once a year usually, but this year I'm going to work straight through so I can move back sooner.'

'You must miss them dreadfully.'

Pam shrugged, 'Of course, but it's worth it. They'll have opportunities that I could never have given them if I hadn't come here.'

Before I could think of anything else to say, Sonia's shrill voice was ordering me upstairs for coffee. I went back reluctantly and sat down.

'Pam's doing a great job with all the children,' I said, as Sonia handed me coffee in a tiny gilt-edged cup.

'She's not bad with the kids, but she's a nightmare at laundry. She shrank my favourite white shirt the other day. I was fuming.'

'Not the Gucci one you got in Milan?' said Maura, looking as if she might just pass out if it was in fact the very same shirt.

'No, the D&G one from New York,' moaned Sonia, as the colour returned to Maura's cheeks. Thank God it wasn't the Gucci one. I looked at Jess, who was concentrating very hard on her coffee cup. I knew she was trying not to laugh.

'So, Emma, how's it going?' asked Sonia. She turned to the rest of the group and reminded them that I had just adopted a little boy from Romania.

'Russia,' I interrupted.

'Pardon?'

'Yuri's Russian, not Romanian.'

'How brave of you,' said Maura. 'What a good person you are to adopt an orphan. He's a lucky boy.'

The other ladies nodded and looked at me as if I was half cracked. It reminded me of the way we all looked at my auntie Doreen when she told us she'd seen a statue of Our Lady swaying in a field down in the west of Ireland. We had nodded and smiled but we all thought she was barking mad.

'Actually,' I said, bristling, 'James and I are the lucky ones to have found Yuri. He's the best thing to happen to us. We adore him.'

'What about his real parents?' asked Juliette.

'What do you mean?' I said, determined to make her spit it out.

'Do you know anything about them? What type of people are they?'

'I've no idea. For all we know the father could be a rapist or murderer and the mother a prostitute,' I answered, laying it on thick.

You could have heard a pin drop.

Jess decided to break the ice. 'But they might also have been lovely people who just couldn't cope with a baby,' she said, squeezing my hand in an effort to get me to calm down. 'Anyway, how's the breastfeeding going, Tamara?'

'I've given up,' said Tamara, looking guilty. 'My boobs were killing me, and when I went to the doctor, I found out I had mastitis, so I told Nigel I was stopping and I didn't want to be made feel bad about it. He really wanted me to do it for six months, but I couldn't. It was making me miserable.'

'Oh, no, Tamara,' said Juliette, looking genuinely upset.

'Don't stop. Go back to it. Honestly, the mastitis will clear up and it's so much better for babies to be breastfed.'

'Why is it so much better?' I asked, clearly the novice in the room.

'Because,' said Juliette, 'breast-fed babies have much lower rates of ear infections, diarrhoea, rashes, allergies and other medical problems than bottle-fed babies. On top of which it's brilliant for bonding with your baby.'

'It also helps you lose weight, quicker,' added Sonia, placing a hand on her washboard stomach.

'Tamara's right to stop if it was making her miserable,' said Jess. 'They're her boobs. Tony was always at me to breastfeed. His mother breastfed him, so I had to follow suit. After four weeks of excruciating pain and cracked nipples I told him he could milk his own nipples if he felt that strongly about it.'

'It sounds awful,' I said, beginning to wonder if I'd be up for it. My pain threshold was fairly low.

'Well, it's not something you have to worry about with an adopted child,' drawled Sonia.

'She will soon enough,' said Jess, smiling at me. 'Emma's pregnant.'

'Oh, how wonderful,' said Tamara, apparently genuinely delighted for me. 'Was it a complete surprise?'

'A total shock, to be honest,' I admitted.

'They always say that once you stop fretting about getting pregnant, it happens immediately,' said Sonia. I wanted to ask her who 'they' were. I also wanted to tell her that there was nothing more annoying when you were trying to get pregnant than some stupid fertile cow telling you to relax.

'Natural or Caesarian?' asked Maura.

'What?' I looked at her blankly.

'Are you going to have a natural birth or go for an elective Caesarian?'

'I'd advise Caesarian. It's much more civilized. The sun roof is the only way to go,' said Sonia, finding herself most entertaining.

'I don't know about that. I liked my natural births,' said Jess, sticking up for Mother Nature.

'But what about all those stitches you had?' Sonia reminded Jess.

'I healed quickly.'

'I agree with Jess,' said Tamara. 'It's not as bad as everyone makes out,' she added, smiling at me.

'I'm still trying to get my head around being pregnant, so it's not something I've given much thought to.' I wanted them all to shut up about their birth choices. I wasn't interested in talking about stitches.

'Won't being pregnant make things difficult for your adopted boy?' Maura asked.

'No,' I said sharply. The last thing I was about to do was get into a conversation about Yuri's well-being with these wenches.

'But the new baby is bound to look like you or your husband, and your little boy will always look like someone else. How are you going to explain it?'

'What difference does it make who looks like who?' said Jess. 'Roy looks nothing like either me or Tony. It's not an issue.'

'But Roy is your natural child. It's different,' persisted Maura.

'No, Maura, it isn't,' I snapped. 'If you had any idea of true love you'd understand that when you love a child – adopted or not – it becomes part of who you are. Yuri couldn't be more a part of me or James than if I had given birth to him – natural or Caesarian – myself. He won't have issues with the new baby because it'll just be his sister or brother. End of story. No big drama. He's our son and the fact that he may or may not look like us is completely and utterly irrelevant and an extremely shallow way of looking at things,' I said, standing up and grabbing my bag. 'On that note, I'm going to love you and leave you. Thanks for the coffee, but I'm going to spend some time with my son now, instead of sitting here listening to your shirt-shrinking dramas, fascinating though they have been.'

I ran downstairs, grabbed Yuri, said goodbye to Pam and rushed out of the door. By the time I got to the car I was shaking with rage. I held Yuri close to me, kissed his pale little face and told him over and over again how much I loved him. He held his hand up to my cheek and gazed at me with his big brown eyes, melting my heart for the millionth time.

Chapter 13

The night before I was due back in work, Yuri woke up every hour on the hour. It was as if he sensed that he was going to be abandoned the next day and was determined to make me suffer. At four a.m., when I had soothed him for half an hour – rubbing his back and singing to him – he finally fell asleep again. I collapsed into bed and went into a coma.

'Waaaaaaah,' I heard in my dream. 'Waaaaaah.' I opened my eyes and looked at the clock. Exactly five a.m. We had moved him into his own room a few days earlier and until now it had been working quite well – he woke up once or twice but had gone back go sleep almost straight away. James was sound asleep beside me, oblivious to his son's crying through the baby monitor, which was conveniently placed on my bedside table.

I dragged myself out of bed and shuffled into Yuri's room. He was standing up in his cot, gripping the bars and crying. At this stage I was really fed up, sleep-deprived and angry. 'Will you hush?' I begged Yuri. 'We've done this already four times. I've got work tomorrow. Give me a break. I'm going to get fired if I arrive in with no sleep and do a bad job. Come on, stop acting up.'

He stared at me and wailed.

I snapped. 'Shut up or I'll send you back to Russia,' I hissed.

'Emma!' said James, choosing this exact moment to finally

wake up and check on his son. 'How could you say something like that to him? Come to Daddy, Yuri, Mummy didn't mean that,' he said, leaning down to pick him up. 'Really, Emma, you should know better.'

'*No!* Don't pick him up,' I said, yanking James back from the cot.

'Have you gone mad?' James glared at me.

I felt guilty about snapping at Yuri, but I was not happy with James rolling up at five a.m., after six hours of uninterrupted sleep, to tell me how to behave. Besides, it was vital – according to all the books I'd read – not to pick up a crying baby when you were trying to get them used to sleeping alone. Obviously if they were in distress you did, but not if they were just kind of whinge-crying and looking for attention, which was exactly what Yuri was doing. If we gave in now, he'd never settle into his new room.

'We can't pick him up. If we do he'll never get used to sleeping on his own and he'll associate crying with us rushing in to comfort him. He has to learn that crying doesn't always work. He'll be fine in a few minutes. He'll settle himself back to sleep. The book says to stay with him so he knows you're there, but not pick him up.'

'Which Fascist book told you that gem?'

'I don't know, I can't remember, I've read so many of them. But they all pretty much said not to give in to your baby's every whim or you'll become a slave to them.'

'Rubbish. If a child cries, it needs to be reassured. It's common sense,' said James and bent down to pick Yuri up.

'James,' I said, in a Clint Eastwood *Dirty Harry* type voice, 'if you pick him up I will kill you. I've spent four nights trying to get him used to this room, and if you break the routine now, he'll never stay here.'

James ignored me and picked up Yuri, who immediately stopped crying. 'It would appear that those books, in which you place so much faith, are wrong.'

I was so angry that I didn't know whether to laugh or cry, but frustration got the better of me and I cried. 'I've been up with him all bloody night. While you've been snoring merrily I've been soothing him back to sleep. I'm bloody exhausted. You're not the only one who has work in the morning. Don't come in here and tell me how to behave.'

'He's a baby. They wake up sometimes. Big deal.'

'Sometimes – fine. Five times in one night, not fine at all. In fact, total bloody nightmare.'

'Will you please stop ranting and cursing in front of him? You're only making him more agitated. He's probably hungry or needs his nappy changed,' said Superdad.

'No, he doesn't, James. He's just acting up. I spend twenty-four hours a day with him, in case you've forgotten. I know his every mood and need. He's not hungry or wet, he's just overtired because he keeps waking himself up. All he needs is sleep, just like his mother.'

'Fine. Go back to bed. Leave this to me.'

I stomped back to bed, but I was too angry to sleep. I spent the next half an hour tossing and turning while I listened to James trying in vain to put Yuri back in his cot. Now that he had been picked up, he had no intention of going back to bed on his own. He roared every time James attempted to lower him in. I have to confess, I was delighted that he was being so bold. At least now James would know how difficult it was.

Eventually after another half an hour of trying unsuccessfully to get Yuri back into his cot, James came into our room, looking demented, carrying Yuri in his arms. I pretended to be asleep.

'Emma,' he whispered, then a little louder: 'Emma.' Finally he practically shouted it.

'*What?*

'Are you awake?'

'Considering the fact that you've just shouted in my ear, depriving me of the only sleep I've had all night, yes, it would seem that I am awake.'

'Well, he won't lie down for me so I wondered if you had any tips.'

'I do have one. You may recall it – don't bloody well pick him up.'

'OK, I admit it might not have been the best idea.'

'Oh, no, James, you were right. Me and my crazy books written by women with decades of child-minding experience are wrong. You and your instinctive parenting are right.'

'Come on, Emma. It's been an hour – help me out here.'

'Do you promise to listen to me in future?'

'Yes.'

'Do you swear that you will not second-guess me, ignore my rules or ruin my routines ever again?'

He nodded.

'Will you appreciate what I do for our son more, now that you've had a tiny taste of what it's like?'

'Darling,' said James, 'I will worship you, hang on your every word and even read your books if you will just get him to stop crying. I've got a splitting headache.'

'Oh, poor you, how awful. I've had one of those since we came back from Russia.'

'I admire you, adore you, am in awe of you – I'll do anything, but please stop the noise,' he begged.

I decided to take pity on him – and on poor Yuri, who was worn out. 'Follow me, watch and learn,' I said, taking Yuri from him. We went back to the nursery where I laid Yuri in his cot. I held his hand, and stroked his cheek, singing to him, until he stopped crying and fell into an exhausted slumber twenty minutes later. When I turned round triumphantly, my not-so-attentive student was fast asleep in the rocking-chair.

We all slept through the alarm. I woke up with a start at half nine and shook James, who bolted out of the door. He had arranged to meet the squad for a training sessions at ten and it would not look good if he was late. While a tired Yuri slept on, I ran around preparing food and packing his knapsack for his first day away from home. I put in enough nappies and food for an army and as many of his favourite toys as I could fit in.

When I woke Yuri he was clinging, as always, to his little grey elephant. I had hoped he'd grow out of it, with all the lovely new toys we had bought, but he loved that elephant more than anything. Just seeing it reminded me that he had been someone else's baby once, which I hated thinking about. But it had been his comforter from the day he was abandoned so I just had to accept that he needed it at all times. I dressed him and put the elephant in the front pocket of the bag where he could see it.

When we arrived, Mum was waiting for us. She told me how awful I looked. 'Well, I didn't get much sleep. Someone was up all night acting the maggot.'

'Still, you should smarten yourself up. You can't go to work looking like a wreck.'

'I'm going to do my makeup in the car. I haven't had a

second to myself this morning, Mum, so please don't start.'

'I just don't want you to let yourself go.'

I couldn't have an argument with her now – she was doing me a favour and I knew she'd do a great job of minding Yuri. If he was with Mum I wouldn't worry about him. I counted to ten. 'I know I look a mess. I'm going to go and do myself up now. I'll see you later.'

As I drove to work, I went to point out a dog to Yuri. But his seat was empty and I was suddenly overcome with sadness. I missed him. This was ridiculous: I'd be seeing him again in three hours, but I was lonely without him. As a lump formed in my throat, I told myself to get a grip.

By the time I arrived at the studio I had gathered myself together. Amanda would not be happy to have a weepy mother on her hands.

Much to my surprise, when I walked in Amanda hugged me. She was not the touchy-feely type. She looked me up and down and nodded. 'Just as I expected,' she said, and sighed dramatically. 'You look tired but happy in that I-love-my-child-so-much-I-don't-care-about-sleep-any-more way. You've moved over to the dark side.'

'I care about the lack of sleep, believe me. But it is amazing.'

'Oh, God, tell me you're not going to bore me with tales of feeding and bowel movements.'

'I promise not to.'

'Is it going all right?' she asked.

'It's hard work, but it's worth it. He's just wonderful. Thanks for asking – and now you've done your bit so you're off the hook.' I decided not to tell her I was pregnant. I'd wait until I was showing. I didn't want to push her over the edge and, besides, she'd have to worry about replacing me again. It was only my first day back in work, and she didn't need to hear that particular gem of information just yet.

Amanda smiled. 'Thank God for that. Please make me look stunning. That silly girl they got in to replace you was obsessed with blusher, even though I told her how much I loathe it.'

'How've you been? How's the love life?'

'Not too bad. You heard John Bradley left his wife?'

I was ashamed to say I hadn't read a newspaper in weeks. This was big news. Four years ago, John Bradley – former leader of the opposition – and Amanda had had an affair, and when the news broke, Bradley was forced to resign. His wife had stood by him and he had bounced back well. Three years after the affair, his party had won the election and he was currently the minister for health.

'No! Has he been calling?'

'Well, I bumped into him at a Christmas fundraiser but the place was crawling with press so he steered clear of me. However, he did call the next day to tell me how well I was looking,' she said, twinkling. 'But I've actually met someone else. David Mason-Holmes.'

'The zillionaire property magnate?'

'The very same,' she said, laughing wickedly. 'He's been whisking me about in his helicopter. We flew to London to have lunch in the Ivy last Saturday, just for the hell of it. It's all very flash, but great fun.'

I groaned. 'Oh, the glamour.'

'You see?' said Amanda, waving her finger at me, 'This is what happens when you don't get married or have children cluttering up your life. And before you tell me how much I've missed by not knowing the joy and beauty of motherhood and how empty and shallow my life is, stop. My friends have been telling me for years.'

'I was actually going to ask you to whisk me off with you on the chopper for a few days so I can feel normal again.' I laughed.

After I had finished her makeup, a happy Amanda was about to walk on to the set when she turned and handed me a bag. Inside were two beautifully wrapped gifts. 'Just a token,' she muttered, and went to tape her show.

I sat down and opened the first one. Inside an elaborate gift box I found a voucher for a full-day treatment at Butterfly, the top spa in Dublin. The second, a blue Tiffany box, contained a gorgeous silver baby rattle. The card read: 'I saw this in an episode of *Sex and the City*. It seems to be the present to give babies, these days. Congratulations on reaching the end of your long journey to motherhood. I'm very proud of you. Just don't bore me about him! Amanda.'

Chapter 14

Having won the European Cup last year, James had been hailed as the best coach Leinster had ever had, a tactical genius and generally a top manager. Several of the big rugby clubs in France and England had tried to poach him with lucrative offers, but James had remained loyal to Leinster. He loved his job and was happy to stay with the team he had so successfully cultivated and nurtured to victory. The only downside to his European win was the pressure he felt now to defend the trophy. He was determined to keep the Cup this year and consolidate his position as the top coach in Europe.

The squad was all keyed up too. They had enjoyed their taste of victory, not to mention the media attention and pay rises that had followed, and were eager to produce some great rugby again this year. Donal, as captain, was head honcho and loved every minute of it. He was also aware that, at thirty-four, his rugby career was coming to an end. This would probably be his last year at the top of his game and he was keen to make it a memorable one.

The first Cup qualifying game was against Glasgow at Leinster's home ground that Saturday. James was like a cat on a hot tin roof the night before.

'But I thought Glasgow weren't supposed to be any good,' I said, as he paced up and down the kitchen.

'Who told you that?' James asked, surprised that I had an opinion. Rugby was not my forte, although I did try to feign interest, and I was desperately proud of James, and had gone to all the big games last year.

'I read it in the paper today. Tom Brown in the *Irish Times* said that Glasgow were not up to much because their star player is injured.' I was delighted to prove that I knew what was going on. Although, truth be told, I had heard it from Dad, who had been at home when I went to pick Yuri up and had read it out to me.

James looked impressed. 'Well, he has a point but Collins being out of the game doesn't mean it's a sure win. They still have a very strong side and their pack is two stone heavier than ours. I'm a bit worried that Kinsella will have trouble scrumming against their prop –'

'James,' I interrupted, before he could dissect the entire Glaswegian team, 'I'm sure it'll be fine. Kinsella will prop up as well as the other fellow and you'll win by a mile. Is pizza OK for dinner? It's the only thing I can face eating.'

'Fine, thanks. Too much rugby detail?'

'You lost me at pack. You know my knowledge is limited to lineups, tries, conversion and penalties. Oh, and drop goals. I like those.'

'I'll shut up then.'

'Well, I think it's important that you switch off when you come home. Otherwise you'd be consumed by rugby.'

'True. How's Yuri?'

'Fast asleep, thank God. Actually, I have a surprise for you.' I produced a shopping-bag. James's face fell. He hated when I bought him clothes. He was only happy in either his Leinster track suit or cords and a V-neck jumper. All of my attempts to make him more chic had ended in disaster. He refused to wear anything that wasn't a plain colour – navy or grey were keen favourites – and comfortable. My biggest victory so far had been to persuade him to wear a beige V-neck jumper.

'Ta-da!' I said, holding up a mini Leinster rugby shirt. It was the smallest one they'd had in the shop and far too big for Yuri, but with the sleeves rolled up it didn't look too bad.

James grinned. 'My very own live mascot.'

'My thoughts exactly. I'm going to dress him up and bring him down to the game. I tried it on him earlier and he looked as cute as a button. He'll be your lucky charm. So you don't need to worry about any packs or props or whatever it is you were talking about.'

The next morning, a focused James left the house early to go over match tactics and lead a final practice session. I busied myself getting Yuri ready and waited for Lucy to pick us up. It was great having her at the games with me. Going with Dad wasn't much fun. He spent the whole time shouting at the referee – normally questioning his parenthood – or muttering about the players under his breath. He only ever spoke to me directly at half-time and then got frustrated because I couldn't analyse the game properly, so he'd end up talking to other Leinster fans seated around us. He always said he thought Leinster was going to lose and at the end of the match when they won he'd say, 'Didn't I tell you they'd win?' Lucy and I kept one eye on the match while we caught up on gossip. Afterwards she'd come into the clubhouse with me to meet the boys and have a few drinks.

Lucy was impressed with Yuri's outfit, but when I handed him to her while I got my things together, she watched him warily.

'It's all right, I gave him toast and cheese for his lunch –

he never throws that up,' I said, laughing as she held him at arms' length.

'Thank God for that. This coat is cashmere and I'm not sure if you'd ever get vomit out.'

Twenty minutes later Lucy was still holding Yuri while I gathered nappies, yogurt, Farley's rusks, soothers and the ever-present grey elephant.

'Come on, Emma, we're going to be late. How much stuff does a baby need? I thought women were high maintenance,' she said, as I stuffed a change of clothes into the baby bag.

'I'm ready. I think I've got everything.'

'Give me the bag and take your son. He's wriggling like a lunatic here. I think he recognizes an amateur when he sees one. He wants his mother, the pro.'

Although it was the first match of the Cup, the stadium was full. The Leinster supporters were out in force to cheer on their winning team. Lucy and I found our seats beside Dad, who was tetchy because we were late. 'I've been holding these bloody seats for over half an hour.'

'The match hasn't even started yet,' I said.

'Turning up just before kick-off! You should be here for the build-up. They need all the support they can get. Glasgow are a good side,' said Dad, with his usual pre-match pessimism.

'Dad, you're the one who told me yesterday that Leinster would walk this, so stop worrying. Now, say hello to your gorgeous grandson,' I said, holding Yuri up so Dad could see his Leinster shirt.

Dad smiled and tickled him. But within seconds he was back in grim-rugby mode. 'There's a lot of pressure on the lads as Cup-holders. It won't be easy.'

'Don't mind Granddad,' I said to Yuri. 'He always gets like this before a game. It's his nerves.'

Dad ignored me and turned to focus on the match.

At half-time, Leinster were up by seven points. The team were playing really well and everyone was happy. Donal was having a great game and had scored a fantastic try in the first minute, much to Lucy's delight. Yuri had been very quiet throughout. He seemed a bit overwhelmed by the crowds of cheering fans. I was worried that he might be frightened by the noise, but he seemed happy to gaze at the coloured scarves and waving flags.

The second half went Leinster's way and they stormed ahead, stretching the lead to thirteen points. With ten minutes to go, Glasgow intercepted a pass and the centre ran down the middle of the field. Donal threw himself at the Scottish player and tackled him to the ground with a thud. Everyone cheered. But Donal remained on the ground, not moving. Lucy jumped up and screamed. James ran on to the pitch with the team doctor. I held Lucy's hand as they rolled Donal over and spoke to him. He was as white as a sheet and clearly in a lot of pain. They stretchered him off.

Lucy was beside herself. 'What do you think it is?' she asked Dad, our rugby expert.

'Looks bad,' said Mr Optimistic. 'Broken collarbone, I'd say.'

'Oh, God,' said Lucy. 'Will that mean he'll be out for the rest of the season?'

'At least.'

'Hold on,' I interrupted, before we all wrote Donal off. 'We don't know. It could be a sprain or something. Let's wait and see before we assume the worst.'

Lucy, Yuri and I went down to the dressing room where we found James, Donal and the doctor. Donal was lying on his back with his limp right arm resting on his chest and a bag of ice on his shoulder. Lucy kissed him. 'Is it bad?' she asked.

'I've dislocated my shoulder again and the doc can't pop it back. I'll have to go to hospital to have it done there.'

'Oh, Donal,' she said hugging him.

'Jesus, Lucy, I'm in agony here, don't go hugging me now.' He yelped as she leant on his sore shoulder.

'Shit, sorry. Will it heal quickly?' she asked.

The doctor shook his head. 'It's a bad dislocation, I'm afraid, and it's a recurring injury. He really needs to have an operation.'

Donal was gritting his teeth. 'I'll be grand. I just need to get it popped back in and get some physio on it and I'll be back playing in a few weeks' time.' Despite his bravado, we could see how upset he was. Even he knew he was out for the season.

Lucy went to the hospital with him in the ambulance. James, Yuri and I followed in the car. 'How bad?' I asked a very grim-faced James.

'Disaster,' he said, thumping the steering-wheel. 'It's over for Donal. He won't play again, not at top level.'

I presumed James was doing a Dad on it by being over-pessimistic. 'Oh, come on, Donal's a big fit guy. Surely he'll bounce back.'

'No, Emma, he won't. This is the third time he's dislocated his shoulder over the last six years. The fact that the doc couldn't pop it back is a bad sign. He'll be out for the rest of the season anyway – his shoulder is in tatters.'

By the time we had arrived at the hospital and parked the

car, Donal had been given a local anaesthetic and they had tried to reposition the shoulder – again unsuccessfully. A surgeon had been called and had told Donal that the shoulder had to be operated on if it was ever to function properly again. Donal was devastated but the surgeon said he had no choice.

Lucy had fainted during the repositioning attempt and was now sitting in a chair beside his bed, her head between her legs.

Donal smiled when he saw us. 'Here, lads, you wouldn't take Florence Nightingale home, would you? She's no bloody use to me.'

'Sod off, you big lump,' mumbled Lucy, and lifted her head. 'I'm going nowhere.'

'What did they say?' asked James.

'They can't get it back in position so I've no choice but to have the operation,' said Donal, looking down to hide how gutted he felt. 'I'm sorry, James, it looks like I'll be out of action for a while.'

James went and sat beside his friend. 'Don't apologize, you idiot. I'm glad they're operating on it. It's long overdue. When you feel better, you can be my assistant coach. I could do with some help training the forwards this year. It'll be great having you on the sidelines with me.'

Donal faked a smile. 'Sounds good to me.'

'OK, folks, Mr Brady needs some rest now,' said a nurse, coming in to shoo us away. We left Lucy behind and went home. James was gutted. His friend, captain and best player was out of action.

Lucy sat on the bed and held Donal's hand. 'It'll be OK,' she said.

'How?' he asked. 'My career is over. I play rugby, it's the only thing I've ever been really good at. What the hell am I going to do now?'

'Well, you could coach with James. He offered you the job.'

'He has a coach for the forwards already – he's just being nice. Jesus, why did this have to happen now when I'd only a year or two left?'

'It's not so bad. Your playing career was almost over anyway. It's hardly even been cut short, really.'

'If you're trying to make me feel better, you're doing a lousy job.'

'Look, Donal, I know it's awful for you, but you would have had to face the end of your rugby career soon anyway. You need to think about what you want to do with the rest of your life.'

'I've only just found out that I have to have a bloody operation. Can I have a few minutes to digest the information before having to choose my new career?'

'Fine. But don't worry about it. I'm earning good money so you can take your time to decide what you want to do next. There's no pressure. At least that's a good thing.'

Donal groaned. 'Jesus, Lucy, I don't want you supporting me. I'm the man, I'll bring home the bacon.'

'Oh, get over yourself, Rambo. I've no intention of supporting you long-term while you sit on your arse. All I'm saying is that you can take your time to recover properly from the operation and figure out what you'd like to do, without worrying about the mortgage repayments. Now, do you want me to get you something to eat?'

Donal shook his head. 'I'm not hungry, I've no appetite.'

'Not even for a Big Mac meal?'

'Well, I suppose I might be able to manage a few bites.'

'That's my boy,' said Lucy, and kissed him. 'It'll be OK,' she whispered, as she went out to get the broken athlete some comfort food.

Chapter 15

Within forty-eight hours of the injury, Donal had had key-hole surgery to fix his shoulder. The surgeon was pleased with how the operation had gone, but Donal didn't really care: his days as a rugby star were over and he had no idea what to do next.

He moved home a day later with a bag full of morphine OxyContin and anti-inflammatory tablets. His arm was in a sling and he was told to move it as little as possible for the next few weeks. After that he'd have physiotherapy and then he could resume light exercise, like swimming, eventually regaining ninety per cent of the movement in his shoulder.

Lucy had taken a few days off work – something she never did – to look after him. Donal was not a good patient. Now that the reality of his situation had sunk in, he was grumpy as hell and shuffled morosely around the house. When he complained about the pain in his shoulder, Lucy got him some pills and a glass of water. When he moaned that the couch was uncomfortable, she plumped and re-arranged the pillows around him until he said grudgingly that it was better. Even though she bought him books, magazines and his favourite series, *The Office*, on DVD, he grumbled constantly about how bored he was.

Eventually Lucy hid in the kitchen and busied herself cooking him dinner – his favourite, home-made lasagne. She was not naturally talented in the culinary field and spent ages trying to get it right, following the cookbook instructions to the letter. When she served it to him, Donal poked at it with his fork.

'What's wrong?' asked Lucy, trying not to snap.

'There's too much of that white stuff on it. I prefer it with more meat and less sauce. I can't eat it, it's all runny. I'll make myself some toast.' He sighed as he struggled to get up.

'No, you won't. Sit there and don't move. I'll make it,' said the perfect wife.

When she came back with the toast, he said there was too much butter on it. 'I like it with just a thin layer of butter. You've drowned it in the stuff,' he complained, scraping the butter off with his good hand.

'Oh, shove it up your arse, you grumpy old fucker,' she snapped, her patience finally running out.

'Charming! I come home after major surgery and get roared at. Where's my sympathy, my comfort and pampering?'

'Pampering? I'm killing myself here to make things easier for you. I know it's difficult, but you'd drive a saint to drink. All you've done so far is complain.'

'Can a man not get a few days' grace? I'm in agony here, so excuse me if I'm not cracking jokes and dancing jigs.'

'I know you're in pain and I don't expect you to be full of the joys of spring. I just think that a positive attitude will help speed up your recovery.'

'What difference does it make how quickly I recover? I won't be playing rugby again regardless, so where's the rush?'

'Come on, Donal, stop being so negative. You've your whole life ahead of you. The world is your oyster – you can do anything you want now. You just have to figure out what that is.'

'I want to captain Leinster to their second European Cup victory,' said Mr Morose.

'Fine. If you're going to be like that, I'll leave you to it,' said Lucy, getting up and clearing the dinner plates.

'Where are you off to?'

'I'm going to work on a proposal I'm behind on.'

'Now?'

'That's the general idea, unless you need me to wipe your brow while you sit on the couch.'

'What'll I do?'

'Watch a movie, read a book, sort out your future, take a bath . . . I don't know, Donal. I can't make all your decisions for you.'

'I thought you were staying home from work to look after and entertain me.'

'Which is exactly what I have been doing, and while it's been a real blast and I hate to tear myself away from your wonderful company, I really need to spend an hour or two working.'

'Well, will you at least get me some socks? My feet are frozen. A cup of tea and some of those chocolate biscuits would be nice too. And put the DVD into the machine for me, will you?'

Lucy bit her tongue and fetched him all of the above. 'Are you all right now? Got everything you need?' she asked, handing him the tea and a plate of biscuits.

'No, not those, I prefer the ones with the chocolate chunks in them. Did you not get any?'

'Donal, chocolate digestives are your favourite.'

'Not any more.'

'Since when?'

'Since I decided to drive you mad. Now, come here and sit down,' he said, grinning at her as he patted the couch. 'That old proposal can wait. You need to put your feet up after your long day playing nursemaid.'

Lucy flopped down beside him. 'Thank God for that. I was about to ram the digestives up your nose.'

'I do have one final request.'

'Oh, God, what now?'

'Any chance you could wear a little nurse's uniform tomorrow? It's a fantasy of mine.'

'You're obviously feeling better,' she grinned, 'but the answer is no. As of this moment I'm resigning from my role as carer. You're on your own.'

That Saturday afternoon when Lucy came in from grocery shopping, she found Donal shouting at the television from his semi-permanent position on the couch. He was hurling abuse at the rugby commentators who were analysing the Munster versus Bath game at half-time.

'That useless fecker Tierney hasn't a clue what he's on about. He keeps getting the players' names wrong and he just said that Andrews transferred to Bath from Harlequins, when even the dog on the street knows he used to play for London-Irish.'

A lightbulb went on in Lucy's head. From her office the following Monday morning, she called the producer of the Saturday sports show on RTÉ. Pretending she was Donal's agent, she brokered a deal for him to be on the regular Saturday rugby panel, commentating on the Cup matches. The producer had met Donal a few times and thought he'd make a colourful addition to the team. Lucy used her finely tuned negotiating skills to land him a very good package. When she hung up, Donal had a new job that she knew he'd like. Delighted, she called him.

'Hello.' He yawned into the phone.

'What are you up to?'

'Let's see now . . . So far today I've got out of bed and shuffled to the couch where I've been watching some hound of a woman being made over by a team of experts and the end result is nearly worse. They're all telling her she's gorgeous but she still looks a fright to me.'

'I've got some good news for you.'

'Go on.'

'RTÉ wants you to be on their rugby panel for the whole season.'

'What do you mean?'

'They want you to commentate on the games. The producer thinks you'd be great. You're young, you know most of the players and you certainly know your rugby. He's mad keen for you to come on board. His name is Colin Dylan and he'll be calling you later to confirm the details. They want you to start this Saturday.'

'And this fella just happened to call you out of the blue to offer me a job? Would it not have been easier for him to call me directly? My number's in the directory.'

'Well, I kind of approached him. I said that now you were injured you were looking to get involved in commentating. He jumped at the chance to hire you.'

'I don't need my wife ringing around begging people to hire me, Lucy. I do have some pride left.'

'I didn't say I was your wife, you dope. I pretended I was your agent and I've negotiated a very good deal for you, so stop being so bloody macho and be grateful.'

'I'd rather get my own jobs.'

'Fine, well, then, call him and tell him you don't want it because you're too busy sitting on the couch watching daytime TV and feeling sorry for yourself,' barked Lucy, and hung up.

Her phone rang. 'I'd like to speak to Donal Brady's agent.'

'She's resigned because her client is an unappreciative arsehole.'

'Any chance you could remind me of her name? As well as being a prize arsehole I've also got a bad memory and I can't remember it. I've to talk to some guy in RTÉ about a job and I don't know what made-up name she used.'

'Caroline Plum.'

'Like the fruit?'

'Yes.'

'Any chance Ms Plum would consider forgiving her client for being an ungrateful oaf and represent me again in the near future? I'd make it worth her while.'

'Oh, yeah, how?'

'By offering her the best sex of her life.'

'Rumour has it you're laid up in bed and can barely make yourself a cup of tea, never mind thrash about having sex.'

'I always rise to the occasion. In fact, I'm rising to it now just thinking about it. Any chance you could nip home at lunchtime?'

'I'll consider it.'

'Lucy?'

'Yes?'

'Thanks.'

Donal went on the panel that Saturday wearing a smart new shirt that Lucy had bought him, his arm in a sling. The other two men were in their fifties. One was a former Irish international player, Pat Tierney, who had the memory of a goldfish and constantly got everyone's names wrong. He spent the afternoon calling Donal David. The other man, Gerry O'Reilly, was a freelance sports journalist and never had anything positive to say about anything. They were commentating on Leinster's second game against Harlequins. Donal was nervous for his team mates: Harlequins were a good side and Leinster needed to win this game.

'So, David, who do you think will win?' asked Pat.

'It's Donal. Leinster have a great chance. James Hamilton has proven himself to be a world-class coach and he's continuing with the same winning tactics he used last year – aggressive play upfront and some new set-plays for the back line.'

'Hamilton is the most overrated coach in the competition,' sneered Gerry. 'One Cup win can be as much fluke as talent.'

'Well, Gerry, having played on the team last year, I can tell you it was no fluke. James's influence on the team and the way we played was enormous. He's a master tactician and the analysis he does on every opponent is phenomenal. I've never worked with a coach I respected so much.'

'Well, obviously you're going to say that – you were the captain until a few weeks ago. Unlike you, I'm coming from an unbiased angle.'

'I'm not being biased, I'm being honest. I played for him and I think I know how good he is.'

Before they could get into a real argument, the match kicked off. Forty minutes later, at half-time, the programme returned to the studio for the panel's opinions. Leinster were down, 10–5.

'They weren't great in that half, were they, David? You'd have to say they don't look like champions today,' said Pat.

'It's Donal – and I think it's a bit early to be writing them off. They had a slow start, but they'll come out guns blazing after the half-time talk. James'll change the tactics to give Leinster the advantage. Just wait and see. I'm not a bit worried about the outcome. They'll win this game.'

'I admire your optimism, but it's totally misplaced,' said Gerry. 'Leinster haven't got what it takes. The out-half is having a terrible game. He's missed two easy penalties and his place-kicking is a joke. He should never have been picked.'

'Ray Phelan is considered to be the best out-half in Europe,' said Donal.

'By whom?'

'By anyone who knows anything about rugby.'

'I've been writing about rugby for thirty years and I can tell you he's overrated.'

'Well, I've been playing with him for six years and I can tell you he's the best I've seen. No one plays at the top of their game for eighty minutes of every match. He'll come out in the second half and kick everything over.'

'The guy should have been dropped months ago. He's useless.'

'Have you ever played rugby?' Donal asked Gerry.

'No.'

'Well, maybe if you had you wouldn't be so judgemental and negative about it.'

'It's my job to be judgemental, and I'm sick of players like you thinking they can become expert commentators overnight. The whole premise of being on a panel is to be non-partisan. You're supposed to be able to analyse a match without bias.'

'It's a lot easier to slate players than to give them credit. I don't think Ray should be dropped just because he's had an average first half in this game – it's the first time he hasn't played out of his skin in ten months. I've never heard such horseshit in my life.'

'Language, David,' warned Pat.

'It's Donal,' snapped Donal. 'My name is Donal and the scrum-half for Harlequins used to play for Edinburgh, not Bath.'

The second half kicked off before Donal could list all the other mistakes Pat had made. As he had predicted, Leinster came out firing and won the match comfortably 25–13. Ray Phelan kicked over four penalties and a conversion. Donal was standing on his chair cheering out of the window, 'Well done, lads,' when the cameras switched back to the panel. He climbed down and, grinning at Gerry, said, 'Well, do you still think Ray should be dropped?'

'Yeah, I do, actually. So he kicked a few balls over. Big deal, he missed a few in the first half.'

'I think you'll find that kicking a penalty from the corner of the pitch in a gale-force wind is actually a big deal, Gerry. Leinster had an incredible second half. They looked like champions to me.'

'I wouldn't get ahead of myself, if I was you,' said Gerry. 'It's early days and they had a bad first half.'

'So you've nothing positive to say about Leinster's win?'

Gerry shrugged. 'They did all right, but it's nothing to get excited about.'

'Well, I am excited. I'm very bloody excited after that performance. I refuse to let you dampen my enthusiasm. It's a great win and I think Leinster are going all the way. Up Leinster,' roared Donal, into the camera.

The phone lines were jammed with people calling in to say how refreshing it was to see a panellist who was genuinely enthusiastic and positive. Donal was a hit – although there was one complaint about his language.

Chapter 16

Although I missed Yuri, I soon began to enjoy being back at work. It felt great to be doing something I was good at again, and to feel useful and confident. I was so unsure of myself all the time as a mother that it was a constant struggle not to feel like a failure. Every time Yuri threw up something I'd fed him, or didn't sleep, or cried for no apparent reason, I blamed myself. Mum seemed happy enough minding him and raking in the cash, and Yuri thrived in her care. Sometimes I even felt a bit jealous — I knew it was ridiculous, but she seemed better with him than I was, and because I lacked self-belief in the mother department I was a bit touchy about it.

One day I went to pick Yuri up as usual at half past three but there was no one there. Mum's car was gone. I let myself in and found a note on the kitchen table saying they had popped out for a while but would be back by four. I made myself a cup of tea and waited. At ten past Mum came bouncing into the kitchen with a very happy-looking Yuri in her arms.

'Hi. Where have you been?' I asked.

'Well, we've just had the best day. I took Yuri to the zoo, didn't I, Yuri? Yes, I did. He just loved it. When he saw all the animals, his face lit up. We may have a zoologist on our hands. He was in his element, but the highlight was definitely the big grey elephant. Yuri was laughing and waving at him. Sure he carries that raggedy old toy one everywhere, so I wasn't surprised when it turned out to be his favourite animal.'

I realize that it was completely irrational, but the fact that she had taken him to the zoo and he had loved it bothered me. Why hadn't I thought of doing that? And, worst of all, I hated hearing that he had loved the elephant most. I wanted to burn that stupid toy. 'Sounds like fun,' I said unenthusiastically. I held out my arms to take Yuri, but he snuggled into Mum's neck.

'He's a bit tired after the exciting day we've had. He was the best boy. You should have seen him, Emma, he was so excited to see the live animals. People kept coming up to me and saying how sweet he was.'

'Did he eat all his food?' I asked.

'No, he didn't like that old vegetable mush you gave me at all. He kept spitting it out, so I fed him brown bread and jam and he gobbled it down.'

My forehead began to throb. I felt as if a vein was about to pop. I knew I was being silly but I had spent ages preparing Yuri's lunches for the week. Every book I read kept crashing on about making your own food, so I had put aside the supermarket organic jars I had been feeding him, and set about cooking him the healthiest meals I could. I felt guilty about going back to work and I thought that preparing him nutritious food would make up for the time I spent away from him.

Annabel Karmel was hailed as the children's food guru, so I had logged on to her website and cooked her well-balanced, super-healthy vegetable purée with tomato and cheese. It had taken me ages to peel all the carrots and I had been very proud of the result. To be told he had hated it, in my current state of paranoia, felt like a personal insult of the most grievous kind. 'You should have made him eat it. It's very nutritious. I'm trying to build up his immune system.'

'Oh, for goodness' sake! If a child spits out food, no amount of persuading will get them to eat it. Brown bread is just as good for him.'

'There's too much sugar in jam.'

'A tiny bit won't do him any harm. Lord, Emma, you're very uptight today.'

I chose to ignore this comment as my uptightness increased by the second. 'What time did you feed him?'

'I'd say about half two.'

'Mum! I asked you to feed him at one. I'm trying to get him into a routine. Now he'll be out of synch again.'

'I don't know what it is about you modern women, always trying to get your babies into these rigid routines. When a child is hungry, you feed it regardless of what time it is. You're all so busy trying to get back to work and do all the things you did before you had children that you don't take the time to get to know them.'

'I do so know, Yuri,' I said indignantly. 'I spent every second with him for the first seven weeks and now I only leave him for three and half hours a day. All the books say that babies need routine and that you shouldn't feed them on demand.'

'Oh, those old books will be the death of you. Every baby is different. What do these so-called experts know? I bet you half of them don't even have children of their own.'

She had a point. I wasn't sure that any of them had their own kids. Still, everyone swore by routines if you wanted to have any kind of life of your own. And, selfish though it may sound, I did want a life of my own. I adored Yuri but

I loved work too. Three and half hours a day wasn't so much to ask for – was it?

'In my day your child dictated your life for the first few years, not the other way round. You girls try to do too much. You can't work, be a mother and a good wife all at the same time. Something has to give,' continued Mum.

'Are you implying that I'm a bad mother?'

'I never said that, just that you're trying to do too much. You look worn out and you need to mind yourself, Emma. Pregnant women shouldn't overdo it. I'm not sure you should be on your feet all day working. I never worked when you were young.'

The fact that my mother had never worked since the day she got married thirty-seven years ago was apparently irrelevant. After having children, she had devoted herself to us, but sometimes when I was growing up, I'd wished she had worked. All of her considerable focus had been on us and sometimes it was a lot to bear. When Babs came along I was thrilled that Mum had something to take her mind off me, my school work, development, growth, hormones . . . and whatever else she chose to home in on.

'In five months' time, I'll have two kids under the age of two. I'm working now to try and save some money and keep my hand in – I love what I do. I know I'll have to give up for a good while when the new baby arrives but I do hope to go back to it eventually.'

'Ridiculous notions,' sniffed Mum. 'And you don't need to worry so much about money. I've opened a bank account for Yuri and all the money you pay me goes into it. In a few months' time it'll have added up to a nice sum so you can use it to buy him anything he needs.'

'Oh, Mum! Thanks,' I said, going over to hug her. 'You're brilliant.'

'Well, I know how bad you are at saving so I decided to do it for you. Now you can stop fretting and when the new baby arrives you can give up that old job and put your children first, like the women of my generation did.'

'I really appreciate that, Mum, but I don't believe working part-time is a bad thing. In fact, I think it was because your generation of women devoted their whole lives to their children that so many of them ended up in their forties at a complete loss for what to do. When their kids were in school all day, the mothers were bored, dissatisfied, restless and, in some cases, depressed. The fact that you had Babs when you were forty meant that you hadn't time to sit around wondering what to do with your life, you were still a full-time mum with a dependent baby.'

'Nonsense.'

'It's true, Mum. You told me yourself that lots of your friends regretted not having gone to college or travelled before settling down and felt that it was too late for them in their forties. I admit that my generation is more selfish. We're having children later because we spent our twenties studying, travelling and experiencing life. So when we do get round to having babies we're used to a certain lifestyle and don't want to give it up. We spend ten years building up a career, earning good money – and once the children arrive we're supposed to give it all up and be happy about it? It's not easy, especially when you like what you do. Having to get handouts from your husband every time you want to buy a pair of shoes or get your hair cut is alien to us, not to mention frustrating.'

'Those women's libbers have a lot to answer for. The

most important thing in life is family. You need to get your priorities straight.'

'Yuri is the most important thing in my life and I intend to do everything in my power to give him a wonderful upbringing, but a happy mother equals a happy child. If that means leaving him for a few hours a day, then so be it. Besides, it looks to me like he prefers being here with you than at home with me.'

'Practice makes perfect, Emma.'

I sighed. The discussion was going round in circles.

'I'm doing my best, Mum. Sometimes I think I'm just not very good at it.'

'All new mothers doubt themselves. It's overwhelming at first. You have to keep at it. It gets better and easier. And you're doing a great job. This little man has thrived in the last few months,' she said, kissing Yuri's cheek.

'Do you really think so?'

'Course I do, pet,' she said, handing him to me. 'By the way, if you're planning on landing the second child on me as well, I'll be looking for double pay. There'll be no two-for-the-price-of-one in this crèche.'

When I got home, James was on the phone to his mother. I always knew when he was on to her because (a) his accent was much more pronounced, and (b) he became all formal. There was lots of 'Yes, Mother, I agree' type of chat.

'Sounds marvellous . . . Yes, I know you're dying to see Yuri . . . Yes, he's settled in nicely now so it won't be a problem bringing him over . . . Super . . . All right, Mother, see you in a few weeks . . .'

I sat down with Yuri. 'Bring him over where?'

'To visit my parents. We're going over the weekend after

137

next. It's my father's seventy-first birthday so it'll tie in nicely.'

'But I don't think Yuri's ready to be taken to a new environment. He'll hate going on a plane again so soon.'

'It's been over two months, Emma, he'll be fine. Besides, it's ludicrous that my family haven't seen him yet. They were a bit put out by being told not to come for Christmas.'

I had banned the Hamiltons from coming to stay with us for Christmas. The adoption people had told us specifically not to crowd Yuri with new faces when he first came home with us. It would be too much for him. He needed to settle in slowly and get used to his new surroundings and new parents, without the cast of *Gandhi* queuing up to see him. 'I was following the social workers' instructions, James. Yuri wouldn't have been able to cope with so many new people all at once.'

'Fine, but now it's time they met him. I'm dying to introduce my son to my family. It'll be great fun. He can get to know his cousins while we're there.'

I didn't want James's nephew Thomas – now six years old and a complete brat – anywhere near my precious son. Mind you, the twin girls were sweet and it would be nice for him to meet them. The thought of the dreaded Imogen, my sister-in-law, made my skin crawl. When James and I first got married she kept telling me to hurry up and get pregnant. When she discovered I was having problems con-ceiving and had tried fertility treatments, including IVF, she told me I wasn't trying hard enough. When she found out we were going to adopt, she endeared herself to me even further by telling me it wouldn't be the same as having children of my own.

'How long do we have to go for?' I asked.

'Three days.'

I groaned.

'Emma, your parents see Yuri all the time. It's about time mine met their grandson. I really don't think it's unreasonable to stay three days.'

'You're right, it isn't. I just hope Yuri doesn't act up because of the change of environment – and Imogen better keep her comments to herself.'

'You'll probably find you get on much better now that you have babies in common. She can give you tips on raising children,' said the ever-optimistic James.

'Tips on how to raise the son of Satan?'

'Emma!'

'Thomas is a brat.'

'I admit he's not the nicest child, but that's a bit strong.'

Not strong enough, I thought grimly.

Chapter 17

Things were going pretty well for Babs. She was now getting the best slots on BFL and the viewers loved her. She was more flirty than the other presenters and also, at times, brutally honest. When she was selling the gardening products, she opened the section by informing the audience that she hated gardening, but if that was what floated their boat, these were the products to buy.

'If I can use this thing to dig up muck then, believe me, it must be good, because I haven't a clue what I'm doing. So if you prefer gardening to clubbing you should either get a life or buy one of these.'

Billy seemed very pleased with her and was paying her a lot more attention now that she had proven herself to be very talented. He was often very flirty with her and Babs basked in their banter. The more she saw of him, the more attractive he seemed. With work going well, the only problem in her life was her living arrangements. She was fed up at Sean and Shadee's – it was really boring, and on the rare occasions she went out with her workmates, Sean insisted on asking her what time she'd be home. It was like being fifteen again. She needed a place of her own, but on two hundred quid a week it was impossible. She asked Billy for a raise every second day, but he reminded her she still had six weeks left on her original contract, but after that, if she was still selling well, he might consider a small one.

Babs came home from work often to find Sean and

Shadee sitting at the table looking at wedding plans. It was all they talked about. If they weren't smooching on the couch declaring their undying love for each other, they were going on about their wedding.

'Oh, God, not more wedding chat. Haven't you finalized it yet?' she said one day, as she grabbed a beer from the fridge.

'How's work?' Sean asked. 'Sold any frozen burgers lately?'

'God, you're a riot.'

'Come on, what vital product are you offering the world now? Weed-killer?'

'Semi-precious jewellery, actually, and I shifted loads of it. I'm definitely on track for promotion soon. Billy thinks I'm brilliant. Anyway, I can't sit around here chatting – I've got to get ready. One of the girls is having a birthday bash in some bar in town.'

'What bar?'

'Dunno, some new place in Soho.'

'Soho's not a safe place to hang out.' Sean frowned.

'Oh, *puuuur-lease*, spare me the big-brother routine. Besides, what are my options? Staying in again with you two? I'd rather stick needles in my eyes,' she said, and flounced off to change.

Half an hour later Babs came out wearing a skintight red mini-dress that left little – if anything – to the imagination. Sean looked up from the couch and choked on his drink. 'I don't think so,' he said.

'*What?*'

'I hope there's a pair of trousers to go with that top.'

'Funny guy.'

'You're not going out to Soho in that.'

141

'I think you'll find that's exactly what I'm doing.'

'Get changed.'

'Get a life,' said Babs, putting on her lipstick.

'Do you want to get propositioned by every sleazeball in town?'

'Sounds a lot better than than sitting in here going out of my mind with boredom.'

'I'm serious. You're not going out like that. You look like a hooker.'

'Well, then, I'll blend right in in Soho, won't I?'

'Babs.' Sean got up and walked towards her.

'Don't wait up,' she said, and sprinted out the door.

The party was in a new bar on Wardour Street called Barcelona. It was crowded with good-looking young people and Babs felt right at home. This was more like it. This was the London she had been expecting – glamour, cocktails and gorgeous people. She made her way over to the corner where a crowd of her colleagues had gathered. Billy was in the midst of it, buying drinks for everyone. His cheeks were flushed and he had a glint in his eye. 'I think you forgot your skirt, love,' he said, and winked at Babs.

'Shut up and buy me a drink. Make it a strong one.'

Billy bought her a blue cocktail that tasted like rocket fuel.

'So, when are you going to give me a raise? I have to get out of my brother's place – it's driving me nuts living there.'

'You have the contract. No raise until the three months are up. After that we can talk about it. But I wouldn't hold my breath, if I were you. We're not flush with cash.'

'Oh, yeah? How come you drive a brand new Porsche, then?'

'Cos I'm the boss.'

'I'm brilliant at selling and you know it. If you don't pay me more, I may have to look elsewhere. I'm sure QVC would like to hire me.'

'You've been on the telly five minutes, love. Don't get ahead of yourself.'

'I know my own worth,' said Babs, flicking her hair. 'You said yourself no one could shift those gardening products but I managed to.'

'Newsflash, Babs: selling a few shovels doesn't make you a celebrity.'

'Admit it, Billy, I'm the best you've seen.'

'Well, you don't lack confidence. What did they feed you over there in Ireland? Super spuds or something?'

'Do I look like I eat carbohydrates?'

Billy looked her up and down. 'You don't look like you've eaten this year. How come you don't have a bloke?'

'Because you don't pay me enough to go out and meet any. Not to mention the fact that living with my brother is the biggest chastity belt of all.'

'Poor Babs, my heart bleeds. Here, let me buy you another drink to make up for your non-existent social life.'

He came back with two more blue cocktails. 'Don't you have to drive back to Brighton tonight?' Babs asked, as Billy knocked back his drink.

'No, I've got a small place near the studio for when I'm out after work.'

'Doesn't your wife mind?'

'She prefers it if I stay in the apartment when I'm pissed.'

'Flash car, a house in Brighton and an apartment in London, but you can't afford to give me a raise?' said Babs, lifting her eyebrows.

'Drink your drink and stop harassing me. You're like a dog with a bone.'

'How often do you use your apartment?'

Billy shrugged. 'Once a week, I suppose. Twice, maybe.'

'So it's empty most of the time?'

'Yes.'

'Well, then, why don't I live in it? I'll be near the studio, I'll pay the bills and it won't be left empty all the time – which is a waste of a good apartment, if you think about it.'

'I can see how this is a really good option for you, darling, but what do I get out of it?'

Babs looked at him through her blue-cocktail haze. Rumour had it that he was a notorious womanizer and had slept with several of the prettier presenters. He was gorgeous – for an older guy – he made her laugh, and she found his confidence irresistible. He was unfaithful to his wife anyway, so it wasn't as if she'd be a home-wrecker. Sod it, she thought. I've got nothing to lose and everything to gain. 'Well, I'm sure we could find something to make it worth your while.'

Billy slipped his hand around her waist. He'd been dying to shag her since he'd seen her bouncing on the mattress.

They left the bar and went back to the apartment. It had one bedroom and a large living room overlooking the river. Babs loved it.

'All right, darling, on your back,' said Billy, and whipped off his shirt to reveal a toned torso.

Babs smiled to herself. This was going to be fantastic. 'What about the champagne and strawberries?'

'This isn't *Dynasty*, love. Come on, get your kit off.'

Babs laughed. This was the beginning of her real London experience. Granted, she hadn't planned on sleeping with her boss, but why not have great sex, free accommodation and guarantee yourself a raise? She lay back and thought of Hollywood.

The next day she woke up to find Billy had gone. He'd left her a note.

Morning, vixen. Can't believe what you talked me into last night. Mind you, if that was a taste of what's to come (no pun intended!) it's all right by me. Be in the studio by ten and don't even think of telling anyone at work about your new living arrangements.

Babs grinned, then walked round the apartment admiring her new quarters. It was minimalist – brown leather couches, cream walls, wide-screen TV, and one or two paintings hung haphazardly on the walls. The bathroom had a lovely big Jacuzzi bath, which Babs couldn't wait to use. She made herself a cup of coffee and sat on the couch, staring out at the river. This was definitely a good move. The sex had been fantastic: Billy certainly knew his way around a woman's body – there was a lot to be said for older men with experience on their side. She had just one problem: what was she going to tell Sean?

She switched on her mobile and saw seven missed calls, all from her brother, increasingly irate as the night had gone on. The three he had left this morning were less angry and more worried. She dialled his work number. 'Hi.'

'Where the bloody hell are you?'

'Chill, Sean. I crashed at a friend's house.'

'Why the hell didn't you ring me to let me know you were all right?'

'I switched my phone off. Look, it's no big deal.'

'I thought something had happened to you – I'm surprised it didn't, wearing those clothes in Soho.'

'I've got some news,' said Babs, deciding to jump right in.

'What?'

'A girl in work is leaving to go to Australia for the year and she's renting me her apartment. She lives right beside the studio and it's really cheap, so I'll be moving out. That's where I am now. I came back to have a look at it last night and ended up crashed out here.'

'What girl?'

'Pippa. She's one of the other presenters.'

'Where's the apartment?'

'I told you, beside the studio.'

'How much is the rent?'

'Seventy quid a week.'

'Seems very cheap. It must be a really dodgy area.'

'It isn't, it's nice.'

'Why is she charging so little?'

'Because her dad bought it for her when she moved to London. They're loaded and she doesn't have any mortgage. My rent is just play-money for her,' said Babs, thinking on her feet.

'I'll need to see it. You're not moving out until I've checked it's OK. I'm not having Mum accusing me of neglecting you.'

Shit. Babs looked around. Would she get away with pretending this belonged to a girl? She'd have to hide Billy's clothes and shaving stuff, but he didn't keep much here so it'd be easy enough. Besides, it'd get Sean off her back once and for all.

'Yeah, fine. You can give me a lift over later with my bags.'

146

'Typical of you to land on your feet. Did you force the poor girl to emigrate so you could have her pad?'

'A certain amount of arm-twisting was involved.'

'Now, why doesn't that surprise me?'

'Oh, even you'd be surprised at my persuasive skills this time.'

'Nothing you do would ever surprise me,' said Sean.

'Never say never,' said the scarlet woman.

Chapter 18

As I had predicted, when we boarded the plane to go and visit James's parents Yuri hated it. He shouted the place down, much to the annoyance of all the unfortunate passengers seated around us. It was a total nightmare. I tried shoving his dummy into his mouth but he just kept spitting it out. I bounced him, cuddled him, read him his favourite *The Hungry Caterpillar* book, sang 'Incy Wincy Spider' over and over again – although I could never remember the last bit so just la-la-la'd it – tried feeding him bread, yogurt and Farley's rusks, all to no avail.

'Do something,' James hissed at me, while he apologized to everyone around us for the racket.

'Like what?'

'Walk him up the aisle or something.'

'Good idea,' I said, thrusting Yuri at his father.

James marched up and down as Yuri continued to howl, then passed him back to me. It was the longest flight of our lives. The fifty minutes felt like ten hours. Eventually when we landed, a frazzled Yuri fell asleep in my arms. His equally frazzled parents waited until everyone else had disembarked before trying to unload the overhead locker.

'I told you he'd hate flying. It's too early to take him on a visit,' I snapped at James, who studiously ignored me as he heaved our bags down.

'Why in God's name can we not put our luggage in the

hold like all normal people?' he muttered. 'This obsession with having everything to hand is ridiculous.'

The thing is, that I never, ever check in my bag if I'm only going away for a weekend. I hate having to wait for an hour after landing, watching people being knocked sideways by enormous Samsonite suitcases hitting them as they are frantically grabbed off the carousel by people half their size. The absolute panic that ensues if – God forbid – your suitcase happens to pass you by in a moment of distraction, is comic. You see very respectable, normal-looking people galloping round the carousel, chasing their oversized suitcases as if their life depended on it. Or those really desperate people who stand beside the plastic flaps, where the luggage comes out, and poke their heads through as if that's going to speed things up.

I like to have my bag with me in the overhead locker. Sure, sometimes it's a bit of a squash to fit it in, but at least I know it's there and if I should decide I want to change my outfit, redo my makeup or give myself a manicure, I can. Not that I ever have, as James points out every time we visit his parents.

Anyway, now that we had Yuri, the two large cases crushed into the overhead locker were full of his things. Gone were the days when I brought six outfits for one weekend. I had barely managed to squeeze in one decent dress. I had decided to bring everything Yuri owned to make him feel at home when we got to James's parents' house. I didn't want him playing up in front of them, and I'd figured that if he had all his familiar toys and books he might remain calm. Judging by the flight, things didn't look promising.

Once we were in the terminal building we headed for

Arrivals, where James's brother Henry was waiting for us. When he saw he us he rushed over, shook James's hand and thumped him awkwardly on the back. They weren't the hugging type of brothers.

'Congratulations, old boy,' he said to James, as Yuri was introduced to him. 'He's a fine fellow. Doesn't look unlike you.' Then he kissed me and congratulated me too. 'So, Emma, how's motherhood? Bloody nightmare in the beginning. Takes a while to get used to. Sleep deprivation is a bit tricky.'

I smiled at him and nodded. I really liked Henry: he was all bluster and what-ho but underneath all that lay a very thoughtful and kind person. 'You can say that again.' I laughed. 'I never thought I'd be able to survive on five hours a night, but somehow I have.'

'Wait until number two arrives – you'll be wishing for five hours,' he said, grinning at me. 'Marvellous news. Delighted for you both. Nice to have a sister or brother for Yuri. Better warn you both – Mother and Father are beside themselves. Dying to meet this little fellow. They've been shopping for weeks so the house is full of toys and bears and clothes. Yuri's going to be spoilt rotten this weekend. Imogen's bringing Thomas and the girls over after school to meet him.'

I sighed. Yuri had had quite enough upheaval for one day. The thought of six-year-old Thomas anywhere near him gave me the shivers. He was bound to cause havoc. An hour later we arrived at James's parents' house. It was a lovely old country cottage set in a couple of acres of well-tended garden. Mr and Mrs Hamilton were waiting for us on the doorstep. Thankfully, Yuri was still a bit groggy from the flight so he didn't cry when he saw the new faces.

Mrs Hamilton held him while her husband hovered in the background beaming over her shoulder at Yuri's pale little face. 'Seems a healthy little fellow,' he announced. 'Bit peaky, but I suppose that's to be expected. Food can't be good in Russia.'

They were clearly relieved to see that he was normal. They must have been expecting the worst.

'I'm sure Emma's been doing a wonderful job of feeding him,' said Mrs Hamilton, endearing herself to me. 'Come in and sit down. We'll have some tea and you can tell us all about our little grandson.'

We walked into a living room that looked like Christmas Day in Santa's grotto. There were beautifully wrapped gifts everywhere. 'A lot of them are his Christmas presents that were too large to post, and we've bought a few other bits and pieces since then,' said Mrs Hamilton, as James and I gasped. 'We felt he needed spoiling after starting his little life in a nasty orphanage.'

'Thanks,' I croaked, trying to retain my composure at their kindness and enthusiasm and feeling guilty for not having allowed them to come over for Christmas. 'It's so sweet of you.'

We spent a lovely hour having tea and scones. While James filled his parents and Henry in on our Russian adventure, I sat on the floor with Yuri and opened his presents. He was delighted and cooed appropriately at the wonderful toys and books. He couldn't have been more angelic. I was incredibly relieved. James's parents were both seventy and I didn't think they'd be able for a screaming baby. So far so good . . .

Until Imogen arrived with the twins and Thomas. The twins, now two, were identical, although I could tell my goddaughter Sophie from Luisa almost instinctively. Thankfully, despite their mother and brother, they had remained sweet-natured. Thomas, on the other hand, raced into the room and dived on Yuri's presents, throwing them about and even breaking one in the process.

'Thomas!' said Henry sternly. 'Leave Yuri's things alone. Come here and say hello to your new cousin.'

Thomas shuffled over and glared at Yuri, mumbled hello, then tore off to smash a few more toys.

James stopped Henry scolding him. 'Leave him be. It doesn't matter – Yuri has too many anyway.'

While the men took Henry's children out to play in the garden and Mrs Hamilton went to put the kettle on again, I was left with Imogen and Yuri.

'Well, he doesn't look at all as I'd expected,' Imogen announced, in her loud, horsy voice. 'I though he'd be like one of those little refugee children you see on television, covered with sores, but he's quite normal. A bit pasty, but not too bad, considering.'

'We think he's the most beautiful child in the world,' I said.

'Wait until you have some of your own. There's nothing like the feeling of having your own child. Your own flesh and blood. A child that is the mirror image of you in every way. It's truly amazing. You'll find out soon enough. I hear you're preggers.'

I nodded.

'Well, of course, I knew it would happen all along. There was no need to rush into that whole adoption palaver. You could have saved yourself and James a lot of trouble. I suppose it's too late to give him back?' she said, sighing at all that wasted time.

'*Give him back?*' I was livid. 'We adore him, Imogen. Why on earth would you even suggest that we give our son back?'

'Temper, temper, Emma. I was only pointing out that you needn't have adopted, after all. I always felt you were too impatient with your fertility treatment. These things take time and look at you now – pregnant.'

'The only reason I got pregnant was because of Yuri. I was so distracted by the adoption that I finally stopped worrying about trying to get pregnant. So if it wasn't for him, I wouldn't be expecting this baby.'

'Nonsense. You would have got pregnant naturally anyway. You were just far too uptight. Still, I suppose it's a good thing that you're being positive about the adoption. Too late for regrets now.'

The only regret I have is allowing myself to be left alone with you, you stupid cow, I thought.

'Did I tell you Thomas has started horse-riding?' she asked, but before I could answer, she droned on, 'He's very talented. They think we may have a future champion on our hands,' said the delighted mother. The horsy genes had clearly been passed down.

'How fab,' I said sarcastically.

'You should try the little Russian when he'd old enough. It's *maaahvelous* for them to be out in the fresh air bonding with the horses.'

'His name is Yuri. Y-U-R-I. If you find it too difficult to remember, I can write it down for you,' I snarled.

'The girls, of course, are thriving. My toddler group simply cannot believe how advanced they are for their age. Quite remarkable, they say, when they hear them talking,' Imogen continued, ignoring me while boring me to death on the amazing talents of her children.

'Yuri does a very good barking sound,' I said, managing to keep a straight face. 'He actually sounds like a dog. It's phenomenal.'

Imogen looked at me as if I were a little unstable. 'Barking sound?'

'Yes, we're very proud of him.'

Before she could commit me to a mental institution, Thomas charged through the door with a stick in his hand and walloped Yuri on the head.

Silence . . . Then bloodcurdling screams. Mine and Yuri's. For once, I didn't hold back. 'You little shit! How dare you?' I grabbed Thomas by the arm and wrenched the stick out of his hand.

'Ow! You're mean and horrible! I hate you!' he cried, as Imogen pushed me away from her precious son.

'How dare you speak to Thomas like that?' she screeched. 'Poor little Tom-Tom. Show Mummy your sore arm. Really, Emma, there's no need to behave like a savage! It was an accident.'

I looked down at the big bump on Yuri's forehead and hissed, 'It was no accident! He's a brat who needs discipline, not bloody horse-riding lessons.'

Mrs Hamilton chose that moment to enter the room with a tray of sandwiches and tea, thus preventing Imogen and me scratching each other's eyes out. Which was a pity, because I felt I had the advantage on her. Granted, she had big muscly arms, but I had blind fury on my side, so I reckon she would have come off worse.

Later that evening, when they had left and Yuri had finally gone to sleep, James and I were getting ready for dinner with his parents. I was still furious about the bump on Yuri's poor little head. 'The little shit! God, James, I nearly hit him. He could have killed Yuri, or knocked him unconscious. Jesus, they should lock him up and throw away the key. I won't have him near Yuri again.'

'Come on, darling, calm down. Yuri's fine. It's just a bump. Kids are always pushing each other about, and Thomas didn't mean anything. It was just high spirits.'

I snorted at this lame excuse. 'He's a horrible little boy. I told you this weekend was going to be a disaster. Look at poor Yuri's head.'

'It's not a disaster. This was one incident and you saw how pleased Mother and Father were to meet their grandson. They couldn't have been more doting or generous.'

He was right. They'd been thrilled. 'Fair enough, they have been wonderful, but I don't want to see Thomas for the rest of the weekend. I don't care what you have to do or say to Henry, but he is not to be anywhere near me or Yuri because, I'm telling you, James, I won't be responsible for my actions.'

'OK, Tiger. Now, breathe deeply and unclench your jaw. I want my parents to see how motherhood has mellowed you.'

'Has it?' I asked.

'I haven't noticed a dramatic change so far, but I live in hope.'

'Oh, shut up,' I said, laughing. 'We can't all be the voice of reason.'

The next day Yuri's bump had gone down and he was in good form. He had only woken up twice during the night so I was very proud of him. We spent a lovely day with James's parents, going for a long walk across wonderfully unspoilt countryside, and Yuri loved being out in the fresh air. He behaved very well, too, except for a small incident when he flung a large amount of mayonnaise over Mr Hamilton's good tweed jacket. Still, in fairness, his grandfather took it in his stride and laughed it off.

That evening was Mr Hamilton's birthday dinner and we were going out with Henry and Imogen to a restaurant in the nearby town. A babysitter had been booked for Yuri, so I decided to take him up early and try to settle him before she arrived, in case he freaked when he saw yet another new face. Yuri, however, overtired from all the fresh air and exercise, had other ideas. Every time I tried to put him down, he began to roar. And I mean screaming at the top of his voice. It sounded as if he was being tortured, not merely put into his travel cot. I tried six times, but he kept freaking out, and I was afraid to leave him crying for ten minutes – as I would have done at home – because I thought James's parents would be shocked. Each time I picked him up, he stopped, but time was ticking by and I was desperate to have him asleep before the babysitter arrived.

Every time I tried to put his dummy into his mouth, he spat it out. The crying and spitting out went on for over an hour until I was at the end of my tether. I looked around for something to help and my eyes fell upon James's tie.

I looped the tie into the ring on the end of Yuri's dummy, I then secured it by tying it in a knot at the back of his head. The dummy was now pasted to his mouth so he couldn't spit it out. I laid him down in his cot. 'I'm sorry, sweetheart, but it's only two minutes while I shower,' I said, feeling like a very bad mother. 'Come on, now, calm down and go to sleep.'

He sat up and stared at me. I looked at my watch. We

were leaving in twenty minutes. I ran into the bathroom and had a speedy shower. When I got back to the room – literally two minutes later – Mrs Hamilton was standing at the cot, looking shocked.

'Emma, what on earth . . . Is he all right?' she asked. 'Is that what they do, these days?'

'Oh, ha-ha – no, not really, it was just for a minute to try to calm him down . . . I was just . . . you know . . . um . . . well . . .' I was at a loss for words. How on earth could I explain it to her? I bent down to undo the tie. Yuri spat the dummy on to the floor and let out the most almighty roar. I picked him up as Mrs Hamilton muttered something about leaving me to it.

A few minutes later, James came in. 'What on earth is going on?' he asked. 'My mother just told me that she found Yuri with a dummy tied to his head?'

'Well, it wasn't quite like that. He wouldn't stop crying – which I notice you completely ignored while you sat downstairs having pre-dinner drinks with your parents – so I had to resort to slightly desperate measures.'

'Like gagging him?'

'No, I just needed him to calm down so I secured the dummy in his mouth for a minute.'

'He could have choked.'

'He was breathing perfectly well through his nose. If you were so concerned you should have come up and helped me.'

'My poor mother came down shaking. We had to feed her a stiff brandy.'

'Well, I'd like a stiff drink myself, but, oh, no, while you and your dad quaff gin and tonics and talk about rugby, I'm left trying to settle a screaming child so that the babysitter won't take one look at him and turn on her heels.'

'Actually, Dad said he thought it sounded ingenious,' said James, beginning to laugh.

'But your mother thinks I'm certifiable.'

'Well, she did say she'd never seen anything quite like it before.'

'What did you say? That I'm just a lunatic, I suppose.'

'No, I said it was family trick your mother had passed down and I used it regularly on you to great effect.'

Chapter 19

A week after we got back from England, I went to meet Lucy and Jess for drinks – well, fizzy water for me, drinks for them. They both commented on my bump, which had suddenly sprouted. I'm not sure if it was the baby or that my appetite had come back with a vengeance. I was permanently starving. With nineteen weeks still to go, at this rate I'd be the size of a house by the time the baby was born. The really worrying thing was, that all I craved was chips, toast lathered in butter, and ice-cream. I had heard of women who craved carrots or liquorice but unfortunately I seemed to need grease in truckloads.

'So, how many weeks are you?' asked Jess.

'Oh, God, not the weeks thing,' said Lucy. 'I hate the way pregnant women do that. Everything's about weeks. For us plebs it just means we have to divide everything by four to try and work out how pregnant you are. Why do months go out the window when you're pregnant? Everyone talks about nine months until they get pregnant and then it's all about forty weeks.'

She had a point – and it was something I used to moan about too.

'Don't worry, I haven't forgotten how annoying it is.' I grinned. 'I'm twenty-one weeks – so, just over five months.'

'You're very neat,' said Jess.

'I won't be for much longer if I keep eating at the rate I am. How much weight did you put on?' I asked Jess.

'For Sally I ate like a horse and put on nearly four stone, which took me over a year to shed. With Roy I was a lot more careful and only put on two.'

'How much is considered normal?' I asked.

'They say two stone is about right,' said Jess.

'Is it really hard to lose?'

'Nightmare.'

'God, I really had better stop eating so much, then,' I said.

'On the positive side, your boobs are sensational,' said Lucy, nodding at my now almost *Playboy*-sized breasts.

I had always had a fine pair of boobs, but they had increased considerably in the last few weeks. I was heading towards Dolly Parton territory. 'I know – they're huge.' I giggled. 'I'll have to get new underwear – I'm spilling out of all my bras.'

'I'd love to have good boobs,' said Lucy, looking down at her fried eggs.

'Yeah, well, I'd love to have your figure,' I said. 'By the way, when will I start blooming?' I asked Jess. 'I'm as pale a ghost and I look like death at the moment. Or is it just bullshit?'

'I found from five months on much more enjoyable and your energy levels go up.'

'Well, if they went down any more I'd be horizontal. I'm permanently tired. I miss energy.'

'Don't worry, you've had a double whammy with Yuri coming along at the same time. You should get that book *What To Expect When You're Expecting*. It's really good – everyone in my mother-and-baby group has it,' said Jess.

I was a bit wary of her books after the ones she had lent me on child-rearing – and as for her mother-and-baby group . . .

160

'I'm not sure about the information thing,' I said. 'I totally overdid it with the research when I was trying to get pregnant and I don't think it did me any good – I was completely obsessed. I'm kind of avoiding all the pregnancy books. I think they'll just make me over-analyse it. I think I'm a less-is-more type of person. And by the way Jess, no offence, but those women in your baby group were hard going.'

'They sound like a bunch of bitches to me. Women with too much time on their hands are dangerous,' said Lucy, who had had a blow-by-blow account of the morning from me, and been furious on Yuri's and my behalf.

Jess bristled. 'They aren't all women with too much time on their hands, Lucy, they're just full-time mums, like me. I admit Sonia can be a bit hard to take, but she means well. She's just got an abrupt manner.'

'Emma said they were all dressed in designer gear at eleven o'clock in the morning,' said Lucy, landing me in it.

'What's wrong with wanting to look nice when you spend most of your time in old clothes covered with dribble? It's fun to dress up once in a while.'

'They were pretty insensitive about Yuri, especially that idiot Maura,' I said, getting a bit hot under the collar as I remembered how rude she was about him being adopted.

'You're the first person they've met who has adopted and they're not used to the idea. They didn't mean any harm. Anyway, it's not as if you didn't make your point. Maura was quite upset about it.'

'Gee, poor old Maura! Maybe next time she won't be so bloody insensitive. What about my feelings, Jess? They were implying that Yuri was some kind of charity case. How the hell do you think I felt?'

'I know you were annoyed – I stuck up for you, remember? But you have to accept that adoption is probably something Maura has never thought about. She was just uninformed as opposed to being deliberately cruel. And you *are* a bit sensitive about it – understandably so,' she said, backtracking when she saw my face darken.

'Pfff, they sound like a bunch of losers to me,' said Lucy.

'They're friends of mine, Lucy,' said Jess. 'I don't slag off your workmates.'

'That's because my colleagues are interesting and don't sit around all day talking about their Filipina maids and designer shirts. Those women spend far too much time drinking coffee and being dissatisfied with everything. You've told us before that they talk a lot about material things.'

'Sometimes they do go on about cars and clothes but, believe me, it's light relief after a week of sitting on the floor reading *Goldilocks and the Three Bears* over and over again, changing nappies and watching *The* sodding *Tellytubbies*.'

'Fair enough. That does sound pretty dull,' admitted Lucy.

I decided to change the subject. We were treading on dangerous territory. Both Lucy and Jess had had a good few drinks and they were singing from different hymn sheets, and probably always would be, on the issue of non-working mothers. Besides, I'd never see those women again, so there was no point in falling out with Jess over them. She was welcome to them and their mindless chit-chat. 'Can we talk about sex for a minute?' I piped up.

'Anytime, anyplace, anywhere,' said Lucy, encouragingly.

'Well, the thing is, between the sleep deprivation with Yuri and my pregnancy, my sex drive seems to have somewhat diminished.'

'Define "somewhat",' said Lucy, cutting to the chase.

'Vastly,' I replied.

'That's completely normal,' said Jess, who hadn't had sex with Tony for eight months after Sally was born.

'It just seems a bit strange, because we've gone from having sex twenty-four-seven when I was trying to get pregnant to having it sporadically.'

'It was the same when I was pregnant with Sally. Although when I was expecting Roy I was a lot randier,' said Jess.

'It's the tiredness I'm most worried about. It's zapping me.'

'Don't be so hard on yourself. You've had a really emotionally, not to mention physically, draining few months,' said Lucy.

'I fell asleep in the middle of it last night,' I blurted out, blushing at the memory.

'*What!*' they squealed, and laughed as they saw me squirm.

'Details, please,' said Jess.

I explained that the previous day I had realized that James and I hadn't had sex in ages, not since New Year's Eve, more than eight weeks ago. The problem was that the relief I felt when I finally collapsed into bed was so enormous that nothing could have enticed me to give up a second of sleep. Not even George Clooney could have persuaded me to offer up sacred sleep. But this was bad: all the books and magazines said it was important to keep up a healthy sex life after having children. I didn't want us to turn into one of those couples where the husband goes around leering at other women because he's starved sexually at home.

I put on a sexy little négligé – that was now not so sexy because my stomach was straining the seams but at least my cleavage looked good – and James came out of the bathroom to find me rolling about, trying to find a position that didn't highlight my expanding midriff.

'Hello,' he said, pleased to see the lacy black number. He knew he was on to a good thing. There was nothing subtle about my efforts.

'Hello, big boy,' I purred, sounding as ridiculous as I looked.

James laughed and hopped in beside me. We kissed and played around . . .

The next thing I knew, James was calling. 'Emma! Emma!'

'What?' I said, opening my eyes.

'Were you asleep?' he asked, appalled.

'Don't be ridiculous, I just had my eyes closed.' My God, I had nodded off. I realized now that I must have fallen asleep right in the middle of sex.

'I can't believe you were asleep.'

'I wasn't.'

'You were practically snoring.'

'I was having a great time. I must have just nodded off for a second.'

'In the middle of sex, Emma,' said James, looking put out. Clearly, having your wife fall asleep during intercourse was not good for a man's ego.

'Yes, but not on purpose. I wasn't bored or anything, I'm just really, really tired. Sorry.' I felt awful. How could I have fallen asleep? It was so insulting for poor James.

'You should have told me you were tired. I thought, with the lacy nightdress, you were up for a night of passion.'

'I was. I am. Come on, let's get back to it. I'm wide awake now.'

'I hardly think that's a good idea. You clearly need a good night's sleep.'

'Come on, it's not as if we'll be here for hours. Chop-chop.'

'Darling, when your wife goes into a coma during sex, it's a passion-killer to say the least. We'll call it a night.'

'No, come on, look, I'm full of beans now,' I said, jumping up and down on the bed. 'Let's go for it. Will I get out the Rampant Rabbit to spice things up?' I asked, referring to the large rabbit-like vibrator that Babs had ordered for me over the Internet when we were trying to conceive.

'To be honest,' said James, looking down at himself, 'the Rabbit might be your best bet this evening. I don't think I'm going to bounce back – as it were – from the shock of finding you asleep.'

'Sorry, James,' I said, hugging him. 'You know it's not that I don't love you or find you incredibly sexy, it's just lack of sleep.'

'It's OK. But you should go to sleep now and try to catch up. I'd like you to be a bit more involved next time.'

Jess and Lucy were roaring laughing by the time I'd finished the story. 'Poor James!' said Lucy.

'I know, I felt awful,' I groaned. 'I need some kind of female Viagra.'

'You'll start feeling more energetic soon,' Jess assured me. 'The first few months of pregnancy are really draining, and with Yuri as well it's no wonder you fell asleep. Are you taking any iron?'

I shook my head.

'Well, you should start. Spatone do sachets that you can dissolve in orange juice. It'll help.'

'I'll get some tomorrow.'

'I'd start with a double dose, if I was you,' said Lucy, winking at me.

Chapter 20

Lucy woke up to a silver rectangle being waved at her. She opened a bleary eye. 'What are you doing?' she asked, as Donal shook it under her nose.

'I thought we had an agreement.'

'What are you talking about? For God's sake, it's eight o'clock on Saturday morning and I've hours of sleep left. Whatever it is, it can wait.' Lucy pulled the duvet over her head.

'Lucy, why are all the weekdays gone out of this packet?'

Lucy frowned. What on earth was he crashing on about at this ungodly hour? She poked her head out. 'What?'

Donal was holding her packet of Nordette contraceptive pills and pointing at the missing days. 'Why are you still taking these yokes? We said we'd try for a baby.'

'No, we did not,' Lucy said, awake now. 'You said you wanted to try immediately and I said I didn't. We never agreed to anything. In fact, we disagreed. And since when do you go around rooting in my bath-bag?'

'I was looking for a nail scissors and I saw these. Lookit, Lucy, you're no spring chicken and it's time these went in the bin.'

'Thirty-six is not that old. Stop telling me I'm past my prime.'

'Can you not stop with these things and give it a shot? I'd make a great father. I've done a good job with Annie and you get on well with her now.'

Lucy snorted. 'Annie's the troublemaker who tried to break us up, remember?'

'Believe me, I remember it well. Let's give it a go, for the hell of it.'

'I just don't feel ready yet. I'm still reeling from the wedding. Can we just stall the ball for a few months?'

'If you're afraid you'll be a bad mother, don't worry. Look at your own – she's a dreadful old boot and you turned out fine.'

'Don't call my mother a boot.'

'You called Annie a troublemaker.'

'Yeah, well, that's different because she was a wench to me for a long time.'

'Every time your mother sees me, she practically hisses,' said Donal.

'I admit she's not your biggest fan.'

'She thinks I'm a joke.'

'Not any more. When I told her you'd given up playing rugby and started a career as a sports presenter, you went right up in her estimation. I think she sees you as the new Des Lynam.'

'I was thinking more Gary Lineker myself. We're both young, good-looking sportsmen with a professional air about us.'

Lucy laughed. Donal seized the moment: 'So, will you stop taking these?'

Lucy paused. 'I'm scared.'

'Of what?'

'Of having kids and becoming one of those couples who fight all the time. I like our relationship the way it is. I like my life. I don't want it to change.'

'It won't, and to be fair, it's not as if we've never had a fight.'

'Yeah, but everyone has the odd row – it's not like the constant sniping that harassed, sleep-deprived parents do.'

'We'll be different. We'll only eat the face off each other once in a while, like we do now. There'll be no sniping. Come on, Lucy, let's at least try.'

Lucy looked at his eager face. He was right: she wasn't getting any younger and it'd probably take a while . . . and she thought she might want a child eventually . . . and it was day twenty-seven in her cycle so she had no chance of getting pregnant if they had sex now. She'd think about coming off the pill later. She wasn't ready just yet, but for the moment Donal needed to be pacified.

She nodded as Donal hopped on top of her to get some practice in.

My bump seemed to be getting bigger by the second, along with my appetite. I called in to Mum's to collect Yuri, having skipped lunch because of some mini-drama on the set at work. The head of the Flower Arrangers' Society of Ireland had arrived for her slot, late and absolutely plastered. The woman could barely stand. She swayed from side to side, precariously carrying an enormous, award-winning floral creation, which looked the worse for wear. Amanda was freaking out because they had allocated twenty minutes to the slot and she had nothing else to fill it. I spent thirty minutes plying the woman with coffee to try to sober her up and she eventually stumbled on and managed to slur her way through the piece, although her attempts to show the viewers how to reconstruct the bouquet she had brought with her were comedic to say the least: she repeatedly dropped the flowers and cut off their heads. Amanda kept having to go to commercial breaks as the rest of us desperately tried to mirror the two flower arrangements.

By the time I got to Mum's to pick up Yuri, I was starving. I headed straight for the bread and was soon buttering myself three large slices of toast.

'You'd want to watch that,' said Mum, shaking her head as she watched me stuff the toast into my mouth.

'Watch what?'

'Eating too much. You don't want to turn into one of those big pregnant girls who let themselves go. You have to be careful, Emma. It's all very well saying you need to eat for two but the truth of it is that if you do you'll end up looking like young Maureen Doherty before the Weight Watchers.'

'I didn't have time for lunch, OK? I'm starving, so I'm having a few slices of toast. It's not as if I've just got up from a large meal.'

'If you pile on the weight while you're pregnant, you'll find it very hard to lose. Believe me, trying to shift those pounds after you've had a baby is very difficult, especially at your age. You need to stay away from those car-bo-hy-drates,' she said, almost spelling the word out for me. 'Apparently that's what does the damage. According to Nuala, if you cut out bread, potatoes and pasta after six o'clock, you'll never put on any weight. She read it in an interview with Catherine Zina-Jones on how she lost all her weight. Nuala's trying it out and she's lost two pounds already.'

'Zeta. How long has she been doing it?'

'Four weeks now.'

'Hardly miraculous.'

169

'She looks well on it and says she feels more energetic. Those carbohydrates are no good for you after six. They won't break down and just stay on your hips. Fruit and veg is what you need, and it'll be good for the baby too. And no crisps or biscuits at all. They are the easiest calories to put on and the hardest to lose, Nuala says.'

'OK, well, I'll –'

'Oh, and the other thing she said was that you have to drink eight litres of water a day, which seems an awful lot.'

'It's eight glasses, Mum,' I said, trying to be patient. Nuala had been on a diet for thirty years. In the past she had waxed lyrical about the cabbage-soup diet, the Atkins diet, the grapefruit diet, Unislim, Weight Watchers, the Fit for Life diet, the Scarsdale diet and Slim-fast. You name it, Nuala had been on it and, as far as I could see, none had worked: she was exactly the same shape. But every time she discovered a new diet, she'd ring Mum up and tell her, in detail, what it entailed.

'I was wondering. I knew it couldn't be eight litres. Anyway, if I was you, I'd stay away from lumps of bread and butter or you'll end up with big hips you'll be stuck with for life. And you're small, Emma, you haven't got height on your side. You're a pear shape like me, so you need to be careful. Your sister's taller, she could get away with it more easily –'

'Speaking of Babs,' I said, interrupting her before she could depress me any further by pointing out the rest of my shortcomings, 'have you heard from her recently?'

'No, nor your brother. It's only eight weeks to the wedding and he still hasn't told me what Shady's mother's wearing so I haven't been able to look round the shops for my own outfit. Whenever I ask him anything about the arrangements, he tells me not to worry, just turn up and smile. Sure I've no idea what type of a day to expect. I posted him a list of the people we want to invite five days ago and I haven't heard a dicky-bird since. I might as well be a distant relation for all the information I'm given. I want you to ring him and find out exactly what's going on. He'll tell you. Then you can let me know. Be sure to ask him what colour Shady's mother's outfit is – or maybe she's not allowed wear colours at all, maybe it has to be black. I know nothing. Totally in the dark I am about my own son's wedding. Is it too much to ask for a little involvement? Well, is it?'

'I'll tell you what. I'll head off now and try to catch him in work. I'll let you know what he says,' I said, backing out of the door with Yuri under one arm before the tirade got worse.

When I got home I rang Sean. 'Hi.'

'Hey, how are you? How's my nephew?'

'Great thanks, getting bigger and cuter by the day. Look, I'm ringing to warn you that Mum's on the warpath. She's feeling very left out of all the wedding arrangements so you might want to give her a buzz and feed her some info before she goes totally mental.'

Sean sighed. 'I got her guest list in the post yesterday. She wants to invite sixty people when I specifically told her that the entire wedding was only going to be eighty. She even has Father Murphy on the list.'

'What?' I said, laughing. Father Murphy was the local parish priest. He was a nice man but by no means a close friend of the family.

'She obviously wants a Catholic priest at the blessing to

try to convert Shadee or something equally awful. Anyway, he's not coming.'

'Who else is on the list?'

'The entire bridge club and every relation we have.'

'What're you going to do?'

'I'll have to call her. She can have twenty-two people max. Shadee's folks have invited eighteen, and we're having forty.'

Yikes! Twenty-two people. That would just about cover the uncles and aunts, leaving no room for friends. Mum was going to freak and I knew that Dad had invited his two partners in the office already. Still, it wasn't my wedding – I had fought enough battles over my own – so I was going to leave Sean to fight his own corner.

'How's Babs? Has she settled into her new place?'

'I think so. It's a nice big one-bedroom apartment over-looking the Thames.'

'Typical of her to land on her feet. Do you think she has any friends to hang out with?'

'She seems to be out all the time. Whenever I call to take her out for a meal or invite her over, she's busy.'

'Have you seen her show?'

'No, she's always on during the day, but she seems to be doing well. She's extremely confident about having her contract renewed and getting a big raise. She keeps telling me it's all in the bag.'

'Well, you know Babs. If anyone's going to get what they want, it's her. You must be glad to have the place back to yourselves.'

'God, Emma, you've no idea. She's impossible to live with. I nearly strangled her on several occasions.'

'Do you think she's seeing anyone? I mean, you know –'

'Do I think she's sleeping her way around London?' said Sean, cutting to the chase.

'Bit harsh.'

'This is Babs we're talking about.'

'Fair enough.'

'I don't know. She's pretty secretive about her social life. Whenever I ask her what she's been up to she just tells me she's having a laugh and enjoying London, unlike me, who's a boring old fart apparently.'

I laughed. 'Oh, well, good to see nothing's changed. I'll give her a call to see how she's doing. You better phone Mum and nip her invitations in the bud before the bridge-club women charter a plane for the wedding.'

Sean groaned. 'I'll have to have a stiff drink before facing that.'

Later that night, when Yuri was in bed, I called Babs.

'Yeah?'

'Charming way to answer the phone.'

'Oh, hi,' she said, sounding exceedingly unenthusiastic to hear my voice.

'How are you?'

'Grand.'

'I'm good too, thanks for asking.'

'So, what's up? Did Mum tell you to call me and make sure I'm not living under a bridge in a cardboard box, mainlining heroin?'

'No.'

'Oh.'

'I'm just ringing to see how you are. It's something sisters do from time to time. It's not that unusual in civilized society.'

173

'Well, I'm fine.'

'Sean said your new place is really nice. Are you OK living on your own? Is it not a bit lonely?'

'Unlike you and Sean, I have a life. I actually like going out after sundown and partying, so no, Emma, I'm not lonely. In fact, I'm having a ball over here. Living in Sean's was doing my head in. Now that I have my own place things have got much better.'

'I hope you're not going mental, are you?'

'Mental?'

'Yes, mental. Overdoing it. Drinking too much. Partying too hard.'

'Jesus, you sound like Mum.'

'Is that a denial?'

'It's more of a sod-off-and-mind-your-own-business.'

'Are you seeing anyone?'

'*Seeing anyone?* What are you? Seventy years old? No, Emma, I don't have a significant other, if that's what you mean.'

'I'm shocked. You're such a charmer – how can they resist you?'

'Hilarious.'

'How's work?'

'Very good, actually, I'm due a promotion soon. My contract's up for renegotiation next month. I'll start earning real money then.'

'How come you're so sure?'

'I just am.'

'Did your boss say it to you?'

'Not in so many words.'

'Well, what did he say?'

'Look, I just know he's going to promote me.'

'Well, you must be doing something right.'

'You can safely say I'm the most dedicated employee he's ever had.'

Chapter 21

Leinster was due to play Bath in another of the qualifying rounds of the European Cup and James, as usual, was up to high-do. With Donal out of the team, James had appointed Ben Casey as captain but he didn't seem too sure of Ben's leadership skills. 'I just don't know if he'll be able to fire the boys up,' he said, chewing on his steak at dinner.

'Well, why did you make him captain then?' I asked.

'Because he's the best player we have and I'm hoping he'll lead by example, if not by rousing speeches.'

'Did Donal really give inspiring team talks?' I asked. 'I thought that was your forte.' I somehow doubted that Donal would be the type to quote Churchill or Lincoln, as James had done when he wrote his pre-Final speech last year. He had spent hours poring over books of quotes. Personally I thought a more direct approach would have been better, but it seemed to have worked: the team came out and played brilliantly.

'I talk to them before they go on to the pitch, but it was Donal who kept them focused during the games. I don't know if Ben has that skill.'

'Well, you could shout from the sidelines. Get one of those megaphone things and roar encouragement through that.'

'I hardly think that's appropriate. Have you ever seen a coach do that?'

'No,' I admitted. 'But, hey, I could start a cheerleading team if you like. Myself and Lucy could come out with pom-poms and dance up and down the sidelines like those American girls at the football games. I've always quite fancied being a cheerleader. I bet you that'd get the boys going.'

James glanced pointedly at my bump and raised his eyebrows. 'Much as I love the idea of my wife swinging her legs about on the sidelines of the games, I'm not sure you're quite cheerleading material in your present condition.'

'Good point. I'll just have to be the coach and Lucy and the other girlfriends could do the dancing. I'd say I'd be a good choreographer.'

I imagined six girls lined up in a row, all dressed in red and blue shouting, 'Give me an L, give me an E . . . Whadda you got? LEINSTER!' and waving their pom-poms in the air. I could watch American football on Sky Sports and copy down some of the routines. It was bound to be easy enough.

'Earth to Emma,' said James, bringing me back to reality. 'I can see you're already planning the first cheerleader session, and while I appreciate the support, I think it might be best left to the Americans.'

'The Leinster Lovelies – isn't that perfect?'

'Tell me you're joking,' said James, beginning to look worried.

'Deadly serious.'

'Darling, it's just not the done thing.'

'Stuff the done thing! Let's have some fun. I'll call myself Busty Hamilton and Luscious Lucy will be the chief cheerleader. Come on, James, give me an L . . .' I said, waving my napkin in the air and giggling as I saw the look of horror on his face.

A few days later we were in Dr Philips's clinic to have a check-up and an ultrasound. I was just over six months pregnant and had heard that I'd be able to see the baby really clearly on this scan so I was very excited. We chatted as Dr Philips took my blood pressure. He asked James about the upcoming game against Bath. Dr Philips, it seemed, was a big Leinster fan and the two men talked of strategy and players' form. Eventually I interrupted them and said I'd like to have my scan.

I lay down on the bed and Dr Philips squirted gel on to my tummy and took out the scanner. The screen was pretty blurry, but we could make out the shape of a baby and the doctor began to point to his/her hands and feet. A huge lump formed in my throat as I stared at my baby wriggling about on the screen. It felt like a miracle. Having given up all hope, I still found it hard to believe I was pregnant and that I was going to have a baby. I beamed up at James, who was hovering in the background peering at the screen. But just as I caught my husband's eye, Dr Philips interrupted: 'So, Donal Brady's out for good, is he?' he asked.

'Afraid so,' said James. 'That shoulder injury has been with him a long time. He should really have had the surgery years ago, but he kept playing.'

'You'll miss him, I'd say. He was a great player.'

'And a great captain.'

'I'll never forget that try he scored against Toulouse – it came out of nowhere. He had a great ability to score from nothing, didn't he?'

James nodded as I gripped the sides of the bed. I wanted to shout at them to stop talking about bloody rugby and focus on the scan. I had waited a long time to see this and I wanted the undivided attention of my obstetrician. I did not want to look at the back of his head while he discussed Donal's talents on the rugby pitch with James. I glared at

James, who carried on, oblivious: 'It was an incredible try. He surpassed himself that day.'

'How do you rate his replacement, O'Hare? He seems a solid enough player,' Dr Philips went on.

Before James could start analysing Peter O'Hare's style of play I butted in: 'So,' I said loudly, 'what are we looking at here?'

Reluctantly Dr Philips returned his focus to the baby and moved the scanner about, pointing out its heart and a leg . . . and then he got distracted again. 'I remember O'Hare playing in schools rugby. He stood out even then,' he said, looking at James as the scanner drifted off to the side of my stomach, where I could see nothing. He might have thought he was good at multi-tasking but he wasn't. Men can't do two things at once. Women can. We can drive and talk on the phone, we can talk while listening to the conversation behind us, we can put our makeup on while getting dressed, and we can iron while feeding a child its dinner. 'So, everything looks OK, then?' I asked.

'He was born to play rugby,' agreed James.

'Naturally talented,' said Dr Philips.

I tapped Dr Philips on the arm. 'What? Oh, yes, Emma, everything looks absolutely fine. The baby's growing well and all its organs are developing as they should. Nothing to worry about at all.'

'Thank you,' I grunted, as he handed me some tissue to wipe the gel off my stomach.

Once we got to the car, I rounded on James. 'For goodness' sake, what was that in there?'

'What?' he said, looking at my red face.

'All that rugby chat. I was trying to get the man to focus

on the scan and you kept crashing on about Donal and Peter.'

'I was being polite. He asked me questions and I answered. I didn't initiate the conversation and I can't help it if the man's a rugby fan.'

'There's a time and place to have rugby chat, and the middle of my scan is not one of them. I was glaring at you to make you stop talking, but you completely ignored me.'

'I was wondering what that was. I thought you looked a bit odd.'

'I wanted you to shut up and stop distracting him. I was trying to get him to explain to me what I was looking at on the screen and to check that the baby was OK, which was pretty hard to do when he had his back to me and the screen for the entire time.'

'What was I supposed to do? Ignore his questions? You can't be rude.'

'Well, you didn't have to be so long-winded and you could have asked him some questions about the baby. That was what we were there for. It was supposed to be a check-up, not a rugby conference.'

'Why are you getting so wound up? Everything's fine, the baby's healthy. Is this your hormones talking?'

'Excuse me?'

'I had a flick through that book you bought – *What To Expect* – and in the chapter on fathers it said that women can be irrational during pregnancy due to hormonal changes but that it's important to be patient and remember that it's not a permanent condition.'

I stared at James. I'd had no idea he'd read it. 'When did this happen?'

'I picked it up the other day when Yuri went for a nap.'

I wasn't sure if I wanted James reading up on pregnancy. He was very factual and always read the small print. I was more of an overall-picture person myself. I didn't want him tormenting me with details that I had overlooked. It was like the car: I drove it until the petrol light went red and started flashing and screaming, 'Fill me up or I'll conk out.' James couldn't understand this: to him it was the behaviour of an alien. When the petrol gauge even considered heading towards the red, he'd drive straight to a garage and have the tank filled. How any sane person would risk their car breaking down because they hadn't bothered to fill it was inconceivable to him. Most of the time I didn't notice the red light until it started flashing. Petrol was not a priority in my life and I found filling up the tank a bore, so I just left it until it reached crisis point and then I'd drive five miles out of my way to the only garage I knew that employed someone to fill the tank for you.

'I learnt a lot from the few sections I read. I presume you're going to breastfeed,' he said, still referring to the book.

'Presume'? What did he mean 'presume'? After the horror stories I'd read and heard I had no intention of breast-feeding. Apparently your nipples got all cracked and bled. Besides which you leaked milk all the time like a cow and then you had that scary-looking machine that I had seen Jess use where you milked your boobs. It was barbaric.

'They say breast is best,' said James.

'Who says?'

'The doctors. Didn't you see the posters up in Dr Philips's waiting room?'

'No,' I admitted, having been far too busy scrutinizing the latest issue of *Now* magazine, which featured very un-

181

flattering photos of celebrities on the beach. It was fantastic: I felt much better about myself after seeing their cellulite.

'It also says in the book that – and I quote – "There is no question that breastfeeding is best for your baby. It provides the perfect food,"' James continued.

That was what bugged me about him. How could he remember precise quotes? Come on, who can actually quote from a book they read the day before? I can barely remember titles. 'So?' I said, sounding like a sulky teenager. 'Who cares what some stupid book says? What do they know? It's just one person's opinion, and Jess said breastfeeding's awful. Really, really painful – excruciating, she said.'

'Just because Jess found it difficult doesn't mean you will. It's better for the baby – safer, prevents allergies and infections, and boosts the child's IQ.'

'And what's in it for me?' I said, dazzling him with the counter-argument of a five-year-old.

'It's also supposed to be beneficial to mothers. It helps you regain your figure more quickly and reduces the risk of cancer.'

'Oh, yeah? What about cracked nipples and mastitis?'

'What's mastitis?' said the resident breastfeeding pusher. I breathed a sigh of relief. For once I knew something he didn't.

'It's when your breasts get infected and your temperature goes through the roof. Apparently you're in agony and then you get depressed and you resent the baby and it's all because you breastfed,' I added, for dramatic effect. I could see I'd overdone it, though, because James was looking suspicious.

'And you have to pump your breasts like a cow if you breastfeed.' I was a little hazy on the details of why and when but it had looked torturous when Jess did it.

'Well, that does sound a little uncomfortable, but breastfeeding is supposed to be a wonderful bonding experience for mother and child and the benefits far outweigh the disadvantages.'

'I've got a great idea. Why don't you try sticking your penis into a breast pump and see if it's a "little uncomfortable" for you or more like a form of torture.'

'Well, if you're going to be immature about this –'

'*Immature!* It's all very well for you to sit there on the sidelines dictating what I should do with my body while you look on. I think you should have hands-on experience of the pain before you go dishing out advice that you read in a book, and making me feel guilty because I don't want to go through any more pain after labour, which, by the way, will probably end up with me having my vagina stitched – externally and internally.'

James winced. 'There's no need –'

'Yes, actually, there is need. I am nipping this in the bud right now. I refuse to be dictated to by someone who has no experience of childbirth or feeding and never will. I'm sorry, James, but you can read all the books you want and quote me reams of passages about the pros of breastfeeding, but when it comes down to it, it's my boobs in the pump, my cracked nipples and my sore fanny, so if I was you I'd stand back and do the silent supportive thing.'

'We'll leave it for now. We can talk about it again when you're calmer.'

'THERE WILL BE NO CALMER. THIS IS NON-NEGOTIABLE. I AM NOT BLOODY BREASTFEEDING SO GET IT INTO YOUR THICK SKULL.'

Calmly James put on his seatbelt and started the car, 'Well, darling, it's good to see that you don't appear to have been in the least bit affected by any hormonal imbalance.'

Chapter 22

Babs stifled a yawn as the producer counted down. She was doing a spot about some new leopard-print mini-dress with Leslie. The dress was cheap and badly made and Babs was sick of flogging crappy products. Besides, Leslie drove her insane. She was totally over-the-top enthusiastic about everything she was selling and Babs thought she sounded insincere and fake.

'Hello, everyone, welcome to BFL's fashion slot. Golly, do we have a treat for you today!' she gushed. 'Leopard-print mini-dresses that will make you look sensational! Don't you agree, Babs?'

'Oh, yes, they're a knockout.'

'As you can see, our lovely model Candice is wearing one and looks so feminine and even, dare I say, sexy?' giggled Leslie, as if she'd just said something really outrageous. Babs rolled her eyes. 'This dress is perfect for a woman who likes her man to treat her well,' continued Leslie.

'Or for a woman who's gagging for a shag,' added Babs, smirking into the camera. 'If you don't have a man and are looking to get lucky, I recommend that you get off the couch and put this dress on with a Wonderbra and a pair of six-inch heels. You'll definitely get laid.'

Leslie recoiled in horror while the cameraman tried not to laugh.

'We also have a, um . . . a . . .' Leslie was flustered now.

'Butterfly tops with matching skirts, which I am lucky

enough to be wearing,' said Babs, pointing to the enormous blue and green sequined butterfly splayed across her chest. It was the most hideous thing she had ever seen. Your granny wouldn't wear it, she thought grumpily. What type of loser would actually want to go out in *this*?

'Yes, that's right,' said Leslie, regaining her composure. 'And how does Barbara look in it? Sensational! I'm so excited about this matching outfit that I'm coming over all funny.' She tittered. 'I've ordered it myself in size medium. I'm going to wear it to my husband's office party.'

'I'm sure it'll go down a treat,' drawled Babs. 'If any of you viewers want to go out looking like you've been attacked by an oversized butterfly, you, too, can buy this outfit for just forty-seven ninety-five. You'll get noticed, all right, but don't expect to score in it. If you have to wear it, save it for church outings or flower-arranging meetings. Do not wear it on a Saturday night or on a blind date. Believe me, guys will go for the girl in the leopard-print mini every time.'

They went to commercial break and Billy stormed on to the set. 'What are you doing?'

Babs shrugged.

'We're trying to shift these bloody clothes. I can't have you sat there slagging them off. The manufacturers are watching this. We need the business and you know the score. Sell whatever you're given, show no favouritism and do it properly.'

'It's the same manufacturer,' said Babs, glaring at him. 'If you'd bothered to check it out, the same people make the leopard-print mini-dress and the gross butterfly top, so it makes no shagging difference to them which they sell more of – it's all profit.'

'The butterfly top is more expensive so just belt up, smile and shift it,' snapped Billy.

'Well, maybe if you paid me more than the slave wages I'm getting, I'd find it easier to sell this shit,' Babs hissed.

'We're back on air,' said the producer.

Leslie and Babs were now moving from clothes to jewellery. Three-stone aquamarine rings that were selling at fifty-five pounds ninety-eight. The stones were set in a gold band, shaped like a snake's head.

'Oh, Barbara, will you look at this ring? It's exquisite,' squealed Leslie. 'It would be the perfect engagement ring. No woman could resist this stunning piece of jewellery. It's like something Elizabeth Taylor might wear.'

Babs put it on and looked at it. 'To be honest, Leslie, if some guy asked me to marry him and produced this sorry excuse for a ring, I'd tell him where to stick it. Look, ladies, if this is all your bloke can come up with, say no. He doesn't love you and the marriage won't last. Dump him, get out the leopard-print mini-dress and head off on the town to find someone new.'

Leslie laughed nervously, 'Oh, Barbara, you are funny. She's such a kidder. Now, folks, this stunning ring can be yours for just . . .'

The section ended with Leslie reading out the product code while Babs sat and sulked. Billy was furious. He dragged her off the set and into his office, then slammed the door. 'What the hell do you think you're doing?'

'I'm sick of selling cheap trash to people who should know better. I've sold more products over the last three months than anyone else and you still haven't given me a raise. I decided to show you what it'd be like if I didn't perform my usual magic.'

'And this is supposed to make me appreciate your talents?'
Babs nodded.

'You sad cow,' said Billy, 'do you honestly think because you shifted some gear that you're the best thing on TV? I have hundreds of birds begging me for jobs. You're just one of many. And, in case you've forgotten, you're living rent-free in my apartment, so if I was you, I'd stop nagging me about a raise. You've got it good, girl, and don't forget it.'

'I think you've got a pretty good deal out of it yourself, Billy. You're not Colin Farrell and you're not running the bloody BBC. You said yourself it's the best sex of your life, so don't try to make out that you're doing me a big favour by putting me up. And as for nagging you about that raise, I haven't even got warmed up yet.'

'I've got a nagging wife at home and I don't need another in the office. You'll have to change your tactics, love. I come to work to get away from it, not to listen to another version.'

Damn. He was beginning to sound really fed up with her and Babs needed to keep Billy on her side. She loved living in the apartment and had the best of both worlds as he was only there two nights a week at the most. Besides, she really liked him: he was fun and he didn't let her walk all over him like all her previous boyfriends had. The fact that he was almost old enough to be her father meant that he gave as good as he got. And he took her to cool restaurants and bars. And the sex was great.

'OK, then, how about a little persuasion of the flesh?'

'Sorry, what was that? I was distracted by a large insect stuck to your tits,' said Billy, grinning as Babs locked the door and peeled off the offending top . . .

*

187

I was trying to feed Yuri, who was flinging his yogurt all over the kitchen and squealing with delight, when the phone rang. I picked it up and tucked it under my yogurt-sodden chin.

'Well?' said Mum.

'Well what?'

'Any news from London?'

'You mean Babs?'

'No, I mean your brother and that fiancée of his. I've heard nothing, and I've left two messages on the phone this week.'

I dodged another spray of food. 'Well, I haven't heard from him either, so he's probably just really busy in work.'

'I've been on the Internet.'

Oh, God, not the Internet again. Whenever Mum went on one of her fact-finding missions on the computer, it always ended in disaster.

'"Iranian wedding ceremonies" is what I typed in and I'm telling you, Emma, it's most insulting. The bride's mother-in-law gets a terrible time, no respect at all, and they encourage these dismissive and insulting customs.'

'Mum, you're going to have to be more specific. I have no idea what you're talking about.'

'Well, according to the information I read, there's a part in the ceremony where the corner of a scarf is sewn together with multi-coloured thread, and this apparently represents the lips of the mother-in-law not being able to speak unpleasant words to the bride. It tells everyone that the bride doesn't want any interference from the in-laws in her marriage. Well, did you ever in your life? The blatant insult of it.'

I tried not to laugh. What a brilliant idea. The Iranians

were geniuses. It was inspired. From the day of your marriage you were making it very clear that you wanted no interference. Oh, the joy for Shadee if Mum's lips were sewn together! 'I'm sure it's just some old tradition that isn't used any more,' I said, opting for the diplomatic approach. I didn't think Mum would appreciate it if I told her I thought it was the cleverest custom I'd heard of.

'It said it still takes place in modern weddings. I can tell you now that if I see any manner of a scarf being produced and Shady within a hundred yards of a needle and thread, I'm leaving that wedding and I'll never speak to her again.'

'Well, maybe that's how it's supposed to work.' I laughed, unable to contain myself.

'This is no laughing matter, Emma. I have never heard anything so rude in my life. And I wouldn't mind but I haven't interfered one iota in their relationship or, indeed, in the wedding plans. Sure how could I? I've been totally excluded. "Just turn up and smile," says Sean to me, the last time I was able to talk to him. That was before he stopped returning my calls. I suppose the scarf is already out over there with the corners sewn together and that's why he's not talking to me. I've obviously already been cast aside with no permission to have an opinion.'

'Come on, Mum, you're jumping to conclusions because of something you read on the Internet. You're not being fair.'

'That's not the half of it. Wait until you hear this. According to the computer, the groom's family is expected to pay all the expenses, and if they can't, they'll be looked down on. Well, when I read that I told your father to get out his cheque book. I'll not have anyone looking down on us. Apparently the higher the social standing of the bride, the more lavish the wedding and presents must be. And it says that an elaborate wedding in Iran today costs about . . .' she paused for maximum effect '. . . one hundred thousand dollars.'

What? She must have read it incorrectly. 'Don't be ridiculous. That's absolute rubbish. You were reading about a royal wedding or something.'

'I was not. I went back and checked it twice and then I got your father to read it. The poor man nearly had a heart-attack. We'll have to sell the house.'

'Hold on a minute. First of all, the wedding isn't taking place in Iran. Second, as far as I know, Sean is paying for the whole thing himself and I can assure you it isn't going to cost anything close to that. They're keeping it small and personal. You can tell Dad to relax.'

'The bride is supposed to be showered with expensive jewellery while the groom only receives a few gifts,' continued Mum. 'And I thought it was supposed to be a chauvinistic society! It seems to me that the girls over there get the best of everything. Lord knows what'll happen to poor Sean. He'll be bankrupt after this and Shady'll be sitting there dripping in jewellery that we've had to remortgage the house to buy her, and me not allowed to say boo to her because my lips are sewn together.'

At least she had come down from selling the house outright to merely remortgaging. This was a good sign. I decided to be firm.

'Stop overreacting. Shadee has never asked for anything. She's a very sweet, undemanding person who is devoted to Sean. Besides, she's lived in London all her life and probably has no interest in any of these traditions. They're getting married in a country house near Brighton, for goodness' sake.'

'Should I give her my mother's diamond necklace? I was keeping it for Barbara, but I won't have Shady's family saying we're not doing our bit. I won't be accused of being tight-fisted. We've always been a giving nation. The Irish are renowned for their generosity and I'll not let the side down. We're ambassadors for our country and I want Shady's people to see that Sean comes from a good family. They may be of high standing in Iran, but we Burkes are of high standing in our own community.'

'Mum, put Granny's necklace away and please stay away from the computer. It's not good for you. You always get wound up and it's not fair to assume that Shadee's family want or expect any of the things mentioned in the article you read, and I can promise you that you won't be having your lips sewn up. So stop giving yourself and Dad heart-attacks about it. I'll track Sean down and get him to give you a call. Now, forget about what you read, it's probably all nonsense.'

'Well, I wouldn't worry too much about your father. He thinks the lip-sewing tradition is priceless. He said he's going to get a scarf of his own and learn how to sew. Oh, if only Sean was marrying young Maureen Doherty from down the road . . .'

I hung up before she got going on that particular topic and contemplated buying a scarf myself . . .

Chapter 23

The Leinster versus Bath match was being played in Bath on Saturday so James headed off to England with the squad on Thursday afternoon. I had decided not to subject Yuri to another flight so I was staying at home and would watch the match on TV. We waved James off at the airport and wished him luck. If Leinster won, they were through to the quarter-finals, so James was understandably nervous and had been analysing the Bath players for weeks. He had spent the last few days muttering about Philip O'Leary not being a good enough mauler.

'Mauler? Do you mean the players are supposed to grope the other team to put them off?' I asked, genuinely shocked. I'd thought rugby was supposed to be a very macho game – I couldn't imagine the team being encouraged to molest the opposition.

James frowned. 'What on earth are you talking about?'

'Mauling. I would have thought it wasn't allowed. What's Philip supposed to do? Pinch the other players' bums to distract them?' I laughed.

James sighed. 'A maul is when the players are trying to get the ball before it touches the ground. You understand as much about rugby as I do about makeup, and I think we should leave it at that.'

'But I want to know more. I want to be able to tell Yuri about it when we're watching the games.'

'I appreciate the enthusiasm, darling, but it would take

too long to explain it to you. I can teach Yuri everything when he's older.'

'OK, but I have one more question.'

'What's that?'

'Who's Gary Owen?'

James groaned.

'You never mentioned him before and now it's all Bath and their Gary Owen this and Gary Owen that, and I just wondered if he's some amazing new player I should know about.'

'A Garryowen is an up-and-under kick.'

I looked at him blankly.

Very slowly, trying not to lose patience, James said, 'It's a punt kick by a player on the attacking side where the ball is sent high over their opponent's head. This gives the team time to charge down the ball.'

'So who is Gary? Did he invent the kick?'

'Garryowen is one of Ireland's most famous rugby clubs. It's based in Limerick and they invented the up-and-under kick, so it's named after the club, not a person.'

'Oh,' I said, still not totally getting the up-and-under concept but not wanting to ask any more questions because (a) James was getting frustrated, and (b) it wasn't really all that interesting. He was right: I was better off sticking to makeup. Besides, I understood the basics of rugby – tries and penalty kicks. James could explain the finer points to Yuri when he was older. 'Well, you learn something new every day,' I added.

James smiled. 'I can see your eyes glazing over. I think we'll leave the rugby talk for the dressing room. Anyway, I have to go. I'm due to talk over some key mauling techniques with Philip before we catch our plane.'

*

Donal was due to commentate on the match from the studio in Dublin, but at the last minute he was sent to Bath to report live from the stadium. Lucy was having a nervous breakdown because Annie was on her way out from boarding-school that weekend and she was going to have to deal with her alone.

'Why don't you call over here and watch the match with me and Yuri? At least it'll kill a few hours and she'll have to behave herself in front of me or I'll tell her off.'

'That'd be great,' said Lucy, sounding relieved. 'She's going to flip when she finds out Donal's gone to Bath.'

'When's she due?'

'I'm collecting her from the station at half twelve. Wish me luck.'

'It'll be fine. Bring her straight here and we'll have some lunch and watch the game.'

'Thanks, Emma, you're a life-saver.'

'If she misbehaves we can get Yuri to dribble on her,' I said, as Lucy laughed.

Annie was standing on the platform, looking thunderous. Lucy's heart sank as she approached. It was going to be a long day. Thank God Donal was due back that evening. She took a deep breath and smiled. 'Hi, Annie, how are you?'

'Pissed off. Donal rang me an hour ago to say he's had to fly to Bath. I wouldn't have bothered coming up but I was on the train already.'

'I know it's disappointing, but he'll be back tonight.'

'What time?'

'He should be landing at about nine.'

'Which means he won't get home till ten and I'm going back first thing tomorrow. I'll hardly see him at all.'

'Well, how'd you like to watch the match in my friend Emma's house? You met her at the wedding – she's married to James Hamilton, Donal's coach at Leinster.'

'I know who James Hamilton is. Anyone who has any interest in rugby knows who he is. I suppose it's better than nothing.'

'Great! Let's head over there now. Emma's offered to give us lunch,' said Lucy, determined not to let Annie get to her. 'She and James have a little boy, Yuri. They adopted him from Russia. He's fifteen months old and very sweet, and Emma's pregnant, which is brilliant for them.'

'I know. Donal told me. You're not getting clucky, are you?' Annie stared at Lucy's stomach for any sign of a bump.

'No, I'm just pleased for my friend,' said Lucy, gripping the steering-wheel and willing herself to remain calm.

'Whatever.'

I opened the door to two long faces. Things obviously weren't going well, then.

'Hi, Annie,' I said, as cheerfully as I could. 'Come on in and meet Yuri.'

She shuffled past me and went to sit on the couch. Lucy sighed. 'Total nightmare. She's furious because Donal's away and she hasn't seen him in six weeks. It looks like I'm being blamed.'

'Don't worry, she'll calm down in a while. She's just disappointed,' I said, trying to sound reassuring. 'Is pizza and salad all right for lunch? I didn't have time to get to the shops.'

Lucy smiled. 'It sounds great. Thanks.'

We followed Annie into the TV room where she was eyeballing Yuri, who was sitting on a rug, flinging toy cars at her and laughing. Several had hit her legs.

195

'Ouch!' she exclaimed, as another made its mark. 'God! Can't you get him to stop?' she asked.

'If I try to stop him now, he'll start roaring. Trust me, it's a lot better for all of us if we leave him to it.'

Yuri, obviously aware that he was being discussed, crawled over and sat at Annie's feet. I bent down. 'Yuri, this is Annie. She's Lucy's –' Suddenly I realized that I had no idea what she was. Lucy's ward? Lucy's niece? Lucy's step-daughter? Adopted daughter? Or, more truthfully, the thorn in Lucy's side. I went for the safe option and said 'friend'.

Annie seemed unimpressed. Yuri was used to being the centre of attention so he was fascinated by the creature who was ignoring him. He grabbed her jeans and pulled himself on to his feet, grasping her knees to balance. She continued to ignore him until he began to dribble all over her. 'Gross! Can you please take him away?' she squealed. 'He's spitting on me.'

'It's only dribble. He's teething so he can't help it, poor little thing,' I said, hurt that she wasn't as besotted by Yuri as I believed everyone else to be. Or, at least, as they all pretended to be in front of me.

Lucy bent down to pick him up. She wiped his face with a tissue and kissed his cheek. He smiled at her. 'Hello, little man, don't you look adorable today?' cooed Lucy as Yuri basked in the attention.

Annie glared at her. 'I thought you said you weren't getting clucky.'

'She's being polite,' I snapped. 'Acknowledging the presence of a child isn't unusual in civilized society. Maybe you should get out of boarding-school more often.'

'Are you pregnant?' Annie demanded, ignoring me completely and staring at Lucy.

'Don't answer that,' I said to Lucy. 'Listen here, Annie, you have no right to be rude to Lucy and ask her personal questions. If and when she and Donal decide to have kids, you should be delighted for them. Lucy is the best thing to happen to Donal so stop giving her a hard time.'

'Just because you've got a baby factory going on here doesn't mean that everyone wants one. I don't want a brother or sister. Especially not one that throws cars around and dribbles.'

'Annie, there's no need to be rude,' said Lucy.

'If you have a kid, Donal won't have time for me any more.'

'Of course he will. Come on, Annie, we've been over this before,' said Lucy, gently. 'Donal will always put you first. You know that. He's told you so a million times.'

Annie sniffed. 'Yeah, but if you have a boy he'll be all delighted and wanting to teach him rugby and stuff.'

'First of all, this is a hypothetical situation you're talking about,. and second, if Lucy and Donal do have a baby it'll be your flesh and blood too, so you'll be as mad about it as Donal,' I said, deciding to step in before she blackmailed Lucy out of ever having kids. 'Now, let's eat our lunch before the game.'

Lunch wasn't exactly a bundle of laughs and for once Yuri's food-flinging was a welcome distraction. When we had finished, Lucy and I cleared away the plates and settled to watch the game. I'd put Yuri down for a nap, so we'd be able to focus properly on it.

Leinster didn't play very well, and with fifteen minutes to go they were trailing by seven points. Donal, in the commentary box, was getting desperate. 'Jesus Christ, Casey, what are you doing?' he roared, as the new Leinster captain

197

dropped the ball that was passed back to him. 'Frank Spencer'd do a better job than that. Come on, lads, get it together.'

Donal's fellow commentator, Pat Tierney, was still getting everyone's names wrong.

'Ah, now, Donal, do I detect a spot of jealousy? Do you think you'd do a better job yourself? Are you wishing you were down there leading the troops instead of Carney?'

'Casey, his names's Casey. Of course I'd love to be play-ing, but overall Casey's had a good game. That was just a bad mistake he made there.'

'Well, folks, it's not looking good for Leinster. Carney just missed a lovely pass for a potential try,' said Pat. 'It looks like it's goodbye to the dream of winning the European Cup again this year.'

'Hold on, Pat. There's fifteen minutes to go. Don't be writ-ing the lads off yet,' snapped Donal. 'Come on, Leinster, get stuck in. Give the bastards a few digs – show them what you're made of. Stop waiting for a loose ball – GET IN THERE!'

Pat sniggered. 'We don't normally have such a partisan commentator so I'll have to ask the viewers at home to excuse Donal's language. He's just a bit overexcited.'

Donal ignored him and whooped as Leinster were awarded a penalty in front of the posts.

'Excellent. If we can get this, all we need is a try to win. Come on, Ray, don't blow it,' he said, as Ray Phelan stood up to take the kick. It sailed over the bar.

'GO ON, YOU GOOD THING,' bellowed Donal into his microphone.

With five minutes to go, Leinster were still four points down and didn't look like scoring.

'Jesus, lads, you couldn't score in a brothel, playing like

that,' hissed Donal, as Peter O'Hare knocked the ball forward, giving possession to Bath.

'Donal, if I could just remind you again, we have young viewers and we really must watch our language,' said Pat, increasingly nervous about what obscenities might come out of Donal's mouth next.

Donal snorted.

Two minutes to go and Leinster had the ball. Phelan kicked a Garryowen up the pitch and the team charged after the ball. Ben Casey got to it first. He passed it to the scrum half, Ivan Green, who whipped it out to Peter O'Hare. He ran towards the line, sidestepping two defenders, and as a third Bath defender caught him in a tackle, O'Hare flung himself over the line, arms at full stretch, just placing the ball in the corner for a winning try.

Donal went ballistic. 'DID YOU SEE THAT? DID YOU BLOODY WELL SEE THAT FOR A TRY? THE MAN IS A GENIUS. I TOLD YOU LEINSTER HAD IT IN THEM. JESUS, MY HEART NEARLY STOPPED THERE! GO ON, YOU BUNCH OF HAIRY MONGRELS, I'D SHAG YOU ALL RIGHT NOW. WE'RE GOING TO WIN THE CUP.'

'I think it's time to go back to the studio,' whispered Pat, as Lucy, Annie and I giggled helplessly on the couch, united by Donal's emotional outburst.

Chapter 24

Donal sashayed into the room and tossed a letter onto the coffee-table in front of Lucy, who was busy painting her nails while watching reruns of *Sex and the City*. He sat down beside her and cleared his throat.

'Ssssh, I love this bit.'

'You've seen this show a million times.'

'I know, but this one's my favourite. It's so sad,' she said, as she watched Miranda standing alone at her mother's funeral while her siblings walked behind the coffin with their partners. Lucy's voice quivered: 'I was Miranda. I always thought I'd end up alone at my mother's funeral while my sisters and brothers had partners to support them.'

'You're an only child.'

'That's irrelevant. I was convinced I'd end up on my own.'

'Believe you me, if you looked like that boot you would have,' said Donal, finding himself very amusing.

'Typical! You're so shallow. Just because Miranda's a successful lawyer and doesn't take shit from anyone, you dismiss her.'

'No it's really got more to do with the fact that she looks like the back of a bus.'

'She's extremely attractive, in a quirky way.'

'Is "quirky" the politically correct word for "plain"?'

'No, Donal, it isn't. Look a little deeper for once. She has a brilliant personality and is a feisty, independent woman. I'd say loads of guys fancy her.'

'Oh, I'd say they're queuing round the block, all right.'

'Looks aren't everything. You could end up with a good-looking mute.'

'Now you're talking.'

Lucy hit his arm. 'OK, so what happens if I end up in a car crash and am horribly disfigured?'

'How bad?'

'Very. Half my face is crumpled and I'm missing an eye.'

'Well, a gorgeous girl like you wouldn't be able to live like that so I'd help you out and smother you with a pillow to put you out of your misery, then go off with the foxy mute.'

'Donal, I'm serious, what would you do?'

'I was being serious.'

'You'd kill me?'

'No, I'd put you out of your misery.'

'Say if I wanted to live?'

'You wouldn't.'

'How do you know?'

'Because you wouldn't want me to suffer with a hound of a wife.'

'Have you looked at yourself in the mirror lately? You're no oil-painting.'

'Well, apparently the ladies find me irresistible,' said Donal, smirking.

'Delusion is not healthy, Donal.'

'I have here some fan mail from a female admirer,' said Donal, picking up the letter and waving it at Lucy.

'No way.'

'Yours truly is a babe magnet.'

'Steady on! One letter is hardly a fan club,' said Lucy, opening it. She read it aloud. '"Dear Donal, it is so refreshing to see enthusiasm from commentators. I'm sick of listening to panellists who have only negative things to say. Keep up the good work and I sincerely hope Leinster win the Cup this year. It's such a pity you won't be playing, you were always exciting to watch. P.S. you look great on TV. I love your shirts they're so sexy. Sarah Talbot." The cheeky cow,' said Lucy.

'What can I say? I'm a sex symbol,' said Donal, leaning back in the couch.

'I don't think Hugh Hefner has anything to worry about yet. But I'm going to stop buying you shirts. You can wear your old checked numbers from now on. Clearly I've been dressing you too well. The neck of that girl Sarah Talbot! Who the hell does she think she is?'

'She's just someone with excellent taste. You should appreciate me more, Lucy. I am a wanted man.'

'Oh, God, I can't listen to this. I'm going for a swim.'

'Drive carefully. You don't want to have any disfiguring accidents,' said Donal, as a cushion landed on his head.

As my bump got bigger and I began to feel increasingly like a hippo I decided to try pregnancy yoga. I kept hearing how wonderful yoga was for pregnancy and how it made you all bendy for the labour and how women who practised it popped out their babies without even a twinge. It sounded good to me, and although I had tried non-pregnancy yoga and found it to be complicated and painful, I presumed that this would be a toned-down version and, hopefully, would involve lots of breathing and relaxing.

I asked around and everyone said, 'You must go to Poppy. She's a genius and has a lovely studio at the back of her house that looks out over the sea.' So I called Poppy and booked myself in. She sounded very nice on the phone, and as I donned my elasticated pink tracksuit bottoms and a tent-like T-shirt, I felt that it was going to be great. I offloaded Yuri on his father and headed off for a couple of hours.

Six other girls were sitting straight-backed and cross-legged on the floor when I shuffled in. I tried to copy their posture but couldn't get one leg over the other without crippling myself so I opted to sit on my knees with my legs tucked under me, which was only marginally less painful. Poppy introduced me to everyone. I was the new kid on the block. They were all very Zen-like and were all in earthy-coloured yoga-wear. I felt a bit foolish in my cerise pink tracksuit, but it was the only thing that fitted me, so I'd really had no choice.

Poppy started the class with some deep breathing, which was quite nice except that she and the rest of the class sounded as if they were choking when they breathed out – it was very loud and offputting. After five minutes of the raspy breathing, Poppy took a stone from her bag and passed it to the girl on her left. 'Now we'll have the section of the class where we talk about our feelings and face our fears.'

I know it's immature and juvenile but I'm just not good with this type of thing. I panic when I have to speak in front of a group of strangers so I began to sweat. So much for a relaxing two hours. Glenda, current holder of the stone, rubbed her tummy as she told us how she had bonded with her baby over the last week and how she felt like a mother already. She was thirty-two weeks gone and said she felt her child would have a lovely personality and would be a caring person who would make a difference in the world. I was still wondering how on earth she had come up with that prognosis when she announced that she had finalized her birthing-pool and was all set for her home birth.

'Home birth!' I squealed. I hadn't intended to say it out loud, but I was shocked. Wasn't that something that they did in *The Little House on the Prairie*? Hadn't we moved on since then? Weren't hospitals where you went to have babies? Was this woman really planning on having her baby in a paddling-pool in the kitchen? Did her husband get into his swimming togs and hop in with her? Would the doctor have to wear goggles and a snorkel?

Six heads swivelled in my direction. 'That's right,' said Glenda, 'I'm having a home birth. Four of the women here are. You should consider it. It's so much better for the baby. There's a day's conference about spiritual midwifery on next Saturday – why not come along?'

'Sure it sounds great,' I said, trying to be casual. How was it better for the baby to be greeted into the world by the Man from Atlantis?

The next stone confessor was Pam. She had breastfed her first child until it was two and was planning on doing the same with this baby. She loved breastfeeding and had been devastated when she'd had to give up because her child's teeth were cutting into her flesh. I looked around at the other girls. Come on, was this for real? Someone else must be finding it a little weird. A child of two sucking at its mother's breast? Was I living in a parallel world where this seemed really odd? I caught Tania's eye. She was sitting to my right and she very subtly raised an eyebrow at me. Aha, a kindred spirit. At least I wasn't alone.

Poppy asked if we were all looking forward to breastfeeding. In turn everyone said yes – even my own hope, Tania, the traitor – and then it came to me and I said no.

'Are you worried about the baby not latching on?' asked Poppy, sweetly.

'Not really. I'm actually thinking about not breastfeeding at all,' I mumbled, feeling shock waves throughout the room.

'Oh' said Poppy, looking bemused. 'Did you have a bad experience last time?'

'We adopted Yuri when he was ten months old so he was already on bottles. I just don't really fancy it to be honest. It looks sore and my friend who tried it said it was horrendous and told me about cracked nipples and mastitis, so I just thought I'd give it a miss.'

'But you do realize that breast is best for baby? What are a few months of discomfort when your baby's health is at stake?' said Glenda.

'Well, my mother didn't breastfeed any of us and we're all OK,' I said defensively.

'That's because she didn't know better. It has been proven that breast milk is best for babies and that it makes them more intelligent.'

'Milk makes them clever?' I asked. Come on, Glenda, give me a break here – milk makes your kid smart? Sure we'd all be hiring wet-nurses before our exams if that was the case.

'It's been scientifically proven.'

'Well, if this child doesn't get straight As in his exams I'll live with it.'

'Why don't we move on to some exercises?' said Poppy, jumping in before Glenda and I got physical and started bouncing our bumps off each other. 'I want you to rock back and forth with a partner.'

Of course no one wanted to partner the freak who wouldn't breastfeed so Poppy had to take me. She was very bendy and I was very stiff. She pulled and tugged at my arms and legs to get me to loosen up. Then she asked if I was doing my Kegel exercises.

'Um, what's that?' I asked, feeling like a complete moron now. Maybe they were right about the breastfeeding. Clearly I was thick due to my mother's negligence.

'They're your pelvic-floor exercises. After you've given birth, your pelvic-floor muscles must receive top priority or you could end up incontinent. It's vital that you strengthen the muscles before and after the birth.'

Incontinent! Christ, this was the most unrelaxing, stressful two hours of my life. Sometimes information can be a bad thing. I didn't want to end up in nappies for the rest of my life. I'd be getting two for the price of one – baby and adult ones. 'What do I need to do? Tell me,' I begged.

'It's very simple. You just need to draw up the pelvic floor. You should feel the sides of the sphincters become tight and the inside passages become tense. Hold for ten seconds, then relax.'

I looked blankly at her. What on earth was she talking about? I had no idea what my sphincters were, so how could I know if they were tight or not? Poppy spotted my distress and laid a hand on my arm. 'OK, Emma, you basically use the muscles you'd use if you were trying to stop yourself urinating. You squeeze those muscles together as if you were stopping your urine mid-flow.'

OK, I understood now. I tried it out. It wasn't as easy as it sounded. 'How often do I need to do these?'

'About fifty times a day every day for the rest of your life. They're very important. The good thing is you can do them anywhere, driving your car, watching TV . . .'

'Have you started your internal vaginal massaging?' asked Pam, the resident dairymaid. 'You'll need to use pure vegetable oil.'

There's only so much a girl can take. I knew my limits,

206

and internal vaginal massaging with cooking oil had pushed me over the edge. I said I felt unwell and hightailed it out of the door. Clearly yoga, in any form, was not for me.

Chapter 25

Lucy called Jess and me, wanting to meet up. She said it was important and sounded excited on the phone. I was convinced she was pregnant. She hadn't been drinking the last two times I'd met her and her boobs had got bigger. I held my breath as she walked into the bar. 'So,' I said, 'what's up?'

'Brace yourselves,' said Lucy, grinning. 'Annie worships me.'

'What?' I asked, startled. 'But she was horrible to you when you came to watch the match with me a couple of weeks ago.'

'I thought she couldn't stand you,' said Jess.

'Yes, well, that was before she had sex.'

'Sex? But she's only a kid,' said Jess, clearly worried about her little Sally.

'Apparently they're doing it younger these days,' said Lucy.

'Why did she tell you?' I asked.

'Because she thought she was pregnant. So, I'm in work last week and my mobile rings . . .' Lucy explained that Annie had called her in a complete state. She was sobbing on the phone and could barely speak she was so upset. Lucy managed to figure out that Annie had had unprotected sex with a boy from a boarding-school half a mile from hers and now she thought she was pregnant.

'When did you have sex?' Lucy asked.

'Two weeks ago,' cried Annie.

'How late is your period?'

'Three days.'

'Look, it's very unlikely that you're pregnant. I'll come and collect you and make an appointment with my gynaecologist and we'll find out. If you are, we'll sort it out. Don't worry, Annie, I'm sure you're just late because you're stressed.'

'Please don't tell Donal. I'm begging you, Lucy. I don't want him to think I'm a slut. I'm not, honestly. I just really liked this boy – he's so gorgeous, everyone fancies him, and when he liked me I was thrilled. All the girls were dead jealous. He said he'd dump me if I didn't sleep with him and I didn't want it to end. It was great being cool for a while. But now I've ruined my life and Donal will hate me.'

'Hey, Annie, come on, now. Donal will love you no matter what happens. But I won't tell him if you don't want me to. Let's just take it one step at a time. I'll think of an excuse to get you out for the day and pick you up first thing in the morning and we'll go to the doctor. Now, get some rest and don't worry.'

'Thanks, Lucy,' said Annie, as she blew her nose. 'I'm sorry for being mean to you.'

'It's OK. See you tomorrow.'

The next day Lucy collected Annie and took her to see the gynaecologist. He did a pregnancy test and declared Annie not pregnant. Then he talked to her about the importance of protection. He said she was very young to be having sex and should be concentrating on her exams. She could worry about boys later. Annie cried with relief.

Lucy took her out for a celebration lunch and Annie poured out her heart to her. She told her how much she missed her parents and how sometimes she felt like a burden to Donal. How she felt guilty because he had had to move back to Ireland when Annie's parents died to look after her. She said she wished she had sisters because she had never had anyone to talk to about girly things.

Lucy told her that she would love to be her surrogate big sister and she could call her any time about anything. Annie hugged her and said she'd never forget today and how Lucy had been so good to her. When Lucy dropped her back to school, Annie leant over and kissed her. 'You're amazing, Lucy. I'm so glad Donal met you.' It was Lucy who was in tears as she drove out of the school gates.

'Oh, Lucy,' I said, welling up. 'That's fantastic. I'm so pleased for you. No more hassle with Annie, it must be such a weight off your mind.'

Lucy nodded. 'You've no idea. I'm thrilled. It will make life so much easier.'

'Did you tell Donal?' Jess asked.

'No. He'd have hit the roof and gone down to skin the boy alive. It's best he doesn't know.'

'Won't he be surprised by your new relationship with Annie?' I asked.

'Well, I told him I'd taken Annie out to lunch and that we'd had an open, honest chat and were now on good terms. He seemed to accept it. You know men, they never ask too many questions.'

We ordered drinks and toasted Lucy's new best friend.

Lucy asked us what we'd been up to, so I told them about my yoga fiasco. Jess said there were far too many breastfeeding Nazis out there and that I wasn't to worry. Lucy said yoga was overrated and I'd be better off swimming as (a) I wouldn't have to talk to other pregnant women, and

(b) you're weightless when you swim so I couldn't do any damage to myself.

'Yes, but I hate changing rooms. I'm just not that comfortable with the whole naked thing.'

'What do you mean?' asked Lucy.

'You know, all that striding around bare-arsed in the changing rooms. I can't focus on a conversation when someone's boobs are in my face.'

'Who are you planning on talking to?' asked Jess.

'Well, people just chat to you. I don't know why, but any time I've been to the pool or a gym – and, let's face it, it's not often – there's always lots of "hell of a class, great workout" chat afterwards. And the women who talk to you are always very comfortable in their own skin so it's Boobs and Pubic Hair City. I never know where to look.'

'I hate that too,' said Jess. 'I always scurry to and from the shower with a big towel round me, then try to put my clothes on under it. I can see the other women looking at me like I'm a freak.'

'I never think about it,' said Lucy.

'That's because you have a great figure,' I said. 'Jess and I have a lot more to hide.'

'Speak for yourself,' said Jess, feigning insult. 'I'm a thin woman in a chubby woman's body.'

'Well, I currently look like Shrek so I'm not comfortable with being naked in front of anyone, not even James. I've actually found myself getting dressed in the bathroom. Whoever said being pregnant was sexy? Come on, what's sexy about your boobs being so big they droop down and stick to your stomach, which has swollen to the size of a basketball?'

'It's that bloody picture of Demi Moore on the cover

of *Vanity Fair* that started all this women-look-beautiful-pregnant lark,' fumed Jess. 'It's bad enough *being* pregnant, without having the pressure to try to look good when all you want to do is wear tracksuits with big elasticated waists and no bra.'

'Not to mention the chest hair.'

'What?' said Lucy, looking alarmed as Jess roared laughing.

I told them I'd come out of the shower a couple of weeks ago and James had said, 'Darling, you've got a black mark on your stomach.'

'No I don't,' I said sighing.

'Yes, you do – just there.'

'No, James, it's not a mark, it's a hairy stripe thing.'

'What?' he said, looking appalled.

'It's a side effect of pregnancy; some women get a moustache down their stomach, it has to do with pigment or something.'

'But it's black and you're ginger.'

'I am aware of the colour, I have noticed that I now have a Tom Selleck special running down my stomach.'

'Is it permanent?' he asked.

'I don't know James, I've never been pregnant before, remember? Believe me I'm not thrilled to be looking like Tarzan's best pal.' And then I told him to drop the subject.

Lucy was staring at me as I finished the story. She looked as horrified as James had. 'So, *is* it permanent?' she asked Jess, who, with two children under her belt, was our resident expert.

Jess shrugged. 'It was one of the only things I didn't get so I don't know, but I doubt it. These things tend to clear up once the baby's born.'

'This is an eye-opener,' said Lucy. 'Can I ask a personal question?'

Jess and I nodded.

'How is the sex when your bump gets big?' she said, looking at my now enormous belly.

Jess laughed. 'When I was pregnant the first time I couldn't do it in the missionary position when I got to about six months because I was too big and it was too uncomfortable. So I told Tony we'd just have to forgo sex for a few months. Not one to be deterred, Tony came up with a plan.' She paused for dramatic effect.

'Well?' I asked, interested to know what the plan had been. James and I were currently not up to much at all.

'Tony, ever the thoughtful and selfless husband, reckoned we should test out different positions and find out which would be the most comfortable for me.'

'Thoughtful of him,' said Lucy, rolling her eyes.

'How did it go?' I asked, keen to find out if there was something in it.

'Needless to say it was great for Tony, and sore for me as he was bashing against my cervix. After a minute or two I told him there was a reason it was called doggy style – because it's only meant for four-legged creatures.'

I admit I was relieved. If Jess had told me it was the best sex of her life I would have felt obliged to try it with James. Right now, all I wanted to do when I got into bed was sleep. I really didn't fancy contorting my body into complicated Kama-Sutra-type positions. Let's face it, I couldn't do a decent yoga move so chances are I'd end up doing myself an injury.

'Was he disappointed?' asked Lucy.

'Very, but he kept suggesting other bendy ways to do it

213

until I locked him out of the bedroom and said I was going to tell his mother her son was sexually harassing me while I was pregnant with her first grandchild.'

'I'd say that took the wind out of his sails.' I giggled.

'You've got to give him credit for trying,' said Lucy.

'I suppose so. Anyway, I'm annoyed with him at the moment,' said Jess.

'What's up?' I asked.

'Last night we were talking about getting a new alarm for the house because the one we have is useless. So the conversation moved on to robbers and what would we do if we got broken into. I asked Tony if he thought he'd turn into Rambo to protect his family and did he have a baseball bat hidden under the bed in case of an emergency . . .'

'Sure what would I need weapons for, I'd just tell them to leave the kids and take you,' he replied.

'Seriously, Tony, what would you do if a robber broke in and said it's the kids or your wife?'

'I *am* being serious. I'd say, "Take the wife, she's all yours."'

'Thanks a lot,' huffed Jess. 'I gave you those bloody kids and now I'm getting offered to a bunch of thugs on a plate to be murdered.'

'Well, I'm hardly going to hand over Sally and Roy. You wouldn't want me to.'

'No, but it'd be nice if you told the burglars to piss off and said you were going to protect all of us, instead of throwing me out the door at the first mention of a hostage. You could at least try to be manly about it.'

'Jess, I'm hardly going to argue with a guy in a ski-mask holding a sawn-off shotgun.'

'It's not bloody Beirut, Tony. Burglars don't carry guns here – they might have a Swiss Army knife if they're really aggressive.'

'Well, I've no intention of finding out, thanks. You knew when you married me that I was a lover not a fighter, so don't expect me to change now.'

'Surely all that testosterone you have would come out in defence of your family.'

'I wouldn't hold your breath.'

'Would you really choose the kids over me?'

'Yes.'

'So that's it! After sixteen years together and seven years of marriage you'd choose the four-year-old and the two-year-old.'

'Yes.'

'So you love them more than me.'

'It would appear so.'

'So,' said Jess, 'I'm not speaking to him.'

'What would you do in the same situation?' asked Lucy.

'I'd feck him out the door so fast he wouldn't know what hit him. Of course I'd save the kids.'

'So why are you giving Tony a hard time?' I asked.

'Because he should have pretended he wouldn't be able to choose. We both know we'd turf each other out, but it still isn't very nice to hear.'

'Do you really love the kids more than Tony?' asked Lucy.

'I still adore Tony, but I love the kids in a more intense, protective way. We've lived, they're only beginning their little lives, you'd have to save them.'

'What about you?' Lucy asked, turning to me.

'I don't know. I've never thought about it,' I said. I didn't want to either. Did I love Yuri more than James? Did James love Yuri more than me? I wasn't sure and, more importantly, I didn't particularly want to find out. Wasn't there enough love to go round? But I was going to check our alarm system. I didn't fancy getting burgled and having to choose or, worse, finding myself outside with the burglars and James's footprint on my back.

Now that I was nearly seven months pregnant the baby had started kicking regularly, which I loved. With my bump getting bigger by the day, I decided to try to explain to Yuri that he was going to have a little sister or brother. I was nervous about getting the wording right so I began gently.

I sat him down, kissed him, then told him I loved him and that he was the best boy in Ireland and Russia. This always made him smile so we were off to a good start. I showed him my stomach and said, 'baby,' then I showed him a picture of a baby and pointed back to my stomach. He smiled at the picture of the baby, which I took to be a good sign. Then I put his hand on my stomach and the baby kicked. Yuri squealed and pulled away his hand. He stared at my stomach, then poked it and the baby kicked again. Yuri giggled, and spent the next ten minutes poking my bump black and blue until the baby got tired of the game and stopped kicking, much to Yuri's disappointment.

'So you see, darling, Mummy's going to have another little baby and you'll have a little sister or brother, but you'll always be my special boy,' I said, smiling encouragingly at him. 'You'll have someone to play with all the time. Won't that be fun?'

Yuri didn't look like he thought it was going to be a barrel of laughs at all. He looked at me, frowned and then turned away and reached over for his elephant. Damn, this was not a good sign. Maybe he thought he was going to be abandoned again. I picked him up to cuddle him but he shrugged me away and continued to chew on the elephant's trunk. He always turned to the elephant when he was feeling upset or vulnerable – which, thankfully, had become much rarer recently.

Did he understand about the baby and feel left out already? Maybe I'd confused him. I was riddled with guilt. What if he had a really hard time when the baby arrived? Would it bring back all the nasty memories of being dumped on the doorstep of an orphanage? Although James did keep reminding me that at two months Yuri probably didn't remember the incident. Still, I was worried that he'd feel left out when the baby was born and that when he grew up he'd always be the 'adopted' son. And then he'd disappear off to Russia to become a painter of angry art because of his mixed-up youth. His paintings would be black and the critics would say his mother must have been an awful witch for him to be so full of *Angst*. He'd tell them all how being abandoned once was bad enough, but twice was unforgivable. Then he'd marry a beautiful ballet dancer called Olga and they'd have a child and he'd understand that I'd done my best, that he'd been loved, and he'd start painting in reds and blues . . .

I'd have to be extra loving and affectionate to him over the next eighteen years so he wouldn't go off the rails. I bent down and whispered in his ear, 'I love you, my little Russian angel. You're the best thing that ever happened to me and nobody will ever take your place in my heart.'

But Yuri continued to ignore me and cuddle his elephant. Dejected, I went to call James. By the time he answered I had worked myself into a hormone-induced frenzy and was sobbing. 'I just tried to uh-uh-uh tell Yuri about the baby and now he thinks he's going to be abandoned again. He looks really sad . . . He uh-uh keeps hugging the elephant.'

'What did you say to him?'

'I just told him that I loved him and that he'd have a playmate soon.'

'How exactly did you phrase it?'

'I just told you.'

'You were probably too blunt. You need to be very careful, Emma. This is a big thing for Yuri to accept.'

'I'm aware of that.'

'You should have waited for me to be there. I'll handle it when I get home.'

'Gee, thanks for the support, I'm really glad I called you now. I feel so much better. I'm off to stick my head in the oven.'

'Calm down, there's no need for drama. He probably didn't even understand. He can't speak, for goodness' sake.'

'He understands lots, James. When I say, "Don't touch that, it's dirty," he doesn't touch it . . . or if I say, "You're the best boy," he smiles. He seems upset. What if the new baby makes him feel left out? He's suffered enough. What if he becomes really messed up because of it and turns into a mad artist who only paints with black?'

'Emma, can you please focus on the issue here and not go off on one of your tangents? We just have to keep reassuring him,' said James. 'He'll be fine. He's settled in so well already, he'll adjust to the baby in no time. I'll have a word with him when I get home.'

By the time James got home Yuri was in bed. He had cheered up when I gave him his bath, but had clung to the elephant when I tucked him in and had only given me a half-smile when I sang 'Incy Wincy Spider' to him. Granted, I had a voice like a cat being swung round by its tail, but it never usually bothered him. He was definitely out of sorts. I felt awful and kept kissing him and telling him I loved him.

James arrived home and went straight in to say goodnight to Yuri. I left them to it, but I could hear him through the baby monitor: 'Now, young fellow, you're not to worry about the new baby because you'll always be our number-one boy. You're as much my son as any biological child could ever be. I have lots of plans for you. I'm going to teach you to play rugby and you're going to be the best out-half in the world and captain England to the next World Cup victory. Or if you prefer you can play cricket for England and bring back the Ashes. You're the best thing that's ever happened to me and don't you forget it. I didn't understand what people talked about when they spoke of the love for a child, but I do now. It's pretty overwhelming, actually. You are my number-one priority and nothing will change that.'

I could hear Yuri snoring as James finished his speech and I realized I'd been usurped. I was relegated to second position. I'd be offered to the burglars on a platter. But, strangely, I didn't mind because I felt the same way. No less in love with James, just overcome with love for Yuri. So much love for such a little person in such a short space of time.

Chapter 26

A few days before Sean's wedding I was in Mum's house trying on the dress I had bought. We were flying out the next day to meet Shadee's family and, needless to say, my mother was up to ninety. Both families were having dinner together the night before the wedding to get to know each other. Sean and Shadee had wisely kept this meeting until the last minute, so that, whatever the outcome, the wedding would go ahead the next day.

'Lord, Emma, that's far too tight on you,' my mother noted helpfully, as I struggled to get the dress over my stomach.

'Damn! It fitted me perfectly three weeks ago.'

'I told you not to buy a dress until a few days before the wedding but, as usual, you wouldn't listen.'

'It's fifty per cent lycra – it's supposed to have lots of room for growth,' I growled.

'Well, you can't wear it, you look enormous.'

'Thanks a lot.'

'For goodness' sake, aren't you lucky to be pregnant? You moaned for years because you couldn't have a baby and now you're giving out because you've a big stomach. Never happy.'

'I'm not giving out and I am extremely grateful to be pregnant. I just don't like being referred to as enormous.'

'Big, then.'

'Lucy and Jess said I'm neat.'

'Neat!' screeched Mum. 'Well, they're good friends, I'll say that for them.'

'*Mum*, you're not helping here. What am I going to do? This is the only decent dress I have and we're going tomorrow.'

'Sure can't you wear a big sheet like the rest of them? No one will notice the difference.'

'I thought we'd agreed that you weren't going to make comments like that any more,' I said, wagging a finger at her.

'For your information, Sean said that one of Shady's aunties, who's coming to the wedding, wears the black sheet and disapproves of Western women.'

'Yes, and Auntie Doreen goes around spraying people with holy water. Neither is clever.'

'Well, your auntie Doreen's from your father's side. Sure they're all a bit touched,' said Mum, condemning Dad's entire family with one sweeping comment.

'Anyway, back to the issue at hand. What am I going to do?' I now had nothing to wear for my brother's wedding and my mother wasn't helping.

'Your sister had better wear that nice frock I sent her in the post. It's got long sleeves and a high neck. I won't have Shady's lot saying my children are badly brought up. I won't be shamed on my only son's wedding day.'

I opened Mum's wardrobe and started looking through it. 'What are you doing?'

'Looking for something to wear.'

'You won't find anything in there that'll fit you,' said Mum, highly insulted at the idea that my big frame would fit into any of her clothes.

'I just thought you might have a floaty dress or a loose top.'

'I'm a size fourteen now, Emma. I've lost half a stone

over the last month by cutting out the car-bo-hydrates,' said Mum, twirling round to show me her new svelte figure.

'I know, Mum. You told me, and you look great. Your outfit is gorgeous and the shoes and hat are perfect. But right now I need you to focus on finding me something to wear.'

'What about the bag? You didn't say the bag was nice. Do you not like it? I thought it was a different colour to the shoes but you made me buy it.'

'The bag is perfect. It came with the shoes. It's a matching set. They are all the exact same colour. And I didn't make you buy anything. You love your outfit. Now, please, help me out here.'

'Why don't you go round to young Maureen Doherty and ask her if she has any of her old dresses from before she joined the Weight Watchers and lost four stone.'

'She was fifteen stone and went around in smocks. I'm not that bloody big.'

Mum sniffed. 'I'll say nothing.'

'What?' I said. 'I'm not that big. Am I? Do I look like Maureen used to?' I was beginning to panic. I looked in the mirror. I was big: big bump, big boobs and, if I was being honest, big thighs and bum too. But my arms were still okayish. Weren't they? Was I kidding myself?

'Sure she has blonde hair,' said Mum, looking at me as if I was stupid. Was that it? Was that where the only difference lay? In our hair colour?

'Did I tell you Maureen's cousin Suzanne bought that house on Talsome Road. Two million euros it cost. But sure didn't she marry Harry Beacon, the beef baron. He's money to burn that fellow. He used to go out with your second cousin Jackie, but it came unstuck. Of course her mother was devastated, she had the hat bought. You remember Suzanne, a plain slip of a thing? But you should see her now, she's got fierce glamorous. Dyed blonde hair and always brown as a berry, has her own sunbed, according to her aunt, and apparently she's had that Botox,' said Mum, whispering the word 'Botox' and shaking her head.

'Good on her, I could do with some,' I said, staring at my wrinkles in the mirror.

'Poppycock! Do you know what's in it? Rat poison! The problem with you girls today is that you want a solution to everything. An injection for this, a pill for that, divorce, abortion. There are no morals any more. Young people today don't take marriage seriously. They get divorced if they have a row. Marriage is a sacred oath and there are tough times, but you put your head down and get on with it. It's not easy – nothing in life is easy. Marrying someone from your own country and religion is hard enough, but when you add opposing cultures and background to the equation you're just –'

'Mum,' I interrupted, 'save the speech for Sean. He's the one getting married in two days. Now, can you please focus on finding me something to wear?'

'Mark my words, Emma, it's not all roses in the garden. There have been times when I've wanted to leave your father, but I stuck it out.'

'Mum, I'm begging you, stop talking and help me,' I pleaded, not wanting to know how many times she had contemplated leaving my father. It was him I felt sorry for: I'd say he had his bags packed every other week.

'Fine, don't listen to me or my pearls of wisdom. You young people think you know it all. Experience, Emma, that's what teaches you about life.'

'I get it. Marriage is difficult and there'll be rocky times ahead. Now, in the name of God, will you please give me a hand finding a dress?'

After going through every outfit in her wardrobe, most of which she tried on for me, describing in detail where she had worn it and who had said what to her in it, I found an old empire line chiffon dress that covered most of my lumps and bumps. The rest I could camouflage with a shawl. It was a pretty nauseating shade of green, but it was too late to get anything else. I'd just have to make do and look like a leprechaun.

When I got home, James was shouting, 'Come on, you can do it,' and whooping at the top of his lungs. Expecting to find him watching a rugby match, I walked in to find Yuri wobbling precariously on his feet. When he saw me he staggered three steps forward, and collapsed on his bum.

'Oh, my God, James, he walked!'

'I know! Isn't it marvellous?' said James, grinning. 'The child is a genius.'

The next hour was spent cheering and clapping as Yuri staggered about like a drunken sailor, fell over and got up again. We were beside ourselves with pride. Our little man was growing up. After we had tucked him into his cot, telling him how wonderful he was and singing a glass-shattering version of 'Twinkle Twinkle Little Star', we went to pack our cases and I tried on my dress for James.

'Now, before you say anything,' I shouted from the bathroom, 'remember that I have no other options. Ta-da.' I twirled round for him.

James swallowed loudly. 'It's really . . . green.'

'Oh, God, that bad?'

'No, not bad, just a shade of green I haven't seen in quite some time. Not since the sixties, I believe. But it looks well with red hair.'

'I realize that the colour is headache-inducing, but focus on the shape for a minute. Does it flatter?'

'Flatter what exactly?'

'My current Hobbit-like shape.'

'Ah. Well, then, yes, it does.'

'In what way?' I asked.

'In a good way,' he fudged.

'Be honest. I can take it. I want you to tell me the truth. It's awful, isn't it?'

'No.'

'Come on.'

'OK, I've seen you look better.'

'How bad?'

'Have you got a coat?'

'James!'

'You asked me to be honest.'

'Yes, but not brutal,' I said, taking off the dress and sighing. 'I look like an Irish heifer.'

James decided the best option was to say nothing so he just shrugged and smiled at me.

I put on my elasticated pyjamas and went to brush my teeth. When I climbed into bed, James was reading Clive Woodward's autobiography in an effort to gain some insight into how he had coached England to victory in the rugby World Cup.

'James?'

'Mmm?' he said, not looking up.

'Should we be having more sex?'

'Pardon?' That got his attention.

'I'm just wondering if we should be a bit more active. We've got very lazy about sex.'

'But you're always saying how tired and uncomfortable you are. And the last time we had sex you kept shouting at me not to crush the baby, which was slightly offputting.'

'I know, and I'm sorry, but you were kind of squashing my bump. Still, the lack of activity can't be much fun for you.'

'It's all right, darling, I'll survive.'

'We could try different positions if you like. I'm not very bendy but I'm willing to try.'

'Really?' said James, perking up.

'Sure,' I said, trying to sound enthusiastic.

Over the next half an hour we tried pretty much every position we could think of. Legs and arms akimbo, we twisted and turned, bent forwards and backwards without much success. We persevered until I fell off the bed during a particularly complicated manoeuvre.

'Ouch,' I squealed, rubbing my arm.

'Are you all right?' asked James, as he helped me up.

'This isn't really working for me,' I said.

'I think we'll call it a night.'

'Sorry, I was hoping we could find a comfy position.'

'It's all right, darling. Actually, I find having sex when you're so pregnant a little strange.'

'In what way?'

'It just seems a bit odd to be having sex when the baby's in there. It can't be pleasant for it.'

'Because of the poking?'

'Yes, I'm rather afraid they may end up with a black eye.'

I laughed. 'Don't flatter yourself.'

'Six and a half inches at full throttle, thank you very much.'

'Is that good?'

'Very.'

'How did you measure it? With a ruler or tape measure?'

'Ruler.'

'Is this a recent event?' I asked, giggling at the idea of James in the bathroom with his ruler out.

'No, I did it years ago.'

'When and why?'

'It was back in the early days of my rugby career. I was only about sixteen and everyone used to slag Stewart – the prop – for being hung like a horse.'

'Did you all go around looking at each other?'

'Communal showers, darling, hard not to.'

'I'd never look at another woman's privates, communal or otherwise.'

'Boarding-school makes you more relaxed about naked-ness. Anyway, when I compared myself to Stewart it was like a hot-dog and a cocktail sausage. So I decided to measure mine. I was concerned that I was stunted and at sixteen all you think about is getting laid, so I was seriously worried about my future.'

'And so you got out the ruler.'

'And realized that I looked smaller than I was.'

'Thank God for that.'

'Best day of my life.'

'Should I call you stallion?'

'If you like, I'd have no problem with it. Might be a bit awkward at family occasions, but I'm game if you are.'

I snuggled down under the duvet. 'James?'

'Yes?'

'You're not going to have an affair because your wife won't put out and you're hung like a donkey, are you?'

227

'Where would I meet my mistress? I work with rugby players, remember?'

'Sure you can meet people in the supermarket, these days. I'm always hearing about affairs starting over the frozen section.'

'To think of all the time I've wasted lurking about by the cheeses.'

'James?'

'Yes?'

'How bad is the dress?'

'Put it this way, darling, I'd have no problem if you wore it grocery shopping.'

Chapter 27

When we landed at the airport the next day, Sean was anxiously waiting for us at Arrivals. He was excited and nervous. Babs was with him, looking bored.

'Jesus, you're massive,' said Babs, eyeing my stomach. 'You look like you've about ten kids in there.'

'It must be great to have the ability to make people feel really good about themselves,' I snapped.

'Can you please not start fighting yet?' groaned Dad. 'We've only just landed.'

Sean put his arm round me. 'Don't mind her, you're blooming,' he said.

'Blooming huge,' giggled Babs.

We trundled out to the car park, suitcases and travel cot in tow, and loaded up the minivan Sean had hired. Then we climbed in and set off for Brighton.

'I can't believe you're getting married tomorrow. It's so exciting. How do you feel?' I asked, as Sean swung the van on to the motorway.

'Good, thanks. Bit nervous, but really looking forward to it. It should be a great day. Shadee's put so much effort into organizing it – she's thought of everything.'

'It'd want to be good,' said Babs, 'You talked about nothing else the whole time I lived with you.'

'Rome wasn't built in a day,' said Dad. 'And how are you, my little ray of sunshine?' He winked at Babs.

'Brilliant. My job's going really well, I've been promoted

to lead salesgirl, everyone in the place loves me and I'm due a pay rise soon.'

'And as humble as the day you were born,' said Dad.

'How's that flat you're living in? I hope you're keeping it clean while the girl who owns it is in Australia. I won't have people saying the Irish are dirty. Have you it nice and tidy?' asked Mum.

Babs rolled her eyes. 'Yes, Mother, I Hoover every night. I never take the Marigolds off.'

'You certainly fell on your feet there,' said James. 'I've never heard of someone paying so little rent. Especially not in that area.'

'Yeah, well, I'm just lucky, I guess,' said Babs, a little defensively.

'You'd sell ice to the Eskimos. I'd say you persuaded that poor girl to go to Australia and give you the place for nothing,' said Dad.

Babs shrugged.

'I hope you packed the dress I sent you,' said Mum.

'The one that looked like something an Amish person would wear? Of course I did. I love it. It's exactly what I would have chosen for myself.'

'Have you a nice sensible pair of shoes to go with it?'

'I found a lovely pair of wellies to match.'

'You cheeky lump,' said Mum. 'I won't have you disgracing us in front of Shady's family.'

'How is Shadee?' I asked Sean, interrupting the bickering.

'Wonderful as always,' said Sean, smiling. 'She's so excited about tomorrow.'

'Where's this dinner on tonight?' asked Dad.

'It's in a little restaurant down the road from the hotel.

It'll just be all of us and Shadee's parents, her brother and his wife.'

'Is the brother's wife a Prussian?' asked Mum.

'Persian, Mum,' corrected Sean. 'Yes, she is. I was a big disappointment to them. They wanted Shadee to marry a Persian too.'

'Disappointment!' said Mum, horrified at the thought that anyone could think ill of her precious son. 'They should be down on their hands and knees thanking God – or yodelling to Allah or whatever it is they do – that their daughter is marrying you. Do they not realize what a catch you are?'

Babs snorted.

'Any lad on the scene in London?' Dad asked Babs.

'Yes, actually. I've met a lovely Nigerian.'

'*What!*' said Mum, giving herself whiplash as her head snapped round.

'Relax, I'm joking. No, I'm not seeing anyone in particular.'

'Just sleeping around, then,' I muttered.

'Jealous, fatso?' she asked, smirking at me.

'How's Yuri? He looks great, is he talking yet?' Sean jumped in.

'No, but he walked last night for the first time. Three steps,' I proudly announced.

'Oh, you clever little boy,' said Mum, kissing him as he cooed at her.

'Crack open the champagne. Aren't they supposed to walk after a few months? Isn't he a bit slow?' said Babs.

'Certainly not,' said James, gravely insulted to have his son's talents questioned. 'He's just doing it in his own good time.'

'We'll have to get him to show us later on. I can't wait to see him,' said his besotted granny, making up for his witch of an aunt.

'Well, it shouldn't take long to demonstrate three steps,' said Babs, yawning.

'Oh, shut up, you contrary cow,' I snapped.

'Children,' said Dad, 'I'd like Shadee's family to think we're civilized people and not a bunch of snarling Rottweilers. Can you please be nice to each other for once?'

'Did I tell you about young Maureen's cousin Suzanne marrying Harry Beacon, the beef baron?'

'Yes, Mum, you did,' said Sean.

'Maureen's lost another stone. Like a matchstick, she is. You wouldn't recognize her, Sean. Stunning she is and a lovely personality to boot.'

'Mum,' said Sean sternly, 'I am getting married tomorrow to a girl that I am absolutely mad about, so can you please give up any hope that you have for Maureen and me? It's never going to happen.'

'Leave the lad alone, Anne,' said Dad.

'All I said was she looks well,' mumbled Mum.

We drove the rest of the way in relative silence. When we arrived we were all impressed – even Babs. The hotel was stunning. It was an ivy-clad country manor with a sweeping driveway and magnificent views of the sea. Shadee was there to greet us, and we sat down for tea and scones.

Mum asked to see Yuri walking, so James propped him up and we all stood around him staring at him. Frightened by all the expectant faces, he fell down and began to howl. The pressure was too much.

'Very impressive,' said Babs. 'He'll be running marathons in no time.'

I picked him up and hugged him. 'He's not a performing seal. He'll do it when no one's gawking at him.'

A few minutes later, when everyone was chatting, I propped him up again and he staggered towards Mum, swaying as he went. She grabbed him on his fourth step as he began to tumble. 'Amazing, my little pet! Just amazing!'

Yuri grinned at his beloved granny. She really was wonderful with him – he could do no wrong.

Shadee told us that she had arranged for her parents to meet us in the bar at seven thirty for pre-dinner drinks.

'I didn't think you lot drank?' said Mum.

'Well, my parents don't, but my brother and sister-in-law do, and I like a glass of wine myself,' she said, smiling.

'Right you are,' said Dad, grabbing Mum's arm and frog-marching her out before she could put her foot in it.

James, Yuri and I found our room and assembled the travel cot. The hotel had organized a babysitter for us so we were looking forward to a night out. I was nervous about the two families meeting and hoped that Shadee's parents were as nice as she was, and that Mum behaved herself.

At seven o'clock there was a knock on the door. It was Dad, looking very fed up.

'Your mother has me driven demented. She wants you to go over – she says it's an emergency. I'm off to the bar for a pint. Sean's meeting me there. The poor lad's a nervous wreck about tonight. Tell James to come down if he fancies a drink.'

I ran over to his and Mum's room. 'What's wrong?'

She was sitting on the edge of the bed in tears. 'I've a ladder in my tights and the other ones don't match my suit. I'll have to stay in.'

'Mum, calm down, it's OK.'

'No, it isn't. It's a disaster. My lovely boy is getting married to a girl I hardly know. He'll never come home now. He'll stay in London or, worse, go off and live in Iran and I'll only see him once a year and if they have children I'll never get to see them. I'll miss out on his life.'

'Come on, Mum! London's an hour from Dublin on the plane. You can go and see him as often as you like. And Shadee's lovely. She makes him really happy. You should be pleased for him. He's never been so happy before. Isn't it better that he's with a lovely girl in London than a girl who makes him miserable in Ireland?'

'Young Maureen Doherty would have made him a lovely wife.'

'*Mum.*'

'I know, I know,' said Mum. 'I'm just sad. It's been so nice having you and James close by with little Yuri, and I'd like to help Sean with his children.'

I wondered if she'd charge him for child-minding. Probably, but since she wouldn't have to worry about saving up the takings for Sean's children – he had a more than healthy bank balance – she'd be a millionaire in no time.

'Look, Mum, get dressed, put on your lipstick and let's go out to celebrate the fact that your son is marrying a wonderful girl. OK?'

She nodded. 'Yes, you're right.'

'I have to go now and put Yuri down. I'll see you in the bar.'

'Emma,' she called, as I was leaving.

I turned round to be hugged or thanked or hailed as a rock of sense.

'You're not wearing that, are you?'

I closed the door and sighed.

Twenty minutes later we were all standing in the bar,

staring at the door, when Shadee and her family walked in.

'Western clothes!' whispered Mum, as Shadee's parents, both dressed in suits, came over to introduce themselves.

'We are so pleased to meet you at last,' said Shadee's mother, a pretty, petite woman. 'We know Sean so well and we were looking forward to getting to know his family. Your son is a lovely boy. You must be very proud of him.'

'Oh, we are,' said Mum. 'Very proud. He's never given us a day's trouble. He was the most good-natured baby you ever saw. And you do know he was the youngest person ever to be made partner at his firm? Of course, he'd never tell you that himself, he's far too modest. Shady is a lucky girl. He's one in a million.'

'Yes, well, as I said, we are very fond of him.'

'Of course, an Irish son-in-law would not have been our first choice,' said Shadee's father, as my mother bristled. 'We had hoped our precious jewel would marry an Iranian boy. The Irish have such a reputation for drinking and violence that we were worried at first.'

'No more than we were when Sean told us he was to marry a girl from Prussia,' countered Mum. 'Sean barely touches the drink. None of us do,' she added, as we all stared into our alcoholic beverages.

'What my wife is trying to say,' said Dad, attempting to rescue the situation before a fight broke out, 'is that we were also concerned about the cultural differences at first. But then we met Shadee and sure she's a lovely girl altogether.'

Shadee's mother nodded. 'It was the same for us. Once we got to know Sean and saw how in love he was with our beloved daughter, we realized that you can't have everything in life. And the most important thing is that Shadee is happy.'

'They're perfect together,' I said, 'and we're so excited about the wedding. It's going to be a wonderful day,' I added, warming to my role as international peacekeeper.

Just as things were beginning to thaw, Babs arrived. 'Sorry I'm late,' she said, strutting into the bar in a skintight gold jumpsuit.

'Bloody hell!' said James, and almost choked on his drink.

Shadee's family stared in shock as the youngest Burke wriggled about, oblivious to the look of horror on everyone's faces.

'Hi, I'm Babs, the only sane member of this family. You must be gutted your daughter's marrying a red-headed Irishman . . . of all the rotten luck. Still, he's loaded so that should make up for it.' She laughed. 'Shadee's a saint for marrying into this family. At least she has the Irish Sea between her and her new mother-in-law. Thank God for geography. I'm parched! Dad, get me a vodka and Coke, will you, and make it a large one? The measures are so small over here it'll take me for ever to get drunk.'

Chapter 28

James, Yuri and I were up at seven the next morning walking by the sea. Yuri had been up since six, bright-eyed and bushy-tailed.

'How do you think last night went?' I asked James, as I shuffled along beside him at the pace of a snail.

The evening hadn't been going too badly until Babs had got drunk and made a pass at Shadee's brother, who had told her politely that he wouldn't touch her with a barge-pole. Babs stumbled out, shouting, 'You should be so lucky,' while the rest of us sat around pretending not to notice. Thankfully, all the parents had gone to bed by then. I really think that seeing her youngest child sexually harassing Shadee's brother would have pushed Mum over the edge.

'Babs is a liability. And that outfit!'

'I'm still trying to figure out how she managed to get into it. It was a feat of engineering,' said James.

'Do you think Shadee's family think we're a disgrace?'

'They seem very keen on Sean, which is the important thing,' said James, ever the diplomat.

'How bad was it when I asked them how they felt about President Bush having invaded their country and captured Saddam Hussein?' I said, blushing at the memory. In my desperate efforts to keep the stilted conversation going, I had somehow managed to get Iraq and Iran mixed up. Of all the times to say something so stupid . . . I was mortified.

'Not your finest hour.'

'Oh, God, James, they must think I'm such an ignorant fool. And then after Mum telling them we hardly drank, Dad gets plastered and starts singing "Danny Boy" and the waiter has to come over and ask him to stop. We're a joke.' I groaned. 'And Shadee's family behaved impeccably. Poor girl.'

'What about me? I have to put up with your family on a daily basis.'

'Yes, but you're used to drink and fast women,' I said grinning at him.

'True.'

'I hope today goes smoothly. I really want Sean to have a perfect wedding.'

'I'm sure it'll be fine, although I can't wait to see what Babs is going to wear.'

'It couldn't be worse than yesterday,' I said, silently praying that it wouldn't be.

Lucy and Donal sat on the plane. Lucy had bought a pile of glossy magazines in the airport shop and was flicking through *Hello!* while Donal had *Now*.

'That Britney Spears has put on a pile of weight,' he said, as he munched a bacon sandwich. 'Those shorts are a bit tight on her.'

Lucy looked at him – his hair was sticking up at right angles and mayonnaise was dripping down his chin. 'Donal, what did your parents put in your porridge when you were growing up?'

'What do you mean?'

'You're the most confident person I've ever met. How did that come about?'

'It came about because I was born with beauty, brains

and talent. You won the lottery of love when you married me.'

Lucy choked on her coffee. 'Have you seen yourself lately?' she said, laughing as she wiped the mayonnaise off his chin.

'I wake up every day, look in the mirror and glory at God's handiwork,' said Donal.

'You must lend me that mirror some time,' said Lucy.

'I hope we've a good table at this gig,' said Donal. 'I don't want to be making conversation with a bunch of Iranians who speak no English. I don't think they play rugby over there.'

'There are more topics of conversation than rugby. You could ask them about their culture, their troubled history, their religious beliefs . . .'

'Or I could sit at the bar with James, drink Guinness and talk about Leinster's next game.'

'Donal! You're not to behave like a caveman today. I want you to make an effort with Shadee's relations. I don't want them thinking all Irishmen are big, ignorant, hairy rugbyites. Be polite and make conversation.'

'OK, if I promise to be Mr Manners himself all day, is there any chance of us joining the mile-high club now?'

'Jesus, Donal, it's nine in the morning not to mention the fact that half of Emma's relations are on this plane.'

Donal shrugged, 'I don't mind an audience if you don't.'

Lucy thumped him on the arm. 'Behave yourself.'

At half past two, we assembled in the lobby to walk across to the Unitarian church. Needless to say, Babs caused a commotion: she turned up in a skintight, backless red mini-dress. Mum had a seizure and refused to leave the hotel until she covered up. My lovely cream wrap was ripped off my shoulders and tied round Babs's bare ones in a big knot.

'For God's sake, I look like a nun,' said the scarlet woman.

Mum pulled the wrap even tighter. 'I'm warning you, Barbara Burke, I want no nonsense out of you today. For once in your life you'll do as you're told. Now, belt up and smile.'

'Do I look OK?' I asked Dad. He looked panic-stricken for a second. I never asked his opinion on my appearance, but I felt like such a frump that I was desperate for any positive feedback, even if I knew it was a lie.

'Very nice, love. The green is, ah . . . um . . . eye-catching.'

'You look like an overweight leprechaun,' sniggered Babs.

'You look great, Emma,' said Lucy, walking in with Donal. She looked lovely as always, if a little tired. She must be working too hard.

Donal seemed uncomfortable when he saw Babs. Obviously the memory of his infidelity still haunted him.

'I'd be very careful if I was you,' I hissed at Babs. 'My hormones are raging today and you might be the recipient.'

'Ooh, Emma, you're really scaring me.'

'I think we should head over to the church,' said James, picking Yuri up and ushering me out of the hotel before a cat-fight broke out.

By three o'clock the church was full, with all our relations to the right and all Shadee's to the left. Only one of Shadee's relatives was wearing a yashmak. The others were all very stylishly dressed: hats and feathers abounded.

Sean stood nervously at the top of the aisle, looking very handsome in a navy blue suit. The organist began to play and Shadee walked down the aisle with her father. She was stunning in a simple knee-length cream dress, with a single flower in her hair. Everyone oohed and aahed. Auntie Doreen tried to throw holy water over her as she walked by but, thankfully, Dad managed to grab her hand in time and Babs ended up being drenched instead. When she squealed, Dad glared at her and muttered that she needed it a lot more than Shadee did.

During the ceremony two of Shadee's friends brought up a variety of gifts, each of which had a specific meaning. They included decorated flat breads, which symbolized prosperity, wild rue for good health, a candelabrum, which represented a bright future, a mirror, in which they were supposed to see the truth of love, a vase with coloured eggs and another with coloured nuts, for fertility.

'We could have done with one of those at our wedding,' I giggled to James. It felt really good to be able to laugh about it all now. I looked down at my beautiful son and my pregnant stomach and silently thanked God.

The ceremony was short and sweet. Dad and Shadee's father both read poems chosen by the bride and groom. Sean and Shadee made their vows, everyone cheered when they said, 'I do,' and we all headed back to the hotel for the reception.

After dinner and a few drinks, everyone relaxed and began to mingle. I made a beeline for Shadee's father to try to make up for my embarrassing *faux-pas* the night before. I cornered him and bombarded him with what I felt were probing questions about his country. After half an hour he said how delighted he was that I had such an interest in Iran and he'd be sure to send me a book that would satisfy my thirst for knowledge. With that he sprinted in the opposite direction and avoided eye-contact with me for the rest of the night.

241

It was about midnight when I went to the loo for the zillionth time. Babs was in the bathroom fixing her makeup and telling one of Shadee's cousins about her nose job. 'You should definitely get one done. Your nose is nearly as bad as mine was. Seriously, I'll give you the name of the plastic surgeon.'

'Is mine really that big?' the poor girl asked.

'Is the Pope Catholic? Yes, it is,' said the plastic-pusher.

As Shadee's cousin scurried out, holding her hand over her nose, I rounded on Babs. 'For God's sake, the poor girl doesn't need a nose job. You've just given her a complex.'

'She wants to work in TV and, believe me, there's no way she'll get a job with that hooter. I was doing her a favour.'

'Why don't you sort out your own life before telling everyone else what to do?'

'I'm sorted, Emma. I have a great nose, a great job and a boss who thinks I'm the best thing ever.'

'I doubt that.'

'He does, actually.'

'Well, I wouldn't get too cocky. Those media types are so fickle – one minute they love you, the next they fire you.'

'He'll never fire me.'

'What makes you so sure?'

'Because he's sleeping with me, and if he fires me, I'll tell his wife.'

I must have misheard her. There was no way she had just said she was having sex with her married boss. Not even Babs was that bad. 'What did you just say?'

'Lighten up. It's a winner for me, I get to live rent-free in his apartment and he takes me out to great restaurants and clubs. Besides, it's only temporary. I'll be moving jobs soon.'

'Oh, my God, Babs. Have you gone *insane*? He's married.

Have you no morals? No heart? What about his wife? What's wrong with you? It's practically prostitution!'

'Shut up, fatso. Go and nag James – he's used to it.'

I grabbed her arm. 'Listen to me. You're behaving like a slut. You have to stop this. Why can't you go out with someone your own age, someone single? Jesus, first you sleep with Donal and now this!'

'Donal wasn't married,' she snapped.

'He was engaged,' I hissed. 'It's pretty bloody close.'

'I presume we're talking about a different Donal?' said a voice I knew too well.

My heart stopped. Please, God, no. I turned to see Lucy glaring at me. She had been in the cubicle and heard it all.

'Don't start freaking out. You'd broken up when it happened,' said Babs, putting on her lipstick.

Lucy moved so quickly that Babs didn't have time to react. She grabbed her by the shoulders and shoved her up against the wall. 'No big deal? No big deal that you shagged my fiancé? Newsflash – it is a big deal. A very big deal. Now, you listen to me, you little slut, if I ever see you near Donal again, you'll need a facelift to repair the damage.' She sounded like something from *The Godfather*. Babs actually looked a bit scared.

'OK, I'm sorry. But it was nothing. He was so drunk he didn't even remember the next day.'

'Great! I feel so much better now. Thanks for sharing that. *Now get out of my sight before I kill you*,' roared Lucy.

As Babs slunk out of the door, Lucy turned to me. 'Were you ever going to tell me?'

'Lucy, it was the night you'd broken up and he was so drunk and upset he didn't know where he was, not to mind what he was doing. You know what Babs is like – she

243

probably hopped on him. He felt so awful the next day and he was so riddled with guilt and you two make such a good couple that I didn't think it was worth telling you because you would have broken up over it and it was just a stupid thing.'

'Would you think it was stupid if James slept with someone else?' she asked, voice shaking.

'Lucy, I agonized over whether to tell you or not and when I saw that Donal was so utterly devastated by it I knew he truly loved you so I decided not to say anything.'

'I'll never trust you again,' said Lucy, tears streaming down her face. 'You're supposed to be my best friend. How could you let this happen? How could you let that little slut near him?'

'Lucy, I wasn't there. Of course I would have stopped it otherwise. The only reason I know about it is because I found Babs in the house when I went over to get your suits for work.'

'In our house? In our bed? Oh, God, I think I'm going to be sick,' she said, and turned back to the toilet to retch.

'Are you OK? Lucy, please, listen to me. It's not as bad as it sounds. Donal was comatose. He didn't even know where he was or what had happened. I thought it best not to say anything. I'm sorry.'

'Well, it's a bit late for that,' she sobbed, and stormed out.

Donal was talking to Shadee's brother, who turned out to be a huge rugby fan. The two men were dissecting the English team when Lucy came over.

'Ah, here she is, let me introduce you to my beautiful wife,' said Donal, as Lucy punched him in the face.

He lay on the floor dazed, as Lucy screamed at him, 'You stupid bastard! How could you sleep with that slut? We were ENGAGED. You've ruined everything! I'll never forgive you for this!'

She ran out, followed by Donal, who was staggering slightly due to his bloody nose and mild concussion.

Chapter 29

Donal got to the bedroom door just in time to stop Lucy locking him out. He pushed his way into the room and closed it behind him. Lucy ran at him and beat her fists against his chest. She was crying so much she was having difficulty breathing. Donal held her arms and gently sat her down on the bed.

'You've no idea what you've done,' she sobbed.

'Lucy, please, listen to me,' he begged. 'I was so devastated we'd broken up that I went out and got blind drunk. I know it's stupid and, believe me, I really regret it. I don't even remember meeting Babs, not to mind . . . well, not to mind the rest.'

'Is that supposed to make it better? You have sex with someone else and because you say you don't remember it it's all right. I can't do this, Donal. I can't be with someone I don't trust. You've ruined everything,' she cried.

'Lucy, I love you. I've loved you since the first time I set eyes on you. Please don't let one stupid mistake ruin what we have. I'm a gobshite. Hit me, thump me, kick me, do anything, but please don't leave me.' He begged, kneeling down and kissing her hands. 'I'll do anything to make it up to you.'

'It's too late,' she said.

'It's not too late. Come on, Lucy, we'd broken up and I did a stupid thing. I'm sorry about that, but don't tell me you're going to let one mistake ruin what we have.'

Lucy pulled away her hands and stood up. 'You cheated on me. If you did it once, you'll do it again.'

'I will never do it again. I swear to you. I swear on my life. Come on, I'll take you away on a romantic weekend and we'll forget about it. We've our whole lives ahead of us. Lucy, please, I'll –'

'I'm pregnant,' Lucy whispered.

'What?'

'You heard me. I'm pregnant. You begged me to have children so I stupidly came off the pill and now I'm pregnant, Donal. Seven weeks pregnant with your baby. So now we have a child and no marriage. Isn't it great? I was trying to find the right time to tell you and I thought this weekend would be perfect. It looks like I was right. What better time to tell your husband you're expecting than ten minutes after you've found out he cheated on you?'

'But, Lucy, that's amazing! Oh, my God, we're going to have a baby.'

He went to hug her. She jerked away. 'Don't touch me. I can't bear the sight of you. I'll be raising this child on my own. Now get out, you lying bastard,' she sobbed, and locked herself in the bathroom.

After talking through the keyhole for twenty minutes, Donal finally agreed to leave Lucy alone for the night. When he came out of his room, James and I were waiting for him in the corridor. He looked devastated.

'What happened?' I asked.

Donal's eyes were filled with tears. 'She says she can't forgive me and she's just told me she's pregnant,' he croaked.

'Oh, mate,' said James, putting his arm round his friend.

Pregnant? Such happy news to come out at such a rotten time. Oh, God, poor Lucy. 'Can I go and talk to her?'

247

I asked. I couldn't bear the thought of her alone. I was worried about her being so upset – it might be dangerous for her pregnancy.

Donal shook his head. 'She said she wants to be on her own and I don't want her getting any more upset. It's bad for the baby. Leave it till the morning. I'm going to stay here in case she changes her mind and wants to talk to me later,' he said, sitting down outside the door.

'I'll stay with you.'

'No, darling,' said James. 'You're going to bed. You need to calm down and rest. You're pregnant too, remember. I'll stay with Donal.'

I waddled back to my room and paid the babysitter. Yuri was sleeping soundly in his little cot. I was struggling out of my green frock when someone knocked on the door. It was Mum. 'What's going on? I heard Lucy thumped Donal and said he cheated on her. Who was he with?'

'Look, Mum, just leave it. Don't be asking questions.'

'It wasn't you, was it?'

'Jesus, Mum, of course not! What do you take me for? Thanks a bloody lot.'

'Your auntie Doreen said she heard Lucy roaring at you so I had to ask. Was it Jess?'

'Mum! Jess would never do something like that.'

'Do I know the girl he was with?'

'Drop it, Mum. I'm warning you. Just leave it.'

'No need to get so touchy. I'm only asking.'

'I'm tired and upset. Can you leave now and let me get some rest?'

'OK, I'll go,' she grumbled. Just as she was about to leave she turned. 'Didn't Sean look handsome today? Shady's a lucky girl. The suit was gorgeous on him, but sure he's such a good figure everything looks well on him.'

'Yes, he did. Now, please, go.'

'I don't know about Shady's dress. It was a bit simple. It could have done with a bit of lace or a frill, don't you think? And what, in God's name, was that nonsense with the friends bringing up the bread and mirrors? Your aunties were all asking me about it. I said it was some kind of a tradition over there. Most peculiar, I must say. Still, by and large her family seems quite normal.'

'Which is more than you can say for ours,' I muttered.

'What's that?' she asked. 'Anyway, didn't I look well? I think the outfit worked. Your auntie Maeve said I was the belle of the ball,' said Mum, twirling.

'Out. Now,' I said, nudging her out of the door. I really wasn't in the mood to discuss her outfit.

'Lord, you're very narky. I suppose it's the hormones. I'll leave you to it. Sleep well.'

I sat down on the end of the bed and sighed. What was I going to do about Lucy? She had always said that trust was the most important thing to her. When her father had cheated on her mother she had seen the hurt and humiliation it caused and she always said that once the trust is broken there's no going back. And now she was pregnant. I wanted to talk to her, hug her, congratulate her, explain that I had genuinely thought I was doing the right thing by not telling her about Donal and Babs. I truly believed that he would never cheat on her again. My mind swirled about. I felt sick. Would she ever forgive me?

*

The next morning I woke up early and went to Lucy's room. Donal was asleep in the corridor. I stepped over him and knocked gently on the door.

'Go away, Donal, I'm not going to talk to you.'

'Lucy, it's me, Emma.'

'Judas!'

'Lucy, please, let me explain,' I begged.

'Go to hell.'

'Can I come in and talk to you? Please. I heard about the baby. It's great news.'

'Yeah, it's great, now that I've found out my husband's a cheat and my best friend's a liar. I can't wait to go through it all alone.'

'Lucy, I'm sorry, really, really, sorry, but I thought I was doing the right thing.'

'Well, you weren't.'

The door opened and Lucy stepped out fully dressed, bag in hand. She tripped over Donal, who woke with a start.

'Lucy, sweetheart, let's go for breakfast and talk this through,' he said, jumping up.

'I've a better idea. Why don't you go to breakfast with your fellow conspirator here and have a chat about how you deceived me?'

'Lucy, come on,' I pleaded. 'Hear us out.'

'No, Emma. Trust is the most important thing to me. You know that and you broke it.'

Her eyes were puffy from crying; she looked pale and fragile. I desperately wanted to hug her. She was my best friend, we had been through thick and thin together, and now she felt I had let her down. I'd really thought I was doing the right thing. At the time they had broken up – granted, only for a short time, but she had left him, suitcase in hand. I had chosen not to tell her about Babs because they were so right together and Donal genuinely had no recollection of what had happened and he was so full of remorse. Was I wrong?

I watched her walk away, followed by Donal, who was limping badly from cramp after a night on the corridor floor. I went back to discuss my next move with James.

'Are you awake?' I asked, poking him in the back.

'I am now,' he grumbled.

'What am I going to do?'

'What time is it?' He looked at his watch. 'Christ, it's six in the morning. Yuri isn't even awake. Mercy, Emma, please. We went over this for two hours last night. I need some sleep. I'll discuss it with you later.'

'But she's my best friend,' I wailed, 'and she hates me. Who am I going to talk to now?'

'Apparently me!' said James, pulling the duvet over his head to block me out.

'Can you believe Babs?' I fumed. 'Sleeping with Donal and now her married boss.'

'Pardon?' said James. His head popped back up.

'The reason Babs is doing so well in work is because she's shagging her boss. Classy, huh?'

'Ambitious.'

'It's prostitution, James.'

'Hardly.'

'Sleeping with someone for free rent, a job and a social life is prostitution in my book.'

'Sounds like the boss is getting a pretty good deal. Nice young thing on the side.'

'He's obviously a sleazeball, who goes around forcing himself on the young girls working for him.'

'Knowing Babs, I'd say it was her idea.'

'She's not that bad.'

James looked at me. 'Didn't you just call her a prostitute?'

I nodded and sighed. 'Yes, you're right, she is that bad. What am I going to do about her? She's out of control.'

'I met lots of girls like Babs when I worked in the City. She's the type who'll always land on her feet. I wouldn't worry about her.'

'Did you ever sleep with your staff?'

'Never, darling.'

'Liar. You told me you slept with your secretary at the Christmas party one year.'

'Me and my big mouth. OK, I did have one episode, but she was single.'

'You told me she was living with her boyfriend.'

'I should be muzzled.'

'Do you think Lucy'll forgive him?'

'Donal will persist until she does,' said James. 'He won't let her go. He's mad about her.'

'I hope you're right, I really do. And, FYI, if you ever cheat on me, I'll chop it off and feed it to a pack of hungry wolves.'

'I do so enjoy these pre-dawn tête-à-têtes,' said James.

Three hours later, we were assembled in the lobby, waiting for the minivan to take us to the airport. Sean and Shadee were getting a later flight to Malaysia, where they were spending their honeymoon.

'So, did you enjoy it?' asked Sean.

'It was amazing, just perfect,' I lied.

'I heard Lucy thumped Donal. What's going on there?'

'Oh, you know those two. They're always fighting about something or other. It's no big deal.'

Sean smiled. 'Good. I was worried she'd found out about his slip-up with Babs.'

'God, no,' I said, fake-laughing. Sean didn't need to know what had happened: he was off on honeymoon and I didn't want him worrying about anything.

As if on cue, Babs strolled in like someone who hadn't a care in the world. 'Is the bus here?' she asked.

'Yes, it is,' I said. I pulled her aside. 'Do you have any idea how much trouble you've caused? Lucy and Donal might be breaking up.'

'It's not my fault. Do I have to remind you that I'm not the one who was engaged? If they've broken up it's Donal's fault for playing away from home.'

'Because of you my best friend isn't speaking to me and her marriage may be on the rocks and apparently you don't give a shit.'

'Honestly? No. It's not my problem.'

'There's no talking to you. Go back to London to your sleazy affair.'

Dad wandered over. 'Are you two arguing again?'

'No, actually, Emma's congratulating me on my progress in work,' said Babs, smirking at me.

'Yes, it's amazing how well she's doing. A true professional,' I retorted.

'Ah, sure we always knew she had it in her. Full of spunk,' said Dad, as James spat his tea half-way across the room.

Chapter 30

The Saturday after Sean's wedding it was the quarter-final of the European Cup. As usual James was up to ninety. Ray Phelan, the place-kicker, had injured himself in the Monday-morning practice session and things were not looking too good. James was not a happy camper. Without a top-class place-kicker, Leinster were vulnerable.

Meanwhile, between working and minding Yuri, I was stalking Lucy. I went to her office four times, but she refused to see me. I called her mobile at least ten times a day, but she hung up every time. She had moved out of the house she shared with Donal and into a hotel while she decided what to do. Donal was beside himself and spent all his spare time in our house moping about and trying to come up with new ways to win her back. He wasn't having any success communicating with her either.

Annie called mid-week, and when she asked Donal to put Lucy on the phone he told her they were having a few problems and that Lucy had moved out for a while.

'What do you mean?' she asked.

'Ah, we just had a disagreement and she's cross with me, so she's taking a few days away to calm down.'

'What did you do to upset her?'

Donal cursed his stupidity. Why hadn't he just lied and said Lucy was away on business? 'Well, I kind of did a silly thing before we were married and she's annoyed with me.'

'How stupid?'

'Very stupid.'

'Were you with another woman?' asked the canny sixteen-year-old.

'Well, kind of.'

'Were you or weren't you?'

'I suppose I was.'

'When you were engaged?'

'Um, yes, but it was when we had broken up that time after you had the fight with her on the phone.'

'You cheated on your fiancée?'

'Technically I didn't cheat. We had broken up.'

'Bullshit, you guys are all the same. You're all arseholes. How could you do that to Lucy? She's such an amazing person! How could you be so stupid?'

'Easy now, there's no need to curse the whole male species. And, in case you've forgotten, you were the reason we broke up at the time and I seem to remember you were delighted about it.'

'Don't blame me because you screwed another woman.'

'Annie, watch your language.'

'Don't get all fatherly on me, Donal. It's a bit late for that. What kind of an example are you, cheating on your wife?'

'I didn't cheat on my wife. I'd never do that.'

'So what are you doing about getting her back?'

'I call her fifty times a day. I've been round to her office and caused a scene trying to get to see her, but the secretary called Security and I got turfed out. I'm trying to come up with another plan.'

'Crap.'

'What?'

'Crap efforts. For God's sake, you have to do something

huge to make her forgive you. You have to do something really romantic to sweep her off her feet. Don't you watch movies? Haven't you seen *Pretty Woman*? Ger her back, Donal. Do whatever you have to do but just get her back. She's brilliant.'

'I know she is. I'll think of something. Now, go and do your homework and mind your language.'

'And you go and keep your trousers on.'

Donal hung up and sighed. Annie's new-found love for Lucy was almost worse than when she had hated her. He knew now that she'd be calling him every night for an update. He'd better get his thinking cap on. Maybe he'd rent that film. What had she said it was called?

The night before the game, James sat on the couch, head in hands.

'What's up?'

'Ray's groin strain hasn't cleared up. He's failed the fitness test. We're buggered.'

'Come on, you've got fourteen other great players. It can't be that big of a deal.'

'Emma, he's the kicker. Without him we'll lose all the penalty and conversion points. It's a total disaster.'

'Can't one of the other guys kick? What about number fifteen, he's always hoofing the ball up in the air.'

'Place-kicking is a completely different skill,' said the pessimist.

'Well, maybe you'll score loads of tries and the kicking won't be so important.'

'The Biarritz pack are bigger than ours. We need the easy points.'

'But are their runners as fast as yours?'

'Their back row is the best in Europe,' he said, as he let out another enormous sigh.

I could see I was wasting my time here and, anyway, I'd run out of positive options. 'Well, then, maybe you'll lose.'

'Thanks a lot. That's just what I need to hear. Very supportive of you, darling.'

'Well, I tried to cheer you up but you bashed down all my ideas. No team can win every game, especially if their best player and kicker is injured. But it doesn't mean you're not a brilliant coach. You're the best in Europe, everyone knows that, and I'm really proud of you. A cook can't bake a great cake without the right ingredients – or whatever the saying is – so if you're down a man, well, it's not your fault if you lose. Would Alex Ferguson be able to win cups if he didn't have Beckham on the team? No.'

'Emma, David Beckham left Man U three years ago, OK? I know you're trying to be helpful but you're actually making it worse. Please stop talking.'

'Fair enough. But don't sit here all night wallowing. You need your sleep before the big game. If you appear confident, the team will too. Go, Leinster!'

James ignored me and went back to watching reruns of Biarritz annihilating Bath. I went upstairs and prayed for Leinster to win.

By half-time Leinster were down 13–5. Biarritz had scored a try, a conversion and two penalties. Leinster had missed two penalties and a conversion, but had scored a try. I sat in the stand with Mum, Dad and Yuri – who was looking very sweet in his Leinster shirt – and bit my nails.

'Well, Dad? What do you think? Will they come back?'

'Sure how can they win with no kicker? It's a disaster.'

257

'But maybe if they score some more tries?'

'No way. That try was a steal. The only reason they scored it was because of an intercepted ball. They'll lose this game. A team needs a back-up kicker, and James should have sorted one out.'

'Don't blame James,' I said defensively, 'He's doing his best.'

'Lord, I'm frozen,' moaned Mum. 'How long more does it go on for?'

'Another forty minutes,' I replied. I was an old pro at this stage. I knew my rugby.

'It's a bit dull, really, isn't it?' said Mum.

'No, it's exciting. You just have to get into it,' I lied, as I shivered in the wind and rain, wishing the minutes away.

In the studio, a dishevelled Donal was arguing with the other panellists. Because of his broken heart, he hadn't slept in a week and was feeling decidedly out of sorts. He had dragged himself to work, but without Lucy's sartorial advice, he had matched a blue jacket with a brown shirt and a red tie. Gerry O'Reilly was slating James and the Leinster team. 'They look like a bunch of amateurs. One player's injured and they fall apart. The coach's decision to run everything is a farce. This side is just not good enough, and Hamilton has a lot to answer for.'

'Hold on a minute,' snapped Donal. 'Don't badmouth the coach. James Hamilton is world class. In case you've forgotten, Leinster are the Cup-holders. They beat everyone last year, something that they'd never achieved before. And it was mainly down to James's coaching. He is an expert tactician.'

'Well, in fairness now, Donal, his game plan isn't working

too well today,' said Pat Tierney. 'I'm generally a fan of John Hamilton's, but I think he's let the team down today.'

'Jesus, Pat, it's James – James Hamilton. How difficult is it to remember names? You're a television presenter, it's your job to memorize them. And James has not let the team down. Leinster wouldn't be here if it wasn't for him.'

'Well, Donal, I think you'll find that television panellists are supposed to be impartial, which is something you seem to have trouble with,' snapped Pat.

Before Donal could answer, the match resumed. Leinster played their hearts out. They scored another try, but missed the conversion and another penalty kick. Biarritz scored a drop goal and two further penalties. The final score was 22–10. The team was gutted. We watched as James went over to congratulate the Biarritz coach, then patted all his players on the back. I could tell by the way his shoulders were slumped that he was devastated.

'Well, Donal, I hope you're not going to take the head off me when I say that the better team won today,' said Pat.

This was the icing on the cake of the worst week of Donal's life. 'It's desperate,' he said. 'A terrible loss. They really gave it their best in the second half.'

'Their best is simply second-rate and that's due to bad coaching,' said Gerry, winding him up. 'Hamilton needs to go. He's useless, and he's let the team down with shoddy leadership.'

'What would a fat fuck like you know about sport?' said Donal, as he stormed off the set, leaving Gerry and Pat open-mouthed.

Donal went straight down to the dressing room to see James. He found him giving the team an after-match talk.

'I want you all to know how proud I am of you. You

259

played your hearts out and that's all a coach can ask for. We were simply outplayed today. It's not the outcome we wanted, but it's been an honour coaching you this season and I fully intend to come back next season and blow the competition out of the water. So, enjoy a well-earned rest and I'll see you back here in two months' time to resume training. Thanks for all your hard work. I'm really sorry that it had to end here today.'

As the team shuffled out, Donal went in and threw an arm round him. 'Hard luck. If Ray had been playing you'd have beaten them. You did your best, though. That was some second-half performance. I thought at one point you were going to win.'

James sighed. 'Ray's not the only player we missed out there. You'd have won a lot more line-outs for us.'

'You're lucky I've retired, believe me. I'd be a liability to the team at the moment. I can't think straight.'

'No luck with Lucy, then?'

Donal shook his head. 'She won't speak to me.'

'Well, thanks to you she won't speak to me either,' I said, walking over to hug James. 'I'm so sorry, James, you were great. Everyone's saying how well Leinster played and how they tried so hard and how brilliant you are.'

James sighed. 'I've no doubt there'll be others calling for my head tomorrow. What did the panel say?' he asked Donal. 'And there's no point sugar-coating it, I'll see it later.'

'That shower of amateurs don't even know what they're talking about,' said Donal, gazing at the floor.

James grimaced. 'That bad, huh?'

'Don't mind them, James. Everyone knows you're a class act,' he said.

'Stupid old farts,' I added. 'What do they know?'

Mum, Dad and Yuri walked in, and Yuri stumbled over to James, bringing a much-needed smile to his face.

'There's always next year,' said Dad.

'Lord, it's very dark and poky in here,' said Mum. 'I'd have thought the changing rooms would be a bit nicer at professional level. You should sort that out, now you've a bit of time on your hands.'

'Put a sock in it,' hissed Dad.

'There's no need to snap at me, I'm only stating the obvious.'

'Let's go for a drink,' I interrupted, before they began to tear strips off each other.

As they walked out, I pulled James aside. 'Yuri wants to say something to you,' I said. 'Crouch down.'

James bent down to Yuri's level and I stood behind him encouraging Yuri to do as we had been practising for three weeks. I mouthed the word and, bless his little heart, he performed beautifully.

Putting his hands up to James's face, he spluttered, 'Bdabda, Bdabda.'

James picked him up. 'Emma, I haven't got time for this. I've no idea what the child's saying. Can't we do this later?'

'For God's sake, he's saying Dada. We've been practising for weeks in case you lost this match. It's supposed to be a moment you never forget – it's supposed to cheer you up and make you feel better.'

'Bdabda,' shouted Yuri, as his father cracked a smile, albeit a small one, and kissed him.

Chapter 31

Billy rolled over and turned off the alarm. 'Bloody hell, my head!' He groaned. 'Why did I let you talk me into drinking cocktails last night?'

Babs grinned. 'Because we were celebrating my promotion. Besides, it was fun.'

'I'm too old for this,' said Billy, as he struggled to sit up. 'I can't keep up with you any more.'

'Ah, stop moaning. It keeps you young.'

'My back's killing me,' he complained, as he shuffled into the bathroom. 'I told you not to make me dance.'

'Don't worry, I won't be doing it again in a hurry. You were an embarrassment,' said Babs, cringing at the memory of Billy sliding across the dance-floor on his knees and trying to twirl her round like some old rock-and-roller.

'Put the kettle on, will you, love? I need a cup of strong coffee to get me going.'

Babs rolled over and went back to sleep.

When Billy came out of the shower he shook her. 'Oi, Lady Muck, I thought I asked you to make coffee.'

'Piss off. I'm too hung over to move.'

'You lazy sod,' he said, pulling the duvet off her. She squealed. 'Get into that kitchen and put on some breakfast. You might try cleaning the place up this morning. It's a disgrace.'

'If you want someone to clean, get a cleaning woman.'

'May I remind you that you live here rent-free? I don't think it's too much to ask for you to throw a duster about once in a while.'

'Sleeping with you is payment enough. Now, go away and leave me alone. I need my beauty sleep.'

'Cheeky. You're on at eleven – don't be late. I need you to shift those bloody ceramic elephants. They're clogging up the warehouse. Put on a short skirt and some extra slap – that should help the sales.'

'Billy, your voice is like a drill in my head. Go to work.'

Ten minutes later the buzzer sounded. Babs ignored it. It sounded again, and this time it didn't stop. Bloody hell, she thought. Billy must have forgotten something. She dragged herself out of bed and stomped to the door. 'Jesus, Billy, I'm trying to sleep,' she said, swinging open the door.

'Well well well,' said a woman Babs didn't recognize. 'So you're his little whore. Nice outfit.'

Babs looked down. She was naked except for a tiny pair of black pants that had 'love me' written in red across the crotch.

'Oh, I'm sorry. How rude of me not to introduce myself,' the woman went on. 'I'm Hilary, Billy's wife and the mother of his two children.'

'Hi, I'm Babs,' said the naked one, proffering a hand.

Hilary pushed past her into the apartment and walked straight to the bedroom. 'So this is where your sordid little affair takes place,' she said, as Babs pulled on one of Billy's shirts to cover herself. 'I knew he was up to no good. How does it feel to know that you're shagging another woman's husband?'

Babs shrugged. 'I'm not the one who's married. I'm not

263

the one with the kids. If you're going to get pissed off with someone, you should talk to Billy.'

'Is that an Irish accent?'

'Yes.'

'Well, you little Irish slut, it's time to pack your things and go home to your mother,' said Hilary. She grabbed Babs by the arm and shoved her towards the wardrobe. 'Start packing now.'

'I'm not going anywhere.'

'You stupid tart. You're not the first slag to catch Billy's eye. This has happened before and I got rid of those sluts too. He's been faithful for the past two years and I intend to keep him that way. So, listen to me very carefully. You will pack your bags and get a one-way ticket home.'

'No, actually, I won't. I've got a job and a life here. I'm going nowhere.'

'Enjoying yourself too much, are you? It must be nice to have an old man looking after you. Not interested in lads your own age? Prefer sugar-daddies, do you? Like sponging off my husband, do you? Well, the party's over. You won't be seeing another penny. Now, get packing.'

'I'm not going anywhere until I've spoken to Billy.' Babs stood her ground.

Hilary walked back into the hall and shouted, 'Terry, can you come up here? I've got a spot of bother.' Turning back to Babs, she said, 'You're messing with the wrong family, love. I dragged myself up from the hole I was born in. Nobody gets in my way.'

Ten seconds later a man – six foot tall and six foot wide – appeared. 'Having trouble?'

'This little tart says she doesn't want to move out. I think she needs to be persuaded.'

'Are you fuckin' with my sister?' asked Terry, picking Babs up and flinging her on to the bed. 'You need to learn some manners. Now, pack your bags and sling your hook, or you'll seriously regret it,' he growled.

Babs opened her mouth to speak, but Terry was too quick for her: he covered it with a hand and hissed in her ear, 'Are you deaf? I said, get the fuck out of here.'

When Babs had thrown a few things into a bag, she was handed a pen and a piece of paper and told to leave Billy a note saying she had had to go home due to a family emergency and wouldn't be coming back.

'He'll call me,' said Babs.

'On what?' said Terry, crushing her mobile phone under his foot. 'And don't even think about contacting him, because if you do, I'll find out, hunt you down and break your legs.'

'How am I supposed to get back to Dublin? I've no money.'

'You'll have to swim,' said Terry, pushing her towards the door.

'Or you could use your talents and shag the pilot,' said Hilary. 'Now get out of my sight, you cheap slag.'

Terry grabbed Babs's arm and shoved her on to the street. He threw her bag after her and told her to make herself scarce.

The phone rang while I was trying to persuade Yuri that broccoli was the most delicious thing he could ever taste, as he repeatedly spat each spoonful back out. Hoping it was Lucy, I lunged to answer it and tucked the receiver under my ear as I continued the 'Yummy yummy, Yuri' game.

'Hello?'

'It's me,' said my sister. We hadn't spoken since Sean's wedding two weeks ago.

'How's the prostitution going?'

'Not so well, actually. I'm in the airport and I need you to buy me a ticket home.'

'Get sick of you, did he? Find someone younger and less of a pain in the arse?'

'No, actually. His wife found out and got her psycho brother to chase me out of town.'

'What do you mean?'

'I mean, he chased me out of the apartment and said he'd kill me if I didn't disappear and go home.'

'Really?'

'Yes. He was like one of those mad soccer-hooligan types. Bald head and tattoo.'

'Did he hurt you?'

'Well, he roughed me up a bit.'

'Are you all right?'

'I'm fine now. Will you just buy me a bloody ticket so I can get out of here?'

'Why can't you buy your own? You've been living rent-free for months. You must be loaded.'

'I'm skint.'

'What did you spent it all on?'

'Stuff.'

'Like?'

'Clothes, shoes, iPod, stuff.'

'So you've indulged yourself completely and now you want me to bail you out as usual? Well, you can sod off. You got yourself into this mess, you can get yourself out of it,' I said.

'Emma?'

'What?'

'We both know you're not going to leave me stranded here, so will you cut the crap and buy me a ticket?'

'Why should I?'

'Because it's your job as my older sister.'

'I swear, Babs, this is the last time. Have you told Mum and Dad?'

'That my boss's wife found out I was sleeping with him and had me run out of town?'

'So they don't know you're coming?'

'No.'

'Don't you think you should tell them you're moving back in?'

'Actually, I was thinking of crashing at yours until I get myself sorted. I'm too old to live with Mum and Dad.'

'Over my dead body.'

'Come on, Emma, just for a few days until I get my own place.'

'I thought you said you didn't have any money? Who are you planning to sleep with here for free accommodation? And, by the way, in case you give a shit, Lucy and Donal have broken up. So, well done, you've now destroyed two marriages.'

'Donal was single when I slept with him and Billy has been cheating on his wife for years. So you can get off your soap-box.'

'Don't you have any self-respect or consideration for others?'

'Jesus, can you give the lecture a rest and just get me a ticket?'

Yuri began to roar. The broccoli was clearly not satisfying his needs and he wanted something decent to eat. Frankly I didn't blame him. I wasn't a fan of broccoli myself. 'I have to go. I'll buy you a plane ticket but don't even think of turning up on my doorstep. You can go home to Mum and Dad and tell them you were lonely or depressed. You're good at lying, so I'm sure you'll think of something.'

As I hung up the phone, James came in to see what the racket was about. 'Why is Yuri howling?'

'Because I tried to give him broccoli and he hates it.'

'Hardly surprising. Does anyone actually like it?' he said, staring at the green mush on Yuri's plate.

'I'm trying to encourage him to eat vegetables. They're good for him.'

'Yuck, Yuri, yucky broccoli,' said James, throwing the dinner into the bin.

'Thanks, James, you're a great help.'

Since the Leinster defeat, James had been moping around the house feeling sorry for himself. Some of the journalists had criticized his coaching skills in their post-match analysis. As a result he was keeping a low profile and was now spending his days following me around, second-guessing everything I did with Yuri.

'Here you go. Have one of these,' he said, offering Yuri the packet of crisps he was eating.

'James, I don't want him eating crisps. They're bad for him.'

'A few crisps aren't going to hurt,' he said. 'Go on, son, tuck in.'

Delighted to be offered forbidden fruit, Yuri grabbed a handful and stuffed them into his mouth.

'He's taken too many, James. He'll choke.'

'Stop fussing – he's fine.'

Yuri began to cough and turn purple. I grabbed him out

of the high chair and thumped him on the back. A mouthful of crisps tumbled out, and he gasped as he sucked air back into his lungs and then as the delayed shock hit him, he began to cry. I glared at James.

'OK, so I won't give him crisps again.'

'Look, James, I know it's been really hard on you losing the match and all, but when I tell you not to give Yuri something it's not because I'm trying to be a pain, it's because I know what'll happen. Why don't you get out of the house for a while and meet Donal for a drink or something?'

'Donal's more depressed than I am. Lucy still won't talk to him. He's hardly the ideal candidate to cheer me up.'

'Well, then, why don't you meet some of the other lads or organize a game of golf or a poker night or something?'

'Because I intend to wallow in self-pity for a while longer. Besides, I enjoy tormenting you.' He grinned.

'Well, if you're not going out, would you mind putting Yuri to bed? I have to book Babs a flight home – her affair has been uncovered. Then I think I'll lie down. I feel a bit funny today.'

'Are you all right?'

'Yes, I'm just tired.'

'How did Babs get caught?'

'Apparently with her knickers down.'

Chapter 32

Lucy arrived to the office to find Annie waiting for her. 'Hi – what are you doing here? Is everything OK? Why aren't you at school?'

'I snuck out to come and see you. I know about you and Donal. He told me what happened.'

Lucy wasn't sure how much Donal had told her so she decided to tread carefully. 'Look, Annie, it's nothing for you to worry about. You need to go back to school and focus on your exams.'

'Please forgive him, Lucy. I know what he did was stupid, but he's miserable and he really does love you and he really is sorry. Every time I call him he sounds worse. Like really, really sad.'

'It's not that simple.'

'I know shagging another woman is really bad, but he said it happened that time when you broke up because of me – which I still feel really bad about – and he doesn't even remember because he was so drunk and he'd never do the dirty on you again. He really means it. I know all guys are arseholes, but Donal isn't. He's a really good person. And you're great together. I know I was mean to you in the beginning, but now I've got to know you I think you're brilliant and I can see how happy you make him. He just sounds so lonely,' said Annie, pausing for breath.

'I'm lonely too, Annie,' said Lucy. And she was, desperately. Living in a hotel out of a suitcase was miserable at the best of times, but at nine weeks pregnant it was truly grim. She loved Donal and she missed him, but he had cheated on her and she couldn't get past that. Once a cheat always a cheat – wasn't that the saying? Her father had cheated on her mother, who had never got over it and was still bitter. Lucy had been five and she remembered the hurt it had caused. Mind you, her father had been with Sandy for twenty years now and, as far as Lucy knew, he hadn't cheated on her. Maybe he'd just fallen out of love with her mother. After all she was a difficult woman. But if Lucy forgave Donal now, so easily, would that make him think it was all right? Would he be tempted to stray again because he knew she was a soft touch? Did she want to bring up a child on her own? Did she want to spend the rest of her life alone because she couldn't forgive this mistake? Donal made her feel special and he made her laugh. When she was with him she felt invincible, safe, happy. Was she throwing it all away for a principle? Her head throbbed and she felt nauseous again.

'Lucy?' said Annie, coming over to her. 'Are you all right? You look like you're going to throw up.'

'I'm OK. It'll pass in a minute. The mornings are always the worst.'

Annie looked at her, and then the penny dropped. 'Oh, my God, are you pregnant?'

Lucy cursed her stupidity. She had presumed if Donal had confessed to Annie about sleeping with someone else that he would have told her about the baby.

'Are you? How many months? When's it due?'

'I'm sorry, Annie. I thought Donal had told you. I'm only two months, and no one else knows.'

'But that's great news,' said Annie, giving Lucy a bear-hug.

'You're OK with it?' said Lucy, trying not to cry. She hadn't had a hug in weeks. She'd been avoiding everyone.

'I knew it'd happen sooner or later,' said Annie, 'and it'll be fun to have a little baby around. I can spoil it rotten. But now you absolutely have to go back to Donal. You can't be separated. Don't let the baby grow up without him. He's a brilliant father. I'd never have got through the last few years without him. You'll be great parents and I'll be a fab auntie. Come on, Lucy, I'm not leaving here until you promise you'll get back with Donal. We're a family now.'

Lucy was having trouble keeping her emotions in check. 'Look, Annie, thanks for coming, I really appreciate it, but you need to go back to school. I promise I'll think about it really seriously,' she said, her voice beginning to quaver. 'I have to go now, I've got a meeting.'

'OK, but I'm going to call you every day until you agree,' said Annie.

Lucy put her into a taxi and waved her off.

The doorbell rang. James went to answer it.

'I'm baa-ack,' I heard Babs shout, and she strode into the kitchen, followed by James, carrying her bag.

'You've got the wrong house. I told you I'd pay for your flight but there was no room at the inn. Go home to Mum and Dad.'

'Come on, it's only for a few days. I'll be fine and I'll even babysit for you.'

'Do you honestly think I'd leave Yuri with you?'

'What's the big deal? All they do is eat, sleep and shit.'

'Mary Poppins herself couldn't have put it more eloquently,' said James. Turning to me, he asked, 'Any reason why you didn't mention your sister was moving in with us?'

'Yes, because she isn't. Come on, Babs, I'll drive you home.'

'I'm not leaving,' she said, taking her coat off and sitting down. 'I don't want to get the third degree at home – you know what Mum's like. She thinks she's Agatha bloody Christie. I'll be followed around for days being quizzed.'

'Serves you right for behaving like a hooker. By the way, I thought you said you'd been roughed up? You look fine to me.'

'Roughed up?' said James.

'Yes, my boss's wife comes from some dodgy part of the East End and her brother – who looked like Mr T from *The A-Team*, except he was white – pushed me around and threatened to kill me if I didn't get out of town.'

James roared laughing. 'So you finally met your match.'

'I'm actually quite traumatized by the whole episode and I think you could at least have the decency to give me a bed for a few days.'

'How is a few days going to change your situation? You've got no money, no job and currently no man to sponge off,' I asked.

'I'm sure Mary Magdalene here will have no trouble sorting that one out,' said James, guffawing at his own joke.

Babs rolled her eyes. 'I've got a plan for a new career.'

'Do tell,' I drawled.

'I'm going to come to work with you tomorrow and talk to Amanda. She loved it when I got the nose job live on her show so I figure she'll be mad keen to have me back, and I wouldn't mind a boob job.'

'Don't even think about it. I like my job and I'm not having you ruining it for me. Besides, Amanda isn't your biggest fan after you threatened to sue her on live TV when you first got your bandages off and your nose looked awful.'

'First, that was all sorted out when the swelling went down and I went back on the show and said I was thrilled with the results. And second, judging by the size of you, I'd say you've only a week or two left before you pop a sprog, so you won't even be around.'

'I've got seven weeks to go, you annoying cow, and you're not to go near the studio.'

'Fine, whatever, I'll think of something else. So, what's for dinner?'

'Your head on a plate.'

That night I woke up to find the bed sheet underneath me soaking. Crikey, I must have peed in my sleep! Then, when I tried to get up. I felt a sharp pain in my gut and a whoosh of watery fluid gushed down my legs. Oh, my God, I was in labour.

'*James!*' I shrieked. 'I'm having the baby!'

'What?' he said, struggling to wake up from a deep sleep.

'Look,' I said, pointing to the bed with a shaking finger. 'My waters have broken. Shit, James, it's too early – I'm seven weeks too early,' I said, beginning to cry. This wasn't right. It was too soon. The baby was too small. Oh, God, please, don't let there be anything wrong, I prayed.

James dived into action, like an army pro. Within minutes he was dressed, had helped me into my dressing-gown and brought me downstairs. He went back up, woke Babs and told her she was about to earn her keep. 'Emma's waters have broken and I'm taking her to hospital. Look after Yuri, and if there are any problems, call me on the mobile,' he said, as he ran back down to me.

Babs followed him, rubbing sleep out of her eyes. 'What's

274

going on? Jesus, are you OK, Emma?' she asked, looking concerned.

Christ, I thought, I must look awful if Babs is worried. I nodded. I was afraid to speak. Pure terror was running through my veins. Was my baby going to die? Why was I in labour so early?

James bundled me into the car. Babs stuck her head in and told me not to worry. 'I'll hold the fort here. Don't sweat it, you'll be fine. Babies are always popping out early,' she said, and squeezed my arm.

James drove like a maniac to the hospital, breaking every red light on the way. Thankfully, at two in the morning traffic was scarce. He rammed the car up outside Reception and charged in to find help.

A nurse came running out with him and helped me into a wheelchair. I was rushed in and, after a preliminary examination by a midwife, I was given something to slow down the contractions while they contacted Dr Philips.

The midwife said that the aim was to keep the baby inside for as long as possible to let the lungs mature. I was put on constant foetal monitoring to make sure the baby didn't go into distress. Everyone looked anxious. I held my breath.

Within half an hour Dr Philips was at my bedside, and although he patted my hand and told me not to worry, he looked pretty worried himself. 'The longer we can delay the birth, the better it is for the baby,' he explained. 'It's quite small still and we'd like to give its lungs a bit longer to develop. But if you do go into full labour, don't panic. Premature babies have a very good survival rate these days.'

Survival! He used the word 'survival'. So it was life and death. There was a possibility that the baby wouldn't make it. I stifled a wail.

'What happens if the lungs aren't developed properly?' James asked.

'We put the baby on a ventilator which does the breathing for them,' said Dr Philips.

'A ventilator?' said James, looking as horrified as I felt.

'Let's not worry about things until we have to. Emma, it's very important that you try to remain calm.;

Keep calm? How could I possibly do that? It was too early. The baby shouldn't be coming now. I'd heard about premature babies dying. We all had. How could this be happening? I had felt fine until today. Why now? Why us?

For two hours I sat in the bed and lurched from hope to despair. 'What if the baby dies?' I asked James.

'Stop it, Emma. Our child is going to be fine,' he said, as though chasing away negative thoughts.

'But what if?'

'Emma, it's going to be all right. We've paid our dues on the baby front. It took us three years to have Yuri and we deserve a break. This baby is going to be fine. It has to be. It will be,' he said, clenching his fists and pacing up and down.

'I really wanted Yuri to have a brother or sister. I don't want him to be an only child.'

'He won't be.'

'At least we have Yuri. Thank God we have him. He's given us the gift of parenthood. Whatever happens, we still have our son,' I sobbed.

'Emma, you have to stop thinking the worst. Of course we're lucky to have Yuri but we're going to have another baby too. Come on, start thinking positively.'

'You're right.' I sat back and closed my eyes. 'You will survive,' I whispered, to my swollen stomach. 'Come on, stay with us.'

'That's the spirit. Another few hours and, hopefully, the contractions will have stopped and we'll be back on track,' said my eternal optimist.

Ten minutes later, I started to bleed. I screamed at James to get Dr Philips.

He came running and performed an ultrasound. 'Emma, this is showing us that clots have formed in the placenta, which is now breaking away from the uterine wall. We're going to have to perform an emergency Caesarian.'

'Is the baby OK?' I sobbed.

'Yes, but it needs to come out now before it gets into distress. The anaesthetist is on her way. I'm going to get scrubbed up. I'll see you in theatre.'

I began to hyperventilate. James held my hand and stroked my forehead. He was trying to be stoic, but I could see the cracks. He was terrified too.

Chapter 33

Dr Philips smiled as he held up our baby. 'It's a girl,' he announced.

James and I stared at our tiny daughter. Her body was curled up and her eyes were closed. She didn't cry. I put out my arms to hold her but the midwife whisked her away immediately to the neonatal intensive care unit.

'What are you doing? Is she all right?' I sobbed.

'She's very small and she needs to be put on a ventilator straight away. Don't worry, she'll get the best care in NICU,' said Dr Philips.

'But she didn't cry,' I croaked.

'It's all right, Emma. She's alive – she just needs help breathing,' he said, as he started sewing me back together.

'I want to see her. I want to see my little girl, please.'

'You'll be taken to her as soon as possible, I promise.'

James, who hadn't uttered a word since the birth, was squeezing my hand so tightly that I thought my fingers would break. His face was ashen. Suddenly his grip loosened and he passed out.

When he came to, he was lying on a bed beside me in a little room down the corridor from the NICU.

'What happened?'

'You fainted.'

'Is the baby all right?'

'I don't know, they won't take me down to see her yet,' I said, crying.

James got up and came over to hug me. 'I'll go and find out.'

He came back with a nurse from Intensive Care who told us that our little angel weighed just three pounds and would need careful monitoring for the next few days. She explained that the baby was on a ventilator and had tubes all over her body to help her feed and breathe.

'It looks a lot worse than it is, so don't be shocked when you see her. I'll talk you through it.'

'But is she all right?' asked James.

'So far she's doing well, but the next twenty-four hours are critical,' said the nurse.

James helped her lift me into a wheelchair and they pushed me down to the NICU where we entered another world. The room was crowded with premature babies in incubators. Alarms were going off and parents, sick with worry, were sitting beside their tiny tube-covered infants. Our little girl was huddled in an incubator with tubes all over her body, up her nose and in her mouth. Her eyes were open and, as we leant over to look at her, James's chin began to shake. He was fighting desperately to be strong.

The nurse patiently explained what each tube and monitor was for. Among them there was a feeding tube and a heart-rate monitor, and the big tube taped to her mouth was connected to the ventilator. 'Premature infants tend to have apnoea. It means there are times when they stop breathing. It can happen once a day or more frequently. The good news is that, as the baby matures, she outgrows it.'

'How will you know if she stops breathing? What if I fall asleep and you're looking after another baby and you don't notice?' I asked, panicking at the thought that she might be overlooked. It was pretty crowded in there and I wanted my baby to get the best treatment possible.

'Don't worry, the monitor will sound an alarm. Babies normally breathe twenty to sixty times a minute and sometimes stop breathing for ten to twelve seconds. The pauses are considered normal if the baby begins breathing again by herself, there's no change in skin colour and no drop in heart-rate. Pauses between breaths that are longer than fifteen seconds or occur with a change in the baby's skin colour and a drop in heart-rate are not normal, and the alarm will give us plenty of warning.'

'How long will she be on the ventilator?' asked James, precariously peaky again.

'We'll be monitoring her progress very carefully and, hopefully, after a day or two we'll be able to take her off the ventilator and see if she's ready to breathe on her own. She looks like a fighter,' said the nurse, smiling at us. 'Have you chosen a name?'

James gave me a watery smile, 'Lara, Lara Hamilton,' he said, as I sobbed over the incubator. Lara and Yuri were the names of the two main characters in *Dr Zhivago*, one of my favourite films. When we found out that our adopted son was called Yuri, I knew it was fate and I'd always hoped that if this baby was a girl we'd call her Lara, but James never seemed that keen on the name.

'Can I pick her up?' I begged, desperate to hold my daughter and kiss her beautiful little face.

The nurse shook her head. 'I'm sorry, Emma, not yet. But you can hold her hand,' she said, opening a little circular door at the side of the incubator.

I put my hand in and held Lara's tiny fingers in mine and felt a rush of love wash over me. It was just like the first time I saw Yuri, the strongest emotion I'd ever felt. She was so small, vulnerable and sick. 'Please, God, please, make her better. Please don't take her away from us,' I whispered, as James put his arm round me. Then I took out my hand and watched as James gently held his daughter's hand and lost control of his emotions.

Babs woke up as her eyelids were jammed open. 'Ow,' she snapped, and Yuri giggled. He had climbed out of his cot and into her bed, having found his parents' empty.

'Bdabda?' he said, pointing to their bedroom.

'What?'

'Bdabda,' he said, waddling over to the room.

'Oh, right, yeah, Dada. Well, he's not there and nor is your mum, so you're stuck with me, I'm afraid. Remember me? Fun Auntie Babs?' she said, waving her arms in the air.

Yuri looked at her quizzically.

'Your mama and dada are gone.'

He blinked, then his lip began to wobble and he started to bawl.

'Oh, Jesus, don't cry. They'll be back. It's not like when your other mother dumped you at the orphanage. They haven't gone for good, just a little while. And guess what? You've got a sister. How cool is that? A playmate. Well, if she makes it that is,' said Babs, suddenly feeling a bit tearful. James had sounded so hollow when he called from the hospital in the middle of the night to tell her what was happening.

Yuri continued to cry.

'OK, Yuri, I'm not holy, but I think we need to pray.' Babs knelt down and pulled him down beside her, rubbing his back to calm him. 'Dear God, please let Yuri's sister have a long and healthy life. Emma and James have suffered enough shit trying to become parents. They deserve a break.'

Distracted by the display of piety, Yuri stopped crying. He struggled to his feet and pulled at Babs's pyjama leg. She followed him downstairs to the kitchen, where he frowned at her and babbled.

'Look, kid, I don't understand baby-talk. You're going to have to help me out here. Are you hungry?'

Yuri shouted, 'Orig, orig.'

Babs looked around. What on earth was he talking about? She wanted to ring James to ask him what his son ate in the morning, but she knew she couldn't. OK, I can do this, she thought. It's a process of elimination. She lifted Yuri up and opened all the cupboards. 'Now, what do you want?'

'Orig,' he shouted, squirming.

'Well, what's that?' she asked, pulling out cornflakes, then bread and yogurt. Eventually she saw him pointing at a box of baby porridge on the counter. 'OK, I get it. Porridge,' she said, showing Yuri the box. He laughed and bounced up and down with excitement and starvation.

She made her nephew a bowl of porridge and gave him a spoon. Most of it ended up in her hair and on the floor. Much to Yuri's delight, Babs's reflexes were slower than his mother's, and he had plenty of time to flick the porridge off the spoon before she reacted.

After breakfast, she took Yuri out of the high chair and brought him upstairs to change him, forced into it by the stench from his nappy. She put him on the floor, took it off and gagged at the smell. She wiped his bum with toilet paper, but as she was reaching for a new nappy, he peed over her.

'Shit,' she said, jumping back and wiping her face. 'You're a bit young for golden showers.' She threw a new nappy on and spent the next ten minutes wrestling him into a jumper and jeans.

As she was pulling on his socks, the doorbell rang. Babs ran down to answer it. 'Where is he?' Mum asked, pushing past her.

'Upstairs,' said Babs, as they heard a thud and then a loud wail.

'For goodness' sake, have you no sense? You can't leave him alone for a minute,' said Mum, rushing up the stairs. They found Yuri in his cot. He must have climbed into it, then on to the chest of drawers and up on to the book shelf, which had toppled him back down. Thankfully, his fall had been broken by the mattress. He was sitting surrounded by books, one of which must have hit him on the side of his head because he was now rubbing it.

Mum picked him up and cuddled him. He was clearly delighted to see her familiar face. 'Gany,' he murmured into her ear, as he clung to her cardigan.

'You're all right, my little pet,' said his devoted granny. 'I'll kiss your head better.' Turning to Babs, she snapped, 'Get dressed, we're going to the hospital to see Emma. I'll deal with your sudden homecoming later.'

'Have you spoken to her?' asked Babs.

'Not as such. She came on to the phone but she couldn't speak, she was so upset. Lord, as if they haven't suffered enough,' said Mum. 'Thank God for this little dote here,' she added, hugging Yuri tighter. 'Come on, now, let's get to the hospital. Emma needs her family round her. Seeing Yuri'll cheer her up.'

While Babs threw on some clothes, Mum packed a bag for Yuri – nappies, spare clothes, some toys and food. Yuri followed his granny around watching her, afraid that if he took his eyes off her she'd disappear too. As she was zipping the bag up, he shouted and pointed to his cot.

Mum saw the little grey elephant. She went to place it in the bag but Yuri grabbed it and clutched it to him. He seemed to sense something was wrong. He needed his comforter.

James and I sat by Lara's incubator and prayed as we never had before. I made a pact with God: if he let Lara live, I'd donate my organs to medical science, go to Africa and build schools, join the church choir, never raise my voice in anger again, be nice to Babs — even though she would try the patience of a saint — and look after my mother in her old age instead of putting her in a home as we children had all agreed.

I leant over and gazed into Lara's eyes. 'Come on, angel, fight.'

James held my hand. 'I can't believe this is happening,' he said. 'We can't lose her, Emma, we just can't.'

I willed myself to be strong. 'We won't. Lara's going to live a long and healthy life.'

'Why is having children so bloody difficult?' he asked.

I sighed. 'Maybe it's because when they do arrive, they bring you so much joy that you have to suffer a bit first.'

'Some people just have sex, get pregnant and have healthy full-term babies. Why the hell do we always pull the short straw?' said James, angrily. 'It's not bloody fair.'

'No one gets away lightly,' I said. 'Everyone has stuff to deal with. If it's not a struggle to have children, it could be ill-health or money worries or bad relationships. We're lucky, James. We've got great families, each other, our health, Yuri and now Lara. That's a lot of blessings,' I said. 'Now, come on, we need to think positively for her.'

'Emma,' said James, staring into the incubator, 'I love you.'

Typical! Just as I was being strong and positive, he disarms me. I sobbed into his shoulder.

Chapter 34

Donal had been up all night, thinking of ways to get Lucy back. He'd had enough – phone calls, flowers and calling into her office weren't working. It was time for something more drastic. He was going to persuade her to come home if it killed him. He picked up a few things he needed, then drove to the hotel where she was staying. He strode purposefully through Reception, ammunition in hand. As he was waiting for the lift to go up to Lucy's room, he caught a glimpse of her in the restaurant having breakfast and reading the paper.

Taking a deep breath, Donal pushed open the glass door to the dining room, walked over to Lucy and set down his CD player. As he pressed play, Christy Moore's haunting voice filled the room – with Donal howling along at the top of his lungs:

> 'Black is the colour of my true love's hair,
> Her lips are like some roses fair,
> She's the sweetest smile, and the gentlest hands,
> I love the ground, whereon she stands.
> I love my –'

Everyone stopped eating and stared over. Lucy had jumped up and switched off the music. 'Jesus, Donal, you're making a scene,' she hissed.

Donal knelt down on one knee and handed Lucy an

enormous bunch of roses, before addressing the other guests. They were mostly tourists, who were amused, if startled, by the spectacle. 'I'm sorry to interrupt you all, but I need your help. I am married to this beautiful creature. Before we got married, we broke up for a few days and I went out and got blind drunk and ended up in bed with another girl. I know it was stupid and, believe me, I regret it. But I love this woman more than life itself and I want her to come home. I can't function without her. I need you to help me convince her to take me back. Lucy, my darling girl, I miss you, I love you, I need you in my life. Please forgive me.'

'Aw, honey, you've got to go back. I'm on my fourth marriage and none of my husbands would ever have done that for me,' said a lady dressed from head to toe in plaid.

'It's so romantic. What a beautiful song. Who was that singing?' asked her friend. 'I must get the CD for my Freddie.'

'Girly,' said an elderly gentleman in the corner, 'this fella must be crazy about you. He's just made a complete ass of himself.'

'Stay away. Once a cheat, always a cheat,' said a voice from the back.

'Oh, don't mind Muriel, honey. Her husband was a sex addict,' whispered the tartan fan. 'This boy loves you. I can see it by the way he looks at you.'

'You are a rock of sense, madam. Please, Lucy, listen to her,' said Donal.

Lucy looked at him. He was a wreck. He looked as bad as she felt. She knew he loved her and that he'd be an amazing father to their baby. He had proven himself already with Annie. But he had cheated on her. Was he a womanizer? She'd never seen him flirt with another woman and he was

287

the first guy she had ever gone out with who had made her feel secure. She was totally herself with him.

Lucy felt a hundred years old. The last few weeks had been a nightmare. She had been sick every day – a combination of morning sickness and emotional upset, exhaustion and, most of all, loneliness. She missed Donal. She loved Donal.

'Any chance you could forgive the poor eejit? He's blocking the door,' said the waiter, struggling under a tray of dirty plates.

Lucy looked down at Donal's expectant face. 'I'd like to go home now,' she said. Donal jumped up, swung her around and the crowd cheered, whooped, and someone took a photo.

As they walked out of the dining room, Donal turned to wave. 'Sorry about the interruption, folks. Enjoy the rest of your stay in Ireland. You'll find the people outside Dublin a lot more normal.'

With that, he escorted his beloved bride out of the hotel.

On the way to his car Donal's phone rang. It was James. Lucy could only hear one side of the conversation. 'Jesus, James . . . Is she going to be all right? . . . How's Emma? . . . Right . . . Hang in there. It'll be OK.'

'What happened?' asked Lucy.

'Emma had a baby girl early this morning –'

'But?'

Donal nodded. 'Yes, it's way too early. She's on a ventilator. It's touch and go.'

Lucy's hand flew to her mouth as she stifled a sob.

Mum, Dad, Babs and Yuri arrived to the hospital and James and I rushed out to see our son. The minute I saw his little face and his big brown eyes, I felt better. He held out his arms and I bent down to smother him in kisses. But when I held him and felt his little cheek against mine, I began to cry and so did he. His eyes were like saucers, he looked scared and confused. He clung to his elephant as tears streamed down his face.

'It's OK, Yuri, I'm so sorry. Look, Mummy's not crying now. Everything's all right. I'm smiling, see?' I said, with the best smile I could muster. Bless his heart, he gave me a watery one back.

'Yuri'd like to see his sister,' said Mum. 'We've told him all about her. Haven't we, pet? Little Lara.'

'Lala,' said Yuri.

'Clever boy,' said James, taking his son from me for a cuddle.

'How are you, love?' asked Mum, as she smoothed the hair back from my face.

'Don't be nice to me, Mum. I'm only just holding it together. If you're nice to me I'll fall apart,' I said, as my voice cracked.

Dad pushed Babs forward. 'There you go, Babs, say something mean to your sister. You're good at that.'

'Piss off, Dad.'

'Language,' said Mum.

'Do you want a drink?' Babs asked me. 'I grabbed a bottle of wine from your fridge in case you needed one. I don't have a corkscrew but I can push the cork in.'

'Have you lost your mind, bringing alcohol into the hospital?' hissed Mum.

'What? It might calm her down,' said Babs.

'Thanks,' I said. 'Maybe later. Come on in and meet Lara.'

James was calming Yuri down, so I brought Mum, Dad and Babs in first.

Although Mum did a good job of hiding it, I could see she was shocked by how tiny Lara was. But she took a deep breath and said, 'Well, Emma, she looks healthy to me. We Burkes are fighters. She's just small, that's all.'

Dad wasn't so subtle. 'Jesus,' he gasped, when he saw the size of his granddaughter.

Babs said nothing. She sat down beside the little round door of the incubator and put her hand in. Lara's tiny hand wrapped round her aunt's finger, and Babs dissolved. For the first time we could ever remember, Babs cried.

We looked at each other in shock.

'Are you all right there Babs?' asked Dad, putting his arm round his youngest child.

'Get off me,' she said, shrugging him off and trying to hide her tears.

'It's OK to be human. We're actually relieved,' said Dad. 'There's no shame in having a heart. It's considered fairly normal these days.'

'Out now, the pair of you, and let my grandson in,' said Mum, ushering them to the door.

They left and James came in with Yuri. He held him up so that he could see Lara in the incubator.

'Look, darling, it's your little sister, Lara,' I said, as Yuri stared down at her. He frowned, glanced at me, then at James. We smiled encouragingly. Then I carefully guided Yuri's hand through the window and placed it on top of Lara's tiny one, making sure he didn't move suddenly and pull out any tubes. He rubbed her fingers, mesmerized. I looked at James. He nodded. Our family, we thought. This is our family. She can't leave us. For the zillionth time I prayed for my little girl's survival.

When we brought Yuri out, the new touchy-feely Babs

said she'd take him to the shop for sweets. As they got into one lift, Donal and Lucy got out of the other. Lucy ran towards me. 'Oh, Emma, I'm sorry,' she said, hugging me.

'I'm so glad you're here,' I said. 'I've missed you.'

'Me too.'

'I'm sorry for not telling you about Babs.'

'I'm sorry for ignoring you. I'm an idiot. You were just trying to protect me. Anyway, it's all sorted now. I've forgiven the big lump. Enough about that! How're you holding up? Can I do anything?'

I wondered. Could my best friend take away my terror of Lara dying? Could she stop the anger creeping up on me as I thought about how unfair it was that James and I had to go through more torture in our quest for parenthood? Just when we thought the hard part was over and we'd got lucky, life had slapped us in the face again. God forbid that we'd ever get complacent about having children. Could anyone help? Lara getting better was the only solution to this problem.

'Just pray,' I said, as she put her arm round me.

When Babs arrived back with Yuri, Donal bristled. But Lucy was amazing. She acted as if nothing had happened. She didn't want to cause any more upset for me or James. Donal, on the other hand, avoided Babs like the plague and stayed glued to Lucy's side.

That evening the doctors said that if Lara had a good night, and her vital signs remained stable, they were going to take her off the ventilator in the morning to see if she could breathe on her own.

'That's great news,' said Mum, when we told them.

'I just hope she can do it,' I said.

'The key is that she has a good night tonight,' said James, as he rubbed his eyes.

'Why don't you go home and have a shower and something to eat, James?' said Mum. 'I'll keep Yuri for the night and Babs can stay with Emma until you get back.'

'You both look exhausted. You should try to get a few hours' sleep,' said Dad.

'I can't leave Lara. I'd die if anything happened,' I said.

'Nor can I,' said James. 'We'll be fine.'

'Donal and I can sit with her,' Lucy offered.

'No, I'll do it,' said Saint Babs.

'Look, guys, I appreciate the offers, but I'm not going to be able to sleep. I'm too worried. You've all been great. Go home and get some rest,' I said.

'Are you sure?' asked Lucy.

I nodded.

'OK, pet. We'll be in first thing in the morning,' said Mum, kissing my forehead. 'Say night-night, Yuri.'

I held my son and kissed his smooth cheeks. 'Goodnight, angel, Mummy loves you. See you tomorrow. Be good for Granny.'

'Sure he's always good,' said Mum.

'I'll come back with you to help put him to bed,' said Babs. Mum recoiled in astonishment.

'Lookit, I don't know who you are,' said Dad, leaning over to peer at Babs, 'but someone's taken my daughter away and replaced her with a human being.'

'Enough, please you're cracking me up,' said Babs, grabbing Dad's nose and pinching it.

'Stop your nonsense, the two of you,' said Mum. 'This child needs to go to bed,' she added, as Yuri yawned.

We waved them off and went back in to sit with Lara.

*

It was a long night. We talked about our journey to parenthood. The naïve way we had started out . . . have sex and get pregnant. We remembered going to the doctor to see what was wrong, being told to relax and just keep at it. We laughed at the time James went to give his sperm sample and I had cut out a picture of Halle Berry in the James Bond bikini to help him along. I talked of how I hated taking the hormone-inducing drugs because they made me so moody, sweaty and miserable. We remembered James injecting me during the IVF attempt . . . how devastated we were when it failed . . . how adoption seemed like the answer to all our problems . . . how that process had nearly finished us, as our lives were dissected and picked apart by social workers . . . how we had fallen in love with Yuri the minute we saw his pale little face on the video, and then how it felt when we went to Russia and held him in our arms for the first time . . . We talked of the joy we felt when I found out I was pregnant . . . how shocked we'd been . . . how thrilled we were that Yuri would have a sibling to grow up with . . . and how terrified we were that we might now lose our little angel.

Chapter 35

I woke up with a start. I was hunched over in the chair, dribble running down my chin. I looked at Lara. She was fine. James leant over and rubbed my back.

'How long was I asleep?'

'Only about an hour.'

'God, I feel awful,' I said.

'You've been through a lot. Physically as well as emotionally.'

I shrugged. What was my pain compared to my little girl's? 'What time are they going to turn off the ventilator?'

'Nine.'

I looked at my watch. It was eight o'clock. 'I'm going to go to the bathroom to freshen up. I'll be back in ten minutes,' I said. I needed to get out of the room. I had to take a moment to gather myself before the ventilator went off.

As I was shuffling down the corridor, I saw Dad, Babs and Sean coming towards me. Sean was carrying a huge pink teddy bear. 'Sis!' he said, hugging me.

'What are you doing here? I thought you were still on honeymoon.'

'Babs called me. We came home a few days early.'

'Ah, Sean, you shouldn't have.'

'I was glad of the excuse. Three weeks on the beach is far too long.'

'Nice tan, though,' said Babs, smirking at Sean's red face

and million freckles. 'I'd say you're an attractive sight in your togs.'

'Good to see the old Babs is back,' said Dad.

'Where's Mum?' I asked.

'Changing Yuri's nappy. He did a huge dump in the car,' said Mary Poppins.

'I'm going to freshen up. I'll be back in five.'

'What time are they turning off the ventilator?' asked Dad.

'Nine,' I said, suddenly feeling weepy again.

'Hey, don't worry, she's got to be a fighter – all the girls in our family are. Look at the two of you,' said Sean.

I nodded and shuffled off to get myself together.

At five to nine, we all stood huddled round the incubator. Yuri was sitting on my knee and James was standing behind us, his hands on my shoulders.

'Lala,' Yuri said.

'Yes, darling, Lala's going to try to breathe now,' I said, crying into Yuri's hair.

He pushed me away. 'Lala,' he said, pointing to her.

James picked him up and Yuri leant over to the little door on the side of the incubator. I opened it and went to guide his hand in, but he pulled it back. In his other hand was the little grey elephant – his only reminder of his life before us. He pushed the trunk, then the legs through the door and placed the elephant beside Lara. It was her turn to have comfort now. She curled her fingers round the trunk.

'Will you look at that?' whispered Mum. 'He's given her his most treasured possession. It's a good omen.'

'Are you ready?' asked the nurse.

James and I nodded.

The ventilator was switched off.

While Lara fought to breathe on her own, we all held our breath. For a second or two there was nothing. I willed her on with every bone in my body. 'Come on, sweetheart, please breathe.'

Her eyes opened and she stared at me. A tiny sigh escaped from her rosebud mouth and, slowly, her chest began to rise and fall. We all breathed with her. I looked around at my family: everyone – old and new – was crying and laughing. Slowly I began to laugh too, as relief flooded my every pore.

One year on . . .

Lara came home after three weeks in hospital. Yuri insisted on sleeping in the same room as her, and the two are inseparable. Lara will go nowhere without her little grey elephant; Yuri is now more interested in trucks.

Lucy and Donal had a baby boy. At two weeks overdue, Lucy threatened to kneecap the obstetrician if he didn't induce her. She gave birth to an eleven-pound baby and has sworn she will never put her body through that again. Donal is besotted and the baby – named Serge after Donal's hero, the French rugby sensation Serge Blanco (Lucy was in too much pain to object) – is permanently dressed in rugby shirts.

While I was tucked away on maternity leave, Babs stalked Amanda until she finally gave in and offered her a slot on her afternoon show. Babs began doing makeovers for middle-aged women. It's become the most popular section of the programme: her bluntness and brutal honesty have hit a nerve and the public loves it.

Shadee got pregnant on honeymoon and had a beautiful baby girl, with her mother's dark hair and her father's blue eyes – as Babs says, it's lucky it wasn't the other way round. They named her Shala, which Mum had decided is actually Sheila and that's what she's calling her. Unbeknownst to Sean, Mum has already christened Sheila under the kitchen tap.

James coached Leinster to the final of the European Cup, where they lost 21–20 in what has been described as 'the best Cup Final ever played.' He has just been offered the job as assistant coach to the Irish team and is currently considering his options.

As for me . . . my cup is full.

X